THE SAINT &
THE MADAM

Lotte R. James

To anyone needing a little light in the darkness, and to all those who think some stories can never be finished. They can, with time, and love.
To RC, who inspired Arthur and kept me company during trying times.
And of course, always, to my mother, BB.

CONTENTS

PROLOGUE

Shadwell, April 25ᵗʰ, 1824

I t was a strange thing, to look at oneself in the mirror, and not recognize the person staring back. Sure, the gold curls that had made her so popular were the same. Her eyes were still the same wide round shape they'd always been, though today their golden hue was darker, like rich honey, and not solely due to the candlelight.

Today, they were full of fear, and sadness.

Determination, and resolve.

Not for the first time, and yet, as never before.

Her features, her form, they were the same as they had been for years now. Sharper than in her youth, but still pleasantly soft and rounded, or so she'd been told a thousand times. Even though, at second glance, perhaps they were that little bit sharper today. That little bit harder. That little bit...

Fiercer.

Lily had been many people in her life. She had been Cecilia Fanshawe of Mapledown Farm. Then for a time, Miss Fanshawe. She had been Lily the tart, and Lily the whore. She had been Miss Lily. She'd been so many variations in between; whatever she needed to be. Whatever others *wanted* her to be. And now...

Now, she felt as if she had become yet another incarnation of herself.

They would have many names for her in time, she was sure, but as she stared at herself in the flickering reflection, she felt that she was simply, *finally*, Lily.

And though Lily was afraid, her heart was steady.

Lily did not tremble. Lily did not question. Lily was strong, and solid, and deadly.

Lily would get it done.

Sarah appeared in the shadows behind her, her brown eyes shining like coals, the lines of worry on her brow deepened by the darkness.

'You sure about this,' she breathed, clutching the black coat tightly in her hands.

'I can't lose him, Sarah,' Lily said, meeting her eyes in the mirror. 'I won't. All I've done tonight... All *we've* done tonight... This is only the next step.'

Only the next step.

Slowly, Sarah nodded, and stepped forward to place the coat on her shoulders. Her hands rested there for a moment; for comfort, for strength, for courage, or perhaps, for all those things. Lily took a deep breath, giving, and taking, all of it.

In the darkness, in the eerie, telling quiet of the night, the grim, gloomy echo of the bells of St. Paul's Shadwell rang the hour of five.

It's time.

I.

A rthur Maximilian Dudley considered himself to be an intelligent man. Even if no one could ever be said to truly know Arthur Dudley, for that name, that man, was merely a mask to the world, it could be said that if anyone was asked, they would undoubtedly say he was an intelligent man. His livelihood, his entire life, everything he had built over the course of it, everything he was, hinged on that very fact. It was perhaps the feature which defined him most of all, though he liked to think he had other attributes as well.

Which was why, on this frosty, frigid, February evening, as he stood across the road from *Miss Lily's*, shuffling from foot to foot to keep them warm despite the slush they currently moved in, he had to wonder, why precisely it was, that he was here yet again.

There was nothing remotely intelligent or reasonable about this. Nothing whatsoever that could justify such reckless, foolish, and frankly ludicrous behaviour. It was the eleventh time in eleven days that he'd come here. Someone was bound to notice; someone had likely already. And though there was a justifiable reason Arthur Dudley could be here, still, it was not clever.

It was why he'd kept his distance since he'd gone into business with Lily; or rather, since his other half had.

St. Nick.

The last thing he needed was for anyone to make a connection between St. Nick and Arthur Dudley. For over twenty years, St. Nick's true identity had remained secret, even as his reputation, power, and influence in the underworld of London, and beyond, grew. To jeopardise that was...

Stupid. Reckless. Likely to get you killed.

The problem was, he couldn't *not* be here.

When he had first turned up here precisely eleven days ago, it hadn't been because he'd planned to come. Because he had thought it would help, or make him feel better, or make him forget. He hadn't planned to come. He had simply stepped outside his door, and ended up at *Miss Lily's*. And when he had realised where he was, well, he'd thought there was really no harm in going in, if only for a moment. Men like him, men and women from all walks of life, came to *Miss Lily's*. It might be noted that he had, but it wouldn't be... *Noticed*.

So no, there hadn't been any harm in going in, if only to have a moment when he didn't have to think about what he'd lost, and how lost he was. How close he felt to giving up, just as he had twenty-nine years ago. A moment, where he could pretend that he was fine, and that nothing at all was any different, and he could see people living, and speak with them, and yes, forget.

So he'd gone in.

Straight to *her*.

Because he had an excuse to see her. Business to discuss. Or at least, that is how it would seem. In truth, Arthur knew deep down he only really wanted to see her. And again, there was no rational reason why he should want to. Why he should seek her out, of all people. Yes, she was beautiful, and young, and whip-smart, and determined, and fierce, and amusing when she was trying to be serious, and just generally so soft, and inviting. But that could be said of a great many women. There was nothing in that description that made *this* woman special.

Even her beauty wasn't in itself *special*. There were generously curved, golden-haired beauties of medium height a plenty. Especially in her trade. Something about that pastoral, youthful freshness paired with particular talents made them a popular offering.

Yet somehow she *was* special.

Maybe it was the way her curls the colour of sunflowers tumbled and bounced and reflected the light just that way. Maybe it was the softness of her features, of her entire self; the round cheeks, dimpled chin and button nose. Maybe it was the way her eyes were like amber, full of old secrets, their colour ever-changing and intriguing.

Or maybe it was just her presence. The quiet strength. The dogged determination. The youthfulness and hope hidden away behind a protective shield. The way she smiled, always as if she couldn't believe that something had made her smile. The fierceness of her conviction.

Perhaps it was all of those things combined.

Whatever it was, he couldn't deny that being with her, it made him feel, *better*.

It got him through the days and hours of the night not spent with her. It got him up in the morning, made him dress, and shave, and do what he had to to keep going. She soothed his pain, and really, after all, wasn't that what women like her were for?

Arthur didn't truly believe that, but he knew it was safer to purport that he did.

Because convincing himself he sought out the company of a prostitute, well, madam now if he were being specific, for the same reason any other person on this earth did, was all he could do. There were things he had relinquished the right to. Things, he was never meant to have. He'd forgotten that, some months ago, but the experience had reminded him of the truth, and for that, he was grateful. There were limits to what he was allowed, and what he could offer to others. Any relationship other than a business transaction, was impossible.

Just as coming here every night for eleven nights was downright *stupid*.

Then go home.

Yes. *Home.* The place that felt like anything but. The place colder than this damned street in the middle of winter. The place meant to be his, but that had nothing of himself to show for it. That was part of the problem. There was nothing left to show of himself. Everything was a mask. Every waistcoat, every bauble, every damned thing he owned and wore, was part of what he had to be. No one, not even his sister, God rest her soul, had known, *would know,* anything but what he chose for them to see and know.

That was how it had to be. The price he paid for the life he led. *Except this.*

In that room, with *her,* he wasn't who he was to the rest of the world. There was no mask, because she had stripped it from him summarily months ago when she'd come knocking on his door making demands.

In that room, with her, he was only himself.

This has to stop.

It did. It would. Soon. When he could bear to spend a night alone in that place called home.

He would stop coming here. Things would go back to the way they'd been.

Soon.

But not tonight.

∞

'It's open,' Lily yelled, louder than she meant to when the knock sounded, and she tried to keep focused on the numbers before her. Maths were definitely not her forte, but she was getting better by the day. Four months ago, the accounts took her the whole night to finish. Now, she could get them done in about three hours, and she was almost there. It wasn't as if she didn't know who was on the other side of the door either; in fact he was the reason she had started the accounts early today. Not that she would ever admit to it.

She may have come a long way, accomplished things many women would never dare to dream possible. But some things, still, *always*, would be beyond her grasp. No matter how much one carved their own path, or challenged the world's expectations, some rules, could never be broken. There was a way to the world, and that was that.

Didn't hurt to dream though. Or rather, to enjoy the little things.

She didn't know exactly why he had suddenly started coming here, after their initial dealings last year, he'd been very clear about the fact that he would only rarely, if ever, come here. Yet the past ten, *no, eleven now*, nights, he'd turned up at her door.

The first few, he'd said he wanted to go over things. Make sure all was in order. Which they had. And then, the excuse had melted away. They hadn't gone over anything. They hadn't really even talked. He had just sat in that chair by the fire, the one that faced her, and he'd drunk the cognac she served him, and that was all. He would stay in that chair until an hour before closing, and then he'd rise, bid her goodnight, and leave. And the thing was, she didn't want to question it.

Well, she did. Because she sensed there was a reason he was here, and not at home, or at least, anywhere other than here. She sensed there was something wrong, and God help her she wanted to know so she could fix it. Or make it better.

But at the same time, she didn't want to know. Because she also sensed that if she *did* know, if by some miracle the man decided to open up to her, not that it would really be that extraordinary considering men confessed to their whores things they would never confess to their priest, except that it *would* be extraordinary because though she may be for all intents and purposes, a whore, she was not *his* whore. So pillow confessions were off the table. Regardless, if he did divulge the great secret behind his sudden nightly visits, she had a feeling there wouldn't be any after that.

And she wanted there to be more.

She liked his company, well, really, his presence. She liked him.

So she would take what little she got, and be grateful, and not question it.

Like a besotted schoolgirl.

Only you're not a girl anymore.

No, she wasn't. Not for a long time now.

'Good evening, Lily,' Mr. Dudley said, in that low, deep voice that barely ever raised above the level of a whisper, yet resonated through rooms; and through her body.

He was only one of a very select few who called her Lily now; most called her Miss Lily, something she encouraged to ensure her status was marked.

No longer a simple whore, but a madam.

Mr. Dudley had tried at first to call her Miss Fanshawe, but that name held a weight she no longer, *ever*, wished to carry, and she had begged him to find something else. They had finally agreed on Lily. Men had often whispered, sighed, relished her name as if it were as sweet as the promises they made her in the dark. But never, had she ever felt it like a caress, as she did when he said it. And that was without any intent. She dared not even imagine what it might sound like in more intimate a setting.

No, you dare not silly girl.

She heard him hang his coat and hat, then wander towards the hearth.

'You were expecting me.'

He sounded surprised, and Lily fought the smile growing on her lips hard, staring down at the unseen numbers before her with such intent they might've burnt up.

She liked to think she could surprise a man such as him.

Or perhaps, just him.

'I was prepared for the eventuality of your visit,' she said, praying she sounded nonchalant, and that none of the ridiculous hope and pleasure she'd felt at the prospect of him returning shone through.

The last thing she needed was for him to be aware of her little attachment to him.

Then he too would think you were as hare-brained as a besotted schoolgirl.

'I despair to think I've become predictable,' he mused, as she heard him settle into his chair, and take the glass she'd poured for him.

'If there is one thing people might accuse you of, Mr. Dudley,' she retorted, casually, and categorically *not* with a smile in her voice as she forced her mind to finish the final tally on the books. 'It would certainly not be predictable.'

'What would they accuse me of, Lily,' he asked, and her heart skipped a little at the sound of the smile in *his* voice.

'I'm sure I don't know.'

Very well, maybe she had smiled a little just then.

Finish the accounts.

'Come now, you cannot simply throw down the gauntlet then refuse the challenge. You are not a woman to retreat so,' he added, and her smile faded as girlish excitement was replaced with another kind altogether.

You need to control yourself.

Tales did not end well for women who lost their minds, lost themselves to men who made them feel... Things. Women who lost sight of who they were, and what they wanted, and how the world worked, all because some man made them feel special, and desired, and made their body respond to them in ways they'd never thought possible, were foolish. And she was certainly not a fool. She was an experienced woman, who knew all about desire, and pleasure, and passion. Well, perhaps not passion exactly. From a personal standpoint.

Which was all likely why she was having such a strong reaction to Mr. Dudley. Because he wasn't like any other man she'd encountered. He was a gentleman who had secrets, yes, but she knew his secrets. Well, the biggest of all, at least. He treated her well, not like a woman, but more like an equal when they were together. An associate.

Because that's what they were.

Business associates.

Really didn't matter what his voice did to her, or that he was handsome. She had known many handsome men. And he wasn't *that* handsome in comparison.

Or at all.

She finished the accounts with a flourish, knowing that she would certainly have to check them after closing, set down her pen, shut the book, and looked over at him, to confirm her hypothesis that really, she was just bored, or starved of real, true attention, and that was all there was to it, and that she was winding herself up over nothing and no one.

Luckily, his soft silver eyes were turned towards the fire, and not on her, so she could make another examination of him freely. Those eyes did have a tendency to draw you in with their kind, hypnotic depths, even when they shifted, coloured with cold fierceness. He did have the strong, square, and symmetrical features that typically made a man *handsome.* His silver and black hair that curled at the front without any aid was all neatly trimmed. He was tall, and well-built, the body of a barrel-chested fighter rather than the lean, trim features of a traditional society dandy, but then, that is what he was, and she liked that strength about him. Tonight, like every other time she'd seen him, he sported a well-cut, but simple three-piece suit, grey superfine today, with a crisp white shirt and tie, though he had done away with the jacket this evening, which he'd never done before, but which she had to admit showcased that strength in his arms she admired.

He did have that charming smile that seemed to grow always from the right side, rather than both at once, adding to its crooked, teasing quality. And sure, those lips, curved into a smile or not, were that thinly plump, well-defined kind that would be both luscious and firm. Then of course his hands, those hands which held all the contradictions of him, strength, and grace, with long, nimble fingers that would surely -

Very well so he is objectively handsome. That's quite enough of that.

Shaking the thoughts straight out of her head where

they didn't belong, Lily refocused on the present and her surroundings, only to find him watching her, that damned charming smile on his face, those damn silver eyes twinkling, and an eyebrow raised expectantly.

He asked you a question you fool, answer it.

Cleverly.

'Odd,' she managed to say finally, pushing the words out with some vigour to ensure she didn't squeak them out. 'They would accuse you of being odd.'

Oh dear Lord.

II.

It wasn't often that Arthur was rendered speechless. Being rendered speechless meant you were surprised, caught off guard, and that your mind did not work fast enough to deal with that surprise. And though he couldn't claim to never be surprised - that was actually one of the things that made life worth living, that made it exciting and interesting - he could however claim to never being caught off guard, and to have a very quick mind.

It was what had kept him alive all these years, what had gotten him to where he was today. And had it been anyone other than Lily who had rendered him speechless, he might've been worried. Instead, it only made him more...

Intrigued. Amused. Excited.

This was not the first time she had rendered him thus either. In fact, this was the second. The first time had been when she had turned up at his door all those months ago, and made her demands. Both times were easily explicable, really, when he thought about it properly. The first time, he had neither expected her, nor what had come out of her mouth. And tonight...

Well of all the things she might've come back with, that he was dull, or proud, or stiff even, she had settled for *odd*. And done it with such a reluctant forcefulness, that he couldn't doubt the truth, or sincerity of the remark.

Taking a sip of the cognac she had left for him - and that was another thing he refused to think on, how good it had felt to know she had been ready for him, waiting even, perhaps - he tried to school himself of the shock, and pretend to be simply, thoughtful. He turned back to the fire, which was much safer than looking over at her, in all her relaxed, soft splendour in the half-light, all simple braids and ink stains and silk dressing gowns over...

Well over what, it was not his business to know.

No matter her profession, she is your associate, and demands respect not ogling.

'Odd,' he repeated. 'How so?'

'I shouldn't have said anything,' she muttered hurriedly, the dismissive note in her voice tearing through him for no reason in particular.

He shouldn't push it, he shouldn't coax her into speaking to him more, after all he had come into her space, her world, and planted himself here because he couldn't face being anywhere else, but really, what if she didn't want him here?

He shouldn't be here.

'Please,' he said before he could stop himself, looking over at her. She stopped fiddling with those account books she was always pouring over, so diligently; more diligently than half the supposed *businessmen* he knew. 'Indulge me. Join me.'

She looked up at him slowly, hesitation, and what he liked to think was longing in her eyes.

After a moment studying him, she nodded, rose, and slowly came to sit across from him, the firelight radiating off her until it seemed like she was glowing.

For a moment he just stared at her, hypnotised, lured by the image, then he shook himself and poured a glass for her, careful not to come too close when he handed it over.

'So, Lily,' he smiled, leaning back, cradling his own drink in his hands just for something to do which wasn't reach out and touch her. 'How am I odd?'

'For one you are a man of means,' she said after a moment,

turning away to examine the dark brown contents of her glass, swirling them around mindlessly. 'But you do not flaunt it, or spend it, other than on houses, the people of Shadwell, and charities. You live in Shadwell though you could live anywhere else, and seem to love it though you are not from here. No one really knows anything of you other than your name, and that you have a sister. Until your... Involvement,' she said diplomatically, throwing him a glance to gauge his reaction, which was simply to incline his head, urging her to continue. 'With Meg Lowell last year, no one had either seen or heard of you with a woman.'

'I would say all that makes me an enigma,' he pointed out, taking a sip of the cognac. He really shouldn't, he was already too warm, too comfortable, too... *Relaxed.* Which was something he'd never really been in his life. Being relaxed got you dead, quicker than stupidity. *Well, perhaps not quicker.* 'Makes me a mystery, perhaps. But odd?'

'Odd for around here,' Lily grinned, raising her glass as if to toast before sampling it.

'I suspect so,' he conceded. He hesitated, knowing he really should leave it here, but he needed to know. Wanted to know. *Her* thoughts. What she thought of him. She who somehow had always seen through him when no other could. 'You, however, know why all that is as it is. Why do *you* find me odd.'

'I don't.'

'You do,' he said, garnering the full attention of those dark amber eyes. 'I heard it in your voice.'

'I don't find you odd,' she repeated, only this time he believed her. She hesitated a moment before continuing, again looking down to her glass before doing so, as if she knew just as well as he did how bad of an idea speaking things such as this was. 'Rather I... Some of the things you do, I find *them* odd.'

'Is not a man his actions in your opinion?'

'Of course,' she agreed. A little frown creased her brow and she looked back up at him with such fervour in her eyes it nearly stole his breath. *Christ, first my speech, now my breath.* Not that it would be the first time for that either. 'But that is not all a man is.'

'Quite,' he said softly. She held his gaze, the fervour slowly fading to make way for... Something he was certainly imagining. 'Tell me them,' he added, clearing his throat, and taking another drink of the cognac. 'What do I do that is so odd?'

'Well, for one, you bought a building and financed a business for a woman you knew nothing of.'

'I knew enough,' he told her before he could stop himself. She had never asked why he'd given into her demands so easily; he had never volunteered the information. As if they'd both somehow known that it made no sense whatsoever, what he had done for her, *with* her; or rather as if they knew something else lay behind the *why*, something that would be dangerous for them both. 'I knew enough to realise it was a wise investment,' he added, hoping to mitigate the damage his mouth had just done. 'And I think I've been proven right.'

'You come to a bawdy house but never indulge in the offerings,' she said, leaning back and pinning him with her stare.

She seemed as relaxed as he was; though in her case her eyes belied it.

As if the questions she was asking now, without actually asking, were ones she had longed to ask for a while.

Which was absolutely not the case; the damn cognac was going to his head now.

'It isn't good business to sample your own wares,' he replied, unable to admit the truth.

He didn't want a whore.

He hadn't for a long while; though they were the only ones he had ever allowed himself to seek pleasure from. The only way to be who he was; and for that very same reason, he had grown weary of the nature of those relationships, if they could be called thus.

Only now, it wasn't solely that which stopped him seeking out companionship.

Not that he was ready to fully acknowledge that either.

'But neither do you sample them elsewhere,' Lily pointed out. She took another sip of her drink, sighed, and measured him up again, deciding whether to speak her mind or not. Though he feared what would ultimately come out of her mouth, he found he couldn't help but wish she would not hold back. 'Tell me, is it women in general you have reservations about, or only whores?'

She lifted an eyebrow, challenging him, even as he saw the fear in her eyes that she had overstepped.

'You know the limits of my life, Lily,' he said, the seriousness, and sadness of that in his voice, whether he liked it or not. 'And as for the ladies of the night... I no longer could quite stand the transactional nature of those encounters.'

'There is always a price to what is given, Mr. Dudley,' she said simply, and yet the bare truth of it rang as if proclaimed by God himself, striking him deep inside. 'Whores are simply more upfront about it, but women, and men, the world over, have sold pieces of themselves for companionship, or safety, or power.'

'So you don't believe in love then, Lily?'

'Do you?' she asked rather than answer. The silence which followed stretched between them like a chasm; a great, deep void which neither could bring themselves to bridge. 'There is a profound sadness about you, Mr. Dudley,' she finally said, so quietly her voice was barely even a whisper. And yet it seemed to reach out over that chasm, inviting him to step and tumble straight into it. 'A longing. A loneliness. I think you're no better than the rest of us,' she sighed with a wan smile. 'You just want to be loved.'

If he'd thought her words a blow before, that was nothing compared to this.

He wanted to run, to scream, to tear off his skin, and rail that it wasn't so, but he had asked, and she had delivered. She had spoken a truth he'd kept buried deeper than any of his other secrets, and seen through every single mask he had ever created, for others, and for himself.

Swallowing hard, he finished his drink, rose, and went to put on his hat and coats.

'Goodnight, Lily,' he said stiffly before he left, refusing to look back.

Swearing, he would never come back again.

Which is for the best, really.

III.

The following night, Lily didn't pour a glass of cognac, and leave it on the table by the chair before the fire. Because she knew that Mr. Dudley would not be back that evening. She stared at what had become his spot, the accounts untouched before her, and in her heart she knew he would never come back, and sit by her fire, and just *be* with her, as he had been before. And that was a good thing. They would go back to the way things were; the way they were supposed to be. They would be business partners once again. Not that they'd ever been anything but.

Only in your own fanciful mind Lily you dimwit.

Yes, it was only in her own mind that they'd ever been something more, because she'd allowed herself to...

Become a besotted little schoolgirl.

So it was good that he would never come again like before, because now she could get over those useless feelings, and focus on what should always be the priority in her life: her business. Her workers. Making *Miss Lily's* the best whorehouse in Shadwell. Who knew, maybe all of London someday; though she doubted she would ever become greater than Madam E. That *Miss Lily's* would ever surpass *The Emporium.* Only, it wouldn't be for lack of trying. And a girl had to have dreams, because without dreams... Life wasn't worth living.

And dreams of building her own success, now those were

good, useful dreams.

Not like - stop it!

For a time, Lily had stopped dreaming. When she'd lost her sister, Kit, when she'd first come to London, when life had taken its toll on her in every way possible. Those times... Those had been the hardest of her life. She'd wondered so often, what the point of living was anyways, if all there was to life was cold nights of terrors, and hurt, and... Well. But she was one of the lucky ones. Sarah had taken her under her wing, gotten her set up and helped teach her how to keep safe, given her a warm bed and friendship. And now...

Now she had her own business, she kept twenty prostitutes safe and warm and fed, and twenty more staff employed. Her business was growing, her clientele was growing, and not just with the sailors and travellers and merchants, but with the lords and men of the West that came to the East End to sample... Everything.

It had been a rough start – local men, sailors, and dockers not used to the slightly elevated rates she set - but particularly not to the obsessive use of French letters and bathing requirements. How many had turned away sneering when told they would be required to *freshen up* before their appointment, even if by their chosen companion for the hour or evening? So many thought her aiming to be above her station, of thinking herself too good for Shadwell. But it was for her employees that she did it all, not because she thought herself better.

Disease killed so many, even those that didn't work the streets. How she had managed to avoid such a fate herself... Was a mystery. Or a miracle. Unwanted pregnancies were yet another risk, more lives put at stake. She wasn't an educated girl, but anyone could see the toll those things took. She'd tried, to look away. Thought about starting over, becoming *a good girl*. Sarah had offered her work at Silver Bell Wharf, working the kitchens there, feeding the hungry dockers who worked for the mad viscount that had fallen for the lighterman's daughter. And it might've been, could've been, a good life.

But try as she might, she couldn't look away. And those daydreams of semi-respectability, hadn't felt... *Right*. The girl in those dreams, didn't feel like who she was at heart. And a whore that may be, but she wasn't ashamed of that. Had never been; even in her worst moments. Then, Marigold had been killed. And she'd known, she had to do something. Not just for herself, but for others like her. Deep down, she'd known she could build a place where workers would be safe, with protection from illness, and violence, with a doctor ready to come at any hour, and food, and warm beds... She'd had a chance, and she'd seized it, and gone to him, and -

Don't think on him.

Only it was blasted difficult, wasn't it, when his absence was so...

Remarkable.

Not even a fortnight, and she'd become accustomed to having him here with her, looking over at her with those eyes, and filling her with warmth, and giddiness, and hope. And now he was gone, and it was all her fault. That was the worst part; that it was her own inability to keep her mouth shut that forced him away. What had she been thinking? Speaking all that nonsense about *oddness* and *love.*

Ninny. Ninny. Ninny.

But in the moment, she'd felt something, *seen* something in him, and her heart had wanted to reach out, she'd wanted to reach out, and touch him, and love him herself, and -

'Miss Lily,' came Bill's voice before the door opened without preamble. The man himself strode in, and one look at his face had her rising before his next words were even spoken. 'We've got a problem.'

∞

'Thank you for your understanding, sir,' Lily said, plastering as bright and seductive a smile on her face as she could, given the circumstances. She curtsied to the wealthy banker before her, luckily only the worse for wear because of a single punch and shove that had left him with a split cheek, and spinning head. And equally luckily, he seemed to view the whole situation as a sort of dashing adventure. 'I am sure Amelia's ministrations will see you set to rights soon enough. And of course your next visit will be entirely our treat.'

'A pleasure, as always Miss Lily,' he bowed, before Amelia came to wrap herself around him, cooing sweet nothings in his ear.

The woman winked as she quietly shut the door, and went on to make better the poor man.

'Fuck,' Lily muttered as she turned away. 'Fuck, fuck, fuck.'

Her best woman, engaged all night in making a situation better that shouldn't have even arisen to begin with.

Another down for who knew how long, and one of her men, to be fired.

A fuckin' mess.

'Where to next,' Bill asked as they strode down the corridor.

'Winston.'

Bill nodded, and they continued to the back stairs.

Then down, and out to the alley behind the house, where Bill had left Winston with two other men. The wretch squirmed and tried to extricate himself from the hold when she and Bill came out into the semi-darkness, the light from the corridor behind them the only thing illuminating the otherwise pitch black.

Lily was pleased to see that Bill and the others had already seen fit to dole out their own brand of retribution, and blood poured freely from Winston's mouth and broken nose. In fact, only those watery blue eyes were recognizable, though he still had enough bite to snarl and rage. She'd never really liked him, he was a skinny, rabid dog, born of St. Giles, but then, it was always best to have those kinds of men on your side.

Or so she'd thought.

'Bitch,' he spat as she approached, some blood even landing on the hem of her silk dressing robe. 'Ye'll pay for this.'

The men holding him yanked him back into submission, but she waved at them, and they stopped, Winston hanging limply between them, his exertions, and the beating, now taking their toll.

She stepped closer, so that she, even small as she was, was towering over him, and steeled herself before speaking. Lily wasn't a violent person, she didn't like violence, but she knew its power.

And she knew any trace of weakness would be exploited, and the respect, the power that she held now, would vanish.

'You listen, and you listen well, Winston,' she said, her tone ice-cold and leaving no doubt of what she was truly capable. 'You are finished here. And if you come within sight of this house, or Joce, you're dead. Not by Bill's hand, not by their hands, but by mine.'

'Ye think ye're untouchable 'cause ye're Saint Nick's whore,' he half-laughed, half-gurgled, his head lifting. 'I'll kill ye.'

'No, you won't,' she said simply, smiling, and bending a little to meet his eye. God he had a hard head. 'Because, and I'll repeat myself so that we're clear, I will kill you first. Look into my eyes, Winston, and tell me I'm wrong.'

To his credit, he did take a good long look.

And what he saw in her eyes, did the trick.

He nodded, a flash of fear mingling with bitterness and hatred.

It was enough to satisfy her.

For now.

'Dump him far away from here,' she ordered the men holding him.

She and Bill watched them slide out of the light, back into the darkness.

'I want someone watching him at all times,' she said, rubbing her arms as a chill swept over her. It was winter still after all, and yet, until now, she hadn't felt the cold. *If it is the cold that makes you shiver…* 'He even thinks about coming here, or to Joce, I don't care what I promised him, you end it.'

'Saint's men?'

'Ours.'

'Aye.'

'You want me to come with you,' Bill asked as she turned to go back inside.

'No. I think it best I speak to Joce alone.'

'Aye, Miss Lily. You gonna tell 'im?' he asked as she stepped into the blessedly warm corridor.

'No, Bill. I'm not going to tell him. It's dealt with.'

She didn't need to turn to see his disappointment - she felt it.

But this was her house, despite who had financed it; who everyone knew protected it. And if Winston was spouting shit like *'Saint Nick's whore'*, it was bound to be going around. She didn't need to give people more reason to think she was just that; that the only power she had was because of a man.

They needed to know she was a force of her own.

'Mr. Dudley ain't been 'round tonight,' he remarked, and *dammit all to Hell, can I not just have one second's reprieve?*

'No, Bill, he hasn't,' she bit back. 'I doubt he'll be 'round again. Now, if you're done talkin' nonsense, I'm goin' to go see Joce.'

'Aye, Miss Lily.'

'Aye, Miss Lily.'

So much, in those three little words. As Lily made her way upstairs, she tried to focus on what was still left to do, rather than on Bill's words. He spoke few of them, and many thought him the brainless thug he appeared to be. But there was so much more to Bill than anyone knew; the man was intelligent, and far too perceptive sometimes.

Always.

And he almost never voiced his disapproval, or talked about anything remotely personal. Yet he had, and it was unsettling. Because he voiced, *sort of*, the things she didn't want to acknowledge.

St. Nick should know about the trouble.

You shouldn't keep things from him.

This likely isn't the end of this - as much as we wish it to be.

Mr. Dudley's visits have been noticed.

So much. *Too much*, on top of the rest.

Lily sighed as she reached the top of the stairs at the third floor, taking a deep breath before continuing to Joce's room.

Responsibility is a right bitch.

Well, she'd wanted it, and now she had it.

Lily entered Joce's room without knocking, to find the doctor had been and gone, and the woman herself sat at the little dressing table across the room. Even in the dim candlelight reflecting off the dark colours, all burgundies and purples, Joce's wounds were visible; even the red marks on her neck. The bastard had done a right number on her, and Lily tamped down the anger, and regret she felt at not having had the boys finish the job on Winston.

No weakness; not even sympathy.

'How long has this been going on,' she said coldly, and the eye which wasn't swollen up met her own in the mirror.

'Two months,' Joce said quietly.

The question was in her hazel eye: *will I be sent away?*

Even if she had actually felt no sympathy, Lily wouldn't be smart to send her away. With those enchanting hazel eyes, chestnut hair, and sweet features, both in face and body, Joce was a good earner; and her French origins made her even more sought after.

But there had to be an understanding.

'This is why we have rules in place,' she said, stepping in closer. 'You understand now?'

'Yes, Miss Lily.'

'You love him?' The girl nodded, and Lily clenched her jaw. 'And I suppose he said he loved you? That he hurt you because you hurt him, that you belonged to him, and only him?'

The eye opened wider, and Lily nodded.

'You face a choice, Joce,' she sighed, crossing her arms, trying to look as much the strong, unhappy madam she was supposed to be. Separating her emotions from her job had always been one of her talents, but when others' lives were in your hands, somehow, it became harder to be convincingly detached. 'You can stay, heal up here, and get back to work when the doctor says you can. Or you can leave, tonight, go find him. It's your life, your choice. But you and I both know… We've both seen it happen before. A man like that doesn't stop. And next time, Bill and I won't be there.'

'I'll stay, Miss Lily,' she said, without hesitation, and Lily felt her heart unclench a little. 'I'll make it right to you, I swear.'

'You just heal up.' Lily made for the door but stopped when she reached it. 'You ring, if you need anything. I'll come see you in the morning. Take some of that laudanum to help you sleep tonight, but don't be takin' it on the regular after that, mind you.'

'Yes, Miss Lily. Thank you.'

Another nod, and Lily slipped back into the corridor.

She hadn't even taken a step before she heard stifled crying, and it took everything she had not to go back in and hug the girl. She would send one of the others. The price of their safety, their wellbeing, was her distance, her strength.

And so she wandered back to her office, to go deal with the accounts.

Strength and responsibility.

IV.

The crumpled note fell from Arthur's hand to the floor as he stared listlessly out of the window. Outside, the sun shone brilliantly, a bright, frosty day that made the garden in the square below sparkle in all its quiet magnificence. He could hear laughter, and the business of the morning on the air, even here, in this tranquil little corner of the East. Before, he'd enjoyed having such a view, and hearing such life. Before, he'd been grateful for it all. And then...

Everything had shattered.

And something in his gut told him it was only going to get worse.

Trouble.

The word taunted him, the scrawled, messy, barely legible letters still dancing before his eyes.

There had been trouble at Lily's. And he had to hear about it from his little birds.

The note hadn't been from her, or even one of hers. It had been from the eyes he kept on her, that even his own men didn't know about. He could lie to himself and think that perhaps later, she would inform him, they were meant to be business partners after all; but he knew she wouldn't. Not because she was proud, or strong, or damned stubborn, and capable of handling it all herself, no. Because he'd been an ass.

Because for the first time in, well, a very long time, he'd been, unsettled. Afraid, almost. Of what she'd seen, sensed in him. As if he were an open book for all to read.

Not all. Just her.

He was the one who had asked, pushed, and she had delivered. And he was the one who hadn't been able to take her words, no, he'd run, and he knew she had been...

Offended?

It felt worse than that, he knew it was worse than that, but offended sounded good for now.

And really, he shouldn't be pondering all this, *again*, as he had most of the night, day, and night, since he'd last seen her. It wasn't like him to get...

Distracted.

Not like him to keep thinking about whatever it was that had happened. It had. It was over, done with. Which was good, because he'd known he shouldn't go back, and this had been the final push to force him to see the truth. He had better things to be getting on with. Lily was more than capable of handling herself. Hell, one only had to look at the way she handled *him* to know that.

Knowing that, didn't stop him from...

Worrying.

The realisation was enough to startle him from his reverie. He rose abruptly, ignoring the untouched coffee and breakfast on the table, and strode to the window, as if a clearer view of his surroundings, and the world beyond, where lay his empire, would make his mind any clearer.

He wasn't used to worrying. He'd thought he was done with it... When he lost the only thing of import he had. He was always *concerned*, for his business, for his tenants, for the progress of this world even, but he didn't *worry*. It served no purpose.

Yet now, he found that he incontestably was. For *her*. Had been, looking back, ever since he'd known her. At first, when she had moved in with Sarah Burgess, he'd thought it the concern he had for all his tenants. But thinking back on those days now, he realised he'd already been worrying. He'd liked her. Who wouldn't? She was brash, and ballsy, rougher at the edges than she was now. But also...

Amusing. Warm. Unafraid.

And he'd worried about her working the streets, as he had no right nor business doing.

Then, she'd come marching up to his door - and he'd only felt surprise.

And relief. That she came to me.

That she knew me.

'Enough,' Arthur muttered, turning away from the window with disgust.

At himself, for being so...

Illogical. Maudlin. Stupid.

Whatever it was that he currently was.

Downing the cup of cold coffee on his way, he strode out, grabbed his coat, gloves, and hat, and went out to take care of the only thing he should ever concern himself with.

Business.

∞

Trouble. It appeared that would be the word he would be faced with ceaselessly today, he thought, as he stood before one of his buildings on Crown Street. *Fucking trouble.* If there was one thing people would say of Mr. Arthur Dudley, landlord to many in Shadwell, it was that he was a good landlord. That he kept his buildings safe, well-tended to; that he was understanding of those who dwelled in them, going so far as to forego the rent, or help with funeral arrangements, as he had in the case of Sarah Burgess' parents.

Therefore, the broken windows, shredded door barely still hanging on its hinges, and threats painted on the facade in bright red paint, *not blood, thank God*, before him, were very much an unusual sight.

Clenching his jaw, his hands curling into fists so tightly the leather squeaked, Arthur forced himself to draw in a deep breath, and release it slowly, before he went any further.

It's getting worse.

Tenants around these parts had been reporting *trouble* for a month or so now. Threats by unknown nefarious sorts, menacing notes, strange noises at night. But nothing compared to this. He'd looked into the matter, of course he had, with all he could, sent men to watch his properties, but *nothing.* Come to think of that - where were the men he'd posted down Crown Street?

Later.

Right now, he had to see to the ten families living here, check that they were well, and that nothing more than property had been destroyed. Later, he could find those meant to be guarding the place, and he could try and think of other ways to find, and stop those threatening people under his care. His protection.

Later.

'Later,' he breathed, the word seemingly hovering in the air along with his breath.

But then the smoky puff was gone, and Arthur made his way into the building.

'Hello,' he called, pushing what remained of the door aside, and carefully stepping into the corridor. It was worse inside, everything from the wall itself, to the sconces, to the individual doors were broken, shreds of it all strewn on the paint-smeared carpet. His anger was like a fire being revived, but he forced it down, and instead called again. 'Mr. Guerin? Mrs. Jenkins? Hello?'

A door creaked above his head, and carefully he made his way to the first step, and stared upwards. A head peeked over the banister on the top floor, which he could barely make out in the gloom.

'Mr. Stein?'

'Mr. Dudley.'

'Where is everyone?'

'Up here, sir,' the older man said sadly, his native French colouring his words more than usual. 'Everyone is up here.'

Arthur nodded, and made his way up.

Later, whoever did this, will pay.

∞

Dearly, Arthur added some time later, as he strode away from Crown Street, from his tenants, from the Thames men; from the death and destruction which shouldn't have bothered him considering his entire life was full of them both, but which, today, most certainly did. Mr. Stein and the others, who had all congregated together in the higher floors, had recounted the hours of fear, and torment they'd been subjected to.

The attack itself had been swift, over before the neighbours could even react, and vicious. Some of the men had tried to confront the masked bruisers who could've been sailors or criminals for all any of them knew, but had only managed to get themselves injured. Nothing grave, *thank God,* but that mattered not. Everyone had spent the night afraid that more would come; or worse would happen. So afraid they didn't even send for him, or the watch, or anyone; they just sat altogether and waited for a new day to arrive.

Just as I once did myself.

Arthur had sent immediately for a doctor, and the River Police, though the man sent to fetch them had not needed to go far for the latter. They'd been on the street already; sent to look into the dead men in a nearby alley.

My men.

Both strangled and stabbed for good measure, left in the muck like refuse.

To their credit, the Thames men were thorough, likely because of Arthur's good standing and reputation. They took notes, spoke to the residents, promised to find answers. But even if they were capable of living up to their promises, which for a variety of reasons, *time, resources, will, corruption,* they weren't, it wasn't up to them.

It's up to me.

It was Arthur's people who had been hurt. His business attacked. His men killed.

So it was up to him to make it right. Some may call him a villain, but for all the ill he'd done in his life, he'd always followed a code. As Mr. Dudley, and St. Nick. Therefore *both* of him would make it right.

Arthur Dudley would see right by his tenants, and by the men sent to guard them. He would see the building repaired, with extra security measures put in place. He would see his men buried and their families taken care of.

And St. Nick, he would see to those responsible being found, and punished.

Yes, I will.

Heading back to the heart of Shadwell, to see to all of it, Arthur realised he couldn't shake off the effect this morning had had on him. He was used to responsibility, used to bearing the weight of it, the feel of it on his shoulders familiar, and oddly, comforting. He was used to hearing and seeing all manner of death and destruction; he'd been raised in it. Raised himself up high in it. It was what he lived, and breathed, and fed off of. It was all part of him. But this morning... Looking into Mr. Stein's and the others' eyes... Seeing the fear, and worry, and hurt lingering in them... He *felt* it, for the first time in a very long time.

It wasn't that he didn't feel normally, he felt things, just not... *Some things.*

He was a man of reason, a businessman, the leader of one of the most successful criminal enterprises in the city; perhaps the country, and no one knew of it. He was intelligent, and clever, Hell, more than twenty years he'd thrived in the shadows, building an empire none other could rival. One had to be intelligent, and rational, and capable of separating themselves from the muck one used to build empires with, to be able to achieve what he had. One had to be able to separate oneself from others, and be above sentiment to be able to make the best decisions at all times. But today, he couldn't seem to shake it off.

The responsibility, the lives in his hands, the fear for others, it all seemed to weigh more than usual. Until it was so heavy he had to stop just off the High Street, and take a moment, to breathe, and *focus*. Stepping to the side, he put a hand against the cool brick beside him, and forced the building supporting him to take some of the weight. Breathing deeply, he let his eyes wander around, see all the people, the life washing like waves against him. Shadwell was good for that; there was always so much life here. Tradesmen, merchants, dockers, doxies, sailors, butchers, and bakers, and children. Yes there was darkness, and danger, and death, and despair, like anywhere. But through it all, seeping up from the streets, was *life*.

There was something so primal here, so vital, he'd fed off it, lived off it for years. So why now, was he seeing it all, smelling it all, tasting it all, as if from a distance? That woman there, selling eels, why could he not hear her? Smell the damned slithering things as they cooked on the fire? That chandler, there, why could he not hear him haggling with some foreman? The horses, the carts, the children running about, the gulls, even, why could he not feel them?

'There is a profound sadness about you, Mr. Dudley...'

An image of Lily, bathed in firelight, a coy smile on her lips, and her golden eyes sparkling danced before his eyes, and Arthur *felt* it. The image, it brought him back from the world he'd been exiled to momentarily, and all at once the sights, the sounds, the deafening cacophony, the dizzying array of it all, hit him like a wave washing high over the deck of a ship.

He didn't understand it.

He didn't wish to anymore.

He would employ his reason for other things.

He would straighten, and walk on, and get everything done that needed doing.

And then, he knew, he would go to her again.

Because though he didn't know why; he knew he needed her, now more than ever.

V.

Even though Lily had tried to convince herself it was simply the weight of responsibility, the toll of *being strong* which had brought about the sullenness she seemed to be mired in, she couldn't quite manage it. Instincts were important when one lived as she did; when one faced the world as she did. It was important to listen to your gut when it told you not to follow this gentleman or that; when it told you to take this road or that. Her gut had saved her life many times. Her gut had given her this place.

And now it was repeating, ceaselessly, *endlessly*, that the reason for her grim mood was not all that she faced, but rather the absence of someone. A certain someone who would come sit in that chair, there, and drink cognac, and just *be* with her.

She tried to shake it off, to do as she had before, to see the beauty in all the little things. She'd tried to focus on the business; she'd hired a new man to replace Winston, Bob, a bruiser Bill vouched for, and Joce was recovering well, in body at least. Her preparations for the first grand party she would throw here, a mask, with for its theme the old Roman New Year, were going well. Several gentlemen of Society had already confirmed their attendance, and excitement. She herself should be thrilled. Everything she had worked for, was coming to fruition.

Yet she was maudlin. On edge, short-tempered, and just, sad.

She *missed* him. His presence. His scent, his -

Stop it. Stop it. Stop it.

This was ridiculous. Throwing down her quill, she got up and paced the office.

Utterly absurd.

She'd never missed a man. There was only one person in this world she missed, her sister, and the man she'd hired was working on that. She didn't mope around and sigh like some forlorn lass because she missed Kit, so why on Earth was she doing it now?

Only it wasn't just that she missed him. It was that she felt guilty, for saying all she had, and she was also worried, because she'd heard there was trouble at one of his houses in Crown Street, and -

You're letting a man control your emotions, do stop it this instant, you -

'Enter,' she growled when a knock sounded, interrupting her thoughts. *For which you should be grateful.* Turning, she told herself to be calm, and professional, and *together*, only when the door opened and she saw who had knocked she froze, her mouth gaping slightly. *You came back.* 'I didn't think you would come back,' she said dumbly, before striding to the desk if only for something to do other than look at him.

One look, and she was back where she started.

Besotted, heart beating, full of... Excitement.

Enough.

There was probably a very good reason he was here, and getting all excited, and letting her heart run away with her again, was beyond foolish, it was plain *stupid.* What she really needed right now was her courage, *and a damned spine*; the courage to apologise, and make it right, so that they could go back to the way things were: a cold, professional business relationship. And there would be no doing that if she allowed herself to look at him, to be ensnared in those silver eyes that seemed to forever make her dream.

If he looked at her, well, that courage would fly right out of the window.

Which is why when she reached her desk, she concentrated hard on ignoring the sound of his footsteps approaching, busing herself instead tidying the already rather tidy desk.

'About the other night -'

'Lily, please, don't,' he said softly. She took a deep breath, her heart still pounding, waiting for whatever would come next. 'There is no need for that,' he added gently, and finally she could breathe again. Perhaps he didn't hate her. Perhaps all wasn't lost. Perhaps they could go back to the way things were, even if that was the last thing she wanted. 'I heard there was trouble,' he said after a moment.

'Nothing I can't handle,' she smiled, daring finally to look up at him. The concern she found gave her stupid little heart too much hope though, so she turned back to the array of papers on her desk, and shuffled them about to put them in order, which they absolutely would not be considering she couldn't see a single word on any of them. Just those eyes, burned into her memory. 'I heard you had some trouble yourself,' she said, hoping her business-like, nonchalant tone was coming across as she wished it to.

'Nothing I can't handle,' he said, a smile in his voice.

'I'm glad. Glad you're... Not hurt,' she said, utter ninny that she was.

Cursing herself, she turned to the bookshelves with a ledger in her hands that may or may not belong where she was about to put it, but froze when Mr. Dudley spoke again.

'My sister is dead.' Shock, fear, and pain for the man behind her turned her around, and she searched his eyes, trying to make sense of the revelation. What had happened? Why hadn't she heard anything? Was he in danger? 'Nothing to do with the business,' he specified, as if he could see the thoughts flashing in her mind. 'She died a fortnight ago. Fever.'

Her heart sank, and twisted all at once within her at the sadness in his eyes.

A profound sadness...

She willed herself to say something, *I'm sorry* was typically what people should say, but she couldn't will the words to leave her body. They were stuck within her, because they felt…

Inadequate. Cheap. Useless.

If she lost her sister, rather, if she learned that Kit was dead, she wouldn't want words, she would want…

Don't.

Wait.

A fortnight?

'You didn't tell anyone,' she said stupidly, frowning.

'Who would I have told,' he shrugged, a hollow smile on his lips.

'I don't know. Meg, perhaps.'

Viscountess or not, they had been engaged once, not so long ago, and were on good terms.

The best terms he'd ever been known to be on with a woman.

Not that she was… Jealous or anything.

'You?' he asked, and she let out a brittle laugh before she could stop herself.

'I am under no illusions about our relationship,' she said, dropping the book back on the desk, shaking her head at her infinite idiocy and carelessness.

The man is grieving and you laugh at him -

'Yet I came here,' he whispered, and her heart tightened again, tears burning her eyes for no reason at all.

Yes, you did.

She wanted to believe it was for another reason than the truth.

'Why not,' she said, pushing away the useless emotions clouding her mind and heart, staring down at the ledger before her as if it might contain the mysteries of the universe. 'There is warmth, and life, and safety,' she continued, with more assurance in her voice, enough to convince herself she was ready to look up at him, and show nothing of that damned terrible hope alive within her. The hope, that he had come to *her*. 'The allure of anonymity.'

'That's not why, Lily. That's not why I came here,' he said, and

God it sounded to her like the same battle was raging inside of him. The same doubts, the same hope tearing through *his* breast. And that longing, and sadness, they were still there, in those eyes that cut her down with a single glance, and with them was pleading. 'Why I couldn't stay away even when I tried. Why I came tonight.'

'Then why did you,' she breathed.

Slowly, as if it took all his strength to move but an inch, he rounded the desk, and came to stand beside her.

It was foolish, she knew it, but she turned to face him, and he raised his hand to her cheek, and traced the lines of it with the lightest and yet most searing touch she'd ever felt.

'What you said the other night,' he whispered, his eyes roving her face, looking at her as if she were precious, and special, and all that she thought him to be. 'That everyone has a price. That everyone wants something... Even you?'

'Even me,' she said, and his eyes came back to meet hers.

'What is it that you want Lily?'

'Something I have wanted for a while now,' she breathed.

She wanted to say the rest, wanted to tell him *you, only you*, but again her voice caught.

As she closed the distance between them, she willed him to see it in her eyes, to see all of it. But she couldn't say it, lay her heart out there for him to rip to shreds because... That was one thing she wasn't quite sure she could survive.

And the truth was, she was under no illusions.

The man was grieving, and yes, from the look in his eyes, he wanted her. But she knew who he was; and men like that... Men like that, even if they did want a woman's heart, they wouldn't want hers.

So for tonight, she would offer him comfort. She had a chance, to give him what he needed, and that was enough. She wouldn't, couldn't, muck it all up with *fantasy*.

An almost imperceptible nod, and she smiled.

'Tell me, Mr. Dudley,' she whispered, slowly leaning in ever closer, until she could feel the cold on his coat. Until her nose was touching his, and she gently nudged it, warming the winter from it, teasing, tempting. 'Is it taking you need? Or to be taken?'

∞

This wasn't why he'd come. None of this was going as he'd planned it. Yes, he'd needed to come back here, to be in her presence, but he'd thought... He'd thought he would just knock on the door to her office, and go in, and maybe they would talk for a moment. He would apologise for being an ass and walking away as he had the other night, and then perhaps they would share a drink, and he'd settle back in the chair by the fire, and just... Watch her.

At no point had he planned to tell her the truth of why he'd come here to begin with. No one knew, and that was fine, because no one needed to know that all he had left, the tiny sliver of family he'd become who he was to protect, to offer a better life to, was dead.

Morgana was dead, and that was that. It was life. And he hurt, so badly, but no one needed to know, because it mattered not. She was gone, and he had to...

Keep going.

But then he'd walked in, and seen Lily again, bathed in firelight as if she washed in it every night to survive, and he'd sworn there was joy in her eyes when she saw him, along with surprise, and unease, and he'd been undone. For the first time since he'd met her she'd been unable to look him in the eye, properly, for more than five seconds, and he'd sensed *something*, something like a desperate attempt to return to what they'd been, and he'd realised he didn't want to. He wanted her to know how she affected him, how he *needed* her, and one thing led to another, and now this?

Lily was offering, *herself*, offering him comfort, and that wasn't what he'd come for, *but God damn it*, he realised it was what he wanted. Needed. Had all along perhaps. Why else did one come to a whorehouse?

For comfort and warmth and life.

And even though he knew it wasn't true, that it wasn't anything but *her* that he needed, he tried to convince himself of it. It had been a long time since he'd been with a woman, and yes, he was grieving, and she was here, beautiful, and soft, and welcoming, and he… Wouldn't resist. Couldn't resist.

Her. Ever.

And it didn't matter that she wanted something from him - she'd been honest about it at least. It didn't matter that she didn't want him, need him, as he seemed to her, because that wasn't what this was. Even if somewhere, in the cavern that held what people called a heart, but which to him was nothing more than an organ, not a concept as they meant it; something whispered and made him want to believe *he* was the thing she wanted. There was something… Something in those wide, trusting whiskey-coloured eyes gazing up at him as if he were the world; that made him want to believe it was more for her too.

It wasn't. He needed to remember that. To remember who Lily was, who he was.

What was being offered, *comfort*; and what wasn't, *more.*

More wasn't for the likes of them, either of them.

He for one didn't deserve more. She did…

Not that I can give it.

'Taking,' he said, surrendering to the vibrant creature before him, so full of life, and youth, and a light he could take for himself, to illuminate the darkness he'd been mired in all his life.

He felt her nose slide against his as she nodded, and he inhaled deeply, taking in her scent, *nutmeg, blackberries and the earth after a Spring rain*, and let it fill his lungs, as one hand slid behind her neck, and the other grasped her hip tight, and brought her flush against him. And it was working, she was giving her vitality to him, he could feel it, seeping through her silky skin, and through the layers of her diaphanous gown, through his fingertips, through every inch of him that touched her.

And then because he could do nothing else, he closed the

infinitesimal distance between them, and captured the lips he hadn't realised until now he had fantasised about, and if he'd had any restraint at all he might've sampled, taken his time, only he didn't. That first touch broke him open, her surrender broke him, the way she melted, and opened, knowing without words what he needed, and so he did as she offered, and he took.

He grasped her so tight, nothing in his body willing to let her go, and he shook; he shook because he was holding back, and he didn't want to hurt her, but also because her taste, familiar, and yet foreign, somehow sweet, and the taste of a thousand wonders he'd never known existed threw him off balance. Threw him into a world he didn't know, and that was terrifying, because knowledge was power. Knowledge was what had given him what he'd built, but he'd never known this indescribable need for another. For the feel of her tongue sliding against his, of their lips moving in savage unison, of her teeth gently scraping across his bottom lip, and her downy curls in his hand. For a taste, for the feel of a body against his, *her body, not a body*, and this need to lose himself in another. He didn't lose himself, and yet he was, lost, and terrified of a million different things.

Needing her.

Wanting her.

Being lost in a world he didn't know.

Losing himself, scaring her, hurting her -

And maybe she knew that, how, well, he didn't want to explore the *how*, because in the next instant her own arms were sliding into his coats, along his waist, and grasping the back of his waistcoat and shirt tight, grasping him as tightly as he did her. It kindled an already raging wildfire within him, and he hadn't thought it possible, but somehow he brought her closer, held her tighter, explored the warm heat of her mouth deeper, until he couldn't breathe, and with a gasp he tore his lips from hers.

Still, he was shaking, and panting, trying to find his footing again, but when he separated far enough from her so that he could look in her eyes again, and saw the same surprise, the same wonder he felt, somehow he felt a little less adrift.

Not alone at sea anymore.

'Don't hold back,' she breathed, grasping the cloth in her hands tightly. 'Take, Mr. Dudley. Take. You won't hurt me. You won't break me.'

'Arthur,' he managed to ground out, her words unlocking a door he'd never known existed either. It was the door to that other world, and he knew it should remain shut, always, but she'd flung it open and what could he do? 'Arthur.'

'Arthur,' she repeated.

It was a plea, a promise; it was another surrender.

And there was nothing for him to do but as she commanded.

∞

If Lily hadn't already been completely lost, if she hadn't already realised how much trouble her heart was in, she would've when Mr. Dudley - *Arthur's* - lips met her own again. She would've when he gave her his name, when it felt like he gave her a piece of himself he never had before; when he gave her his own surrender even as he took.

She'd known she was in trouble before - *besotted like a damn school girl* - but she'd not known really, how one lost their head when another person touched them. She should've, should've known the danger, but she was past caring about the danger. She just wanted him, his touch, his scent, his taste, the feel of him against her, clutching her as if she was the only thing keeping him alive.

It made her head spin, made her dizzy, and irrational, a pool of goo at his feet. She'd heard people talking about feeling this, but she never had. Never felt like when another slid his tongue against yours, when he nigh-on devoured you with a passion she'd never expected, never known, and still looked at you with wonder, as if you were a treasure, that there were answers to questions she'd never dared ask, just there, within reach.

And when he took a little step and turn so that he could hoist her onto the desk, and tore off his coats, before his hands started to rove everywhere, moving her skirts so there was room for him between her legs, obeying her command to let go, and take what he would, *my soul if you wish it*, she was glad that she was in trouble. Because trouble was the most exceptional thing she'd ever felt. To be needed, to be touched by this man, it was a dream she'd never thought to dream, and yet that was real.

He was everything she'd fantasised about, but more, because he was here, in her arms, and she could touch him, and undo his trousers as he made quick work of the top of her gown, growling as he nearly ripped it in an effort to release her from it, his lips moving from her own to trail across her face, her eyebrows, her cheeks, her jaw...

And there was such tenderness in those touches beside the desperate savagery, such worship as he made his way down to her neck -

'Please,' she gasped. 'Not there,' she said, and he stilled, and she hoped it wouldn't be the end of it - but she needed him to know, she didn't want to just suffer through it as she had for so long. She wanted to enjoy this, it was her one chance to have it, to have him, and she didn't want to *bear* it. 'Not there.'

He gazed up at her, and nodded, before kissing her so gently, so sweetly, a cry sounded in her chest.

A cry of pain, because it was, torment, it hurt to feel that sort of care, and maybe it hurt him too because he broke away again and resumed his way down to her breasts, passing by her neck but stopping along her collarbone, until finally his mouth was taking a nipple and suckling, and she ran her fingers through his hair and clasped him tightly to her even as her other hand finished the job of releasing him from the confines of his undergarments and trousers.

With a grace and power she'd never thought possible, he grasped one of her hips tight as his lips made their way to the other nipple, lavishing it with the same affection as the first, his tongue swirling around it, working it to its peak, and he slid her forwards enough so that she could position his length, *so silky and potent, and impressive*, her mind noted vaguely, right where he belonged, at the entrance to her warm, slick depths, more than ready for him. His other arm slid behind her back, holding her steady, and he thrust in, no longer holding anything back from her.

Lily's head fell back, and she trusted him, to hold her, to not let her fall, and inside her chest, her heart broke open a little further, welcoming his dominion over it, yet bleeding a little from him having torn it open. But it healed itself, as he stroked inside her, quicker, harder, faster, with desperate frenzy, sewing it, *her*, all the pieces of everyone she'd ever been back together into a whole.

Gripping her even tighter to himself, on he went, his mouth peppering kisses anywhere he could, and she opened further for him, in heart and in body, offering him everything again, and so he took, and took, and took, until they were a heaving breathing mass of delicious, molten flesh, and he stilled, his peak reached inside her.

And she held him there, and held him close against her breast, stroking his head gently when it fell to her bosom, and let everything about that moment seep into her, into her bones and her soul so that it would be hers, always.

They remained there for what could've been an eternity for all she knew or cared, and then he removed himself from her, and fell to his knees, and took his handkerchief and cleaned himself off her, and it was then, as a little tear escaped her eye, that she realised she was in the most trouble a girl could be in.

She was in love with a man who could never be hers; who could never love her.

Strangely enough, heart-breaking though it was, she wasn't afraid.

Because she knew it could never have been otherwise.

VI.

'I shouldn't have done that,' Arthur ground out, trying to pull himself together as he rose, the sweet temptation before him, so glorious in her abandon it took all he had to not pull her close again. Take her again. What he'd just found... *No.* He couldn't go back there. Undiscovered worlds that tore him open like clawed fiends. And it was badly done, all of it, he'd lost himself, lost control, and he'd not even...

Satisfied her.

Though by the look of her one wouldn't have thought. By the way she held him, kept him close as he came back down... One would've thought he'd given her the world.

Enough.

The woman was incredible, and she felt like Heaven. She took him with such generosity, with such openness... But there wasn't anything *more* to it. He had to keep reminding himself of that. Because not only did *he* not deserve it, or even want it, she certainly did not want it either. She was...

Say it.

A whore.

No, she didn't practise that trade anymore, but she was. It was what she'd been, what she called herself. She knew how to give men the comfort they needed, and so she had, and he was grateful for it. But she was young, and intelligent, and strong, and feisty, and damn determined, and... He was old. Worn up by life, and with nothing to give but what he just had.

Right.

What he'd done, he'd abused her trust, and behaved like any other man, and he was better than that. She deserved better than him, and it didn't matter that he needed her, she neither wanted nor needed him. Beyond what he could do for her. Beyond what his power could do to assure her safety, her position.

Right.

Glancing back at her amidst the wreckage of her desk, papers and inkpots all asunder, not that he'd noticed or even thought to be careful before, how could he when she was all he could -

Stop.

He noticed the regret in her eyes as she straightened, covering herself from his gaze, and it was like ice-water, pulling him from his well of self-hatred.

'I only meant, you deserved better than this,' he said gently, willing that regret to go away.

She softened, and smiled, amusement sparkling in her eyes now.

'I've been taken against walls,' she said wistfully, and the blatant reminder of her past, of who, and what she was, tore at him a little. Not because of how it made him see her, it was as much a part of her as anything else, and he wouldn't change a damned thing except how annoying she could be on occasion; but because it reminded him of what *he* was then. *A client.* He nodded, and fastened his trousers. 'On tables, and chairs, the floor, and in beds. I've learned one thing. It's not the place, that matters, Mr. Dudley. It's the intention.'

He finished straightening his shirt, and nodded again.

'Arthur,' he corrected.

He shouldn't.

Not when he would have to erect barriers again between them, because there weren't enough already. Not when they could never be Arthur and Lily, two old chums, or lovers, or whatever other people could be.

The thing was, he wanted to hear it on her lips.

One last time.

'Arthur,' she repeated with an uncertain smile he wasn't sure he'd ever seen before.

God, it is better than I imagined.

Which was certainly not good.

Everything about her was tempting him to believe there could be more, that there was more, but he knew well and good it couldn't be. And he now had to do the last thing he wanted, which was to ensure he knew where precisely they stood. Whilst also thanking her, and *not* telling her all he had felt.

Christ.

'Lily, I...'

'There is no need for that,' she smiled gently, twisting her hair into a knot as she slid off the desk.

'Right,' he agreed. *Back to business then.* Well. Good. 'I should go.'

'You could stay a while,' she offered casually, glancing over to the drinks cabinet. 'Have a drink.'

'I need to go,' he amended.

'Of course,' she said lightly.

The look of disappointment that flashed across her face belied her words however, and nearly undid his resolve.

Leave.

'I will come back,' he heard himself promise. Because he would. In time. At some point. This was partly his business after all, and just leaving it, *her*, was impossible. He just couldn't deal with *this*, right now. 'We can discuss whatever it is you want then,' he added, going to find his hat.

When had it even come off?

'What?'

'We can discuss what you want when I come back,' he said, turning back to her.

She looked so confused, frowning, staring at him as though he were a dunce.

'What I want,' she repeated, and God her voice was so hollow. *Oh no.* 'Of course,' she said slowly, understanding washing over her along with pain. *No, no, no.* 'My price. For this,' she said, with a bitter laugh, gesturing between them. *What did you do, you idiot?* There was a sheen in her eyes that looked an awful lot like tears, and his gut churned, and that thing that he refused to call a heart twisted inside him at the sight of her pain. 'Once a whore, always a whore, right, Arthur?'

No.

'Lily -'

'Don't,' she warned. He had hurt her, beyond repair, he knew it, but still she stood strong and proud. 'Whatever you're thinking of saying, or doing just now, don't. It's not necessary. I understand completely.'

No, you don't...

'Lily, please -'

'Go,' she breathed, her voice cracking, cutting him like daggers. 'Just, go.'

Leaving was the last thing he wanted to do.

But he did.

Because she asked him to.

And because he knew, that even though he hated what had happened, hated that he'd hurt her, it was likely for the best in the end.

A clean break.

∞

As soon as the door closed, Lily did something she hadn't done in a very, very long time. Not since they'd taken Kit from her. She crumpled, all her strength, her will to fight, gone, and she sobbed. She sat on the floor, right there, beside her desk, and buried her face in her hands, and cried, and cried, and cried.

Every tear helped a little, helped expel, lessen the hurt from the gaping wound she bore from his words. When they'd been together, he'd cut open her heart, and that had hurt, but in a good way, only this... It felt as if he'd slashed daggers across her chest, across her belly, until all that was left were gaping wounds.

It wasn't as if she didn't know what she was, didn't know all that meant she couldn't have. It wasn't as if she didn't know he was far, far above her in so many ways. She might've realised that she loved him, but it wasn't as if she expected him to make similar declarations. But to her, at least, they had shared something...

Special.

She hadn't, for one second, been Lily the Tart, or Miss Lily. Only herself, Lily, a girl like any other, and he'd only been a man, not a hardened criminal or businessman. He hadn't been St. Nick or Mr. Dudley - but *Arthur*.

True, she *was* the one who had said she wanted something, and not specified *what* - but she'd thought for the smallest second that he'd understood her. Known that even if she couldn't admit she wanted *him*, that he would at least *know* she wanted him. That she wanted to be with him as they had. She'd thought he'd seen her as something other than a whore.

Something other than what you are.

It had never bothered her before, that word. She used it freely, because it took away others' power with it. She'd never been bothered by any other of the myriad words people shouted at her when they weren't shouting *for* her. Some said it was the oldest profession in the world, and truth be told, she was good at it. She could sense what people needed, become who and what they needed, and give it to them. She could feed herself, and her sister, for a time at least, and she had only herself to rely on. She chose her hours, and her clients, and yes, there was danger at every corner, but that was the world they lived in. There was danger working in the kilns, and danger working the wharves, and danger working the fields. She'd never been ashamed of being a whore.

Until now.

And maybe it wasn't so much shame as... Anger.

Anger at all that meant she couldn't have.

Which was stupid, really, because she'd known that before

now - known that when she'd offered herself to Arthur - *Mr. Dudley* - but she hadn't quite felt it in all its searing, gory truth.

Lily had always been a dreamer - but a practical one. She made sure her dreams were within her reach. That they were... Achievable.

Make money. Find Kit.

Make more money and build a home for Kit and I.

Start a business, help the others like me. Make a safe place.

Be successful enough to make sure she or anyone else in her care or protection would never be without again.

Be with Arthur, if only for a moment, even though I know he can't be mine.

They were good dreams.

Simple dreams, but good ones. They were what got her up every day, and kept her going past all the terrible things she'd endured and done. They were her reason to keep going. And none had ever really been snatched away so viciously, so cruelly before.

That's what made her hurt so badly, what made her angry. That Arthur - *Mr. Dudley goddammit* - hadn't allowed her to keep her silly little dream.

Yes, well, it's gone now. No use cryin' over spilt milk and all.

Right.

She was... Stronger than this. Better than this simpering, and crying, and behaving like a heartbroken idiot. Yes, it hurt. Life bloody well hurt. And sitting here, sniffling, and leaking like a flowerpot, achieved nothing.

So what that he'd snatched away her little dream? She was glad of it, she told herself, wiping her leaky nose on her sleeve as she crawled to her feet. In fact, she wasn't angry at him, she was grateful. That he'd reminded her where they stood. Now, she could move on from her foolish little love for him, and do what she was supposed to be doing all the while she was mooning at him.

Right.

Rubbing her eyes with the palms of her hands, she shook

some sense back into herself. She had work to do. So she would go clean up, wash the man right off her, and then... She would get back to work.

Dreams of love are not for you.
Dreams of love are for fools.

VII.

'**M**orning Bill,' Lily said brightly as he strode in, just like every other morning, to have their daily meeting. She always had one with the workers, later, before the doors opened, and after they'd all recovered from the night before, and she always had one with Bill, who'd become her right hand. She'd been grateful more than ever for him the past four days, a steady rock to cling to in a stormy sea.

After her little... Moment on the floor five nights ago, she'd picked herself up, and done as she knew she had to. She'd gotten back to work, and become Miss Lily yet again. The anger, the pain still fresh in her breast, were good. They drove her onwards.

And whenever she was feeling a bit low, a bit listless, a bit... Sad, she had Bill.

Bill, who made sure everything ran smoothly with her security men, and St. Nick's, and the rest of her staff. It was strange really, how much she'd come to rely on him.

How much she trusted him considering how they'd met, and how little she truly knew of him.

'Good mornin', Miss Lily,' Bill said, tearing her from those dark days.

'We've a lice problem in the top bedrooms,' she began when he reached her desk. 'I might need your help cleaning things from there later, and if you can help the girls move to the spare bedrooms - though make sure they understand no linens. I don't want a repeat of Christmas. And we've got that extra whiskey coming in a couple days - late - I'll need you there, make sure it gets here in one piece. I'm to Sarah's to see how the mask costumes are going.'

'Aye, Miss Lily. If I can ask - why'd you want me on the whiskey? The other lads -'

'There's trouble brewing,' she said, finally turning her gaze from the papers before her, more bills and letters and accounts that she was actually grateful for as they kept her mind busy, *mostly.* That feeling, in her gut, that she couldn't shake, that kept her mind busy too. 'I can feel it. And I think you can too, Bill.'

He nodded, and she felt inordinately relieved that it wasn't just her.

That she wasn't imagining things - not that she wanted trouble - but that someone else felt the change in the air. The whisper of things to come on the wind.

The restlessness - like that before a storm.

'Ye should know Winston's been runnin' his mouth about gettin' Joce back,' he offered, and she let that sit for a moment, trying to determine if *that* was what she felt coming. 'And givin' ye what ye deserve.'

No... Winston isn't the storm that's brewin'... It's somethin' else...

'Somehow I'm not surprised,' she sighed, focusing on the conversation at hand rather than imaginary tempests. 'Just... Keep eyes on him. Yours, when you can.'

'What about you?'

'What about me?'

'I'm watchin' him, I ain't watchin' you. Ye should ask Saint Nick's men -'

'I can watch my own back,' she said, harsher than she meant.

Sighing, she turned her gaze back to the paperwork.

'Ye alright, Miss Lily?'

'Yes,' she snapped again.

Damn it.

'Ye seem... Well ye ain't glowin' no more.'

'Glowing,' she repeated dumbly, staring up at the man as if he had three heads.

Which he didn't, but still - Bill was being... Odd.

Glowing?

'Aye. For a time there, ye seemed happy.'

Because I was, she thought grimly, disappointed that she was so transparent, and that despite all her promises, and all her efforts these past days, she couldn't just... Move on.

Still letting a man take hold of your emotions.

Even Bill noticed.

Which was saying something indeed.

'If we survive all this year is set to bring us,' she shrugged, forcing a dismissive, carefree, entirely false smile on her face. 'I'll be happy again.'

The bruiser who was so much more than he looked narrowed his eyes and pursed his lips as if desperately wanting to say something, but instead of giving into his own urges, he simply nodded.

'Until later, Miss Lily.'

'Later, Bill.'

She stared at the empty doorway long after his form had disappeared from it.

Didn't matter what Bill said. That she *had* been glowing, and happy, for an instant. That time was over now. And if she truly wished to *move on*, and make what she dreamed of herself, well, she would have to start moving.

To Sarah's then.

What an excellent notion.

∞

It had been four days. *Four.* Since he'd left Lily looking as if he'd carved out her heart, and stomped on it; left her bleeding right there on the rug she'd chosen especially for her office. There weren't many things he'd ever felt truly guilty for in his life. Because most terrible things he'd done had been about necessity. He never took a life without reason - never hurt anyone without reason. The world was a harsh cruel place, and yes, he was someone who in some ways made it so. Or rather, perpetuated it.

To survive and ensure the survival of many others.

For he'd also tried to do good. Tried to have a code, a rulebook to ensure he wasn't as bad as the rest of them; wasn't as bad as those who had forged him into what he was, and taught him all he needed to know about the world. Those who truly dealt in horror, and pain, as if true demons of Hell on Earth. The only thing he'd ever really felt guilty about was lying to his sister about who he truly was. Where the money came from. But that too, had been done out of necessity.

What he'd done to Lily...

That had been born of his own need to pull back. To be the man of reason he was, to keep *himself* safe. It hadn't been intentional, no, but still, it gnawed at him. Like a little rat in his soul, gnawing away at the tiny sliver that was still untainted. Good, in some way.

He felt like a bastard. Like a man he'd sworn never to be.

Lily, she was... Despite all she'd likely seen in her life, her strength and fierceness, a lioness; underneath, he knew, *felt* her sweetness. The innocence of her heart, and soul. She was *good*. In every possible way. A sweet, kind soul, and he'd... Hurt her. It was like kicking a puppy, or a child. It wasn't bloody right.

And you are a bloody right bastard.

It tormented him as not much had ever tormented him before.

The worst part?

He still knew however terrible what had happened was, it was for the best. They had crossed a line, and they needed to cross right back over it to where they each belonged. There was something happening in Shadwell, and his business, *businesses*, were at the heart of it. He needed a clear head, and focus, and not to be...

Well, there was no room in his life for anything other than business. In truth, it was how it had always been, and how it would always be. Sure, he'd thought about, *hoped* really, for a little something more, but that hadn't been meant to be, and that was for the best. People in his life, in any capacity, ran the risk of being hurt, and not just in spirit.

The River Police hadn't found anything to lead them to the culprits of the attack on Crown Street, and neither had his own men. Not that Arthur was surprised. Particularly not when the bodies of five men washed up on the banks of Rotherhithe, members of Waterman Tom's crew. He didn't know how, but he knew, those had been the men to attack his house in Crown Street. Though he also doubted Waterman Tom, rival though he may be, to be behind all this. Even involved. It didn't quite sit right - not that he wouldn't look into it further.

Someone is cleaning up their mess as they go along.

No loose tongues; no clues.

And there had been more attacks. On his legitimate holdings - again, he was lucky no one had been injured, his men actually able to take on the attackers, though sadly that meant they had killed them - and on his illegitimate ones. One of his smuggling routes upriver had been compromised, he'd lost twenty men, and that outlet west. Someone was after him, *both of him*, and he didn't bloody well have a clue as to who or why.

It felt... Big. Larger than any enemy he'd faced before. It felt coordinated. And the only whispers he actually heard - were from the Wapping and Rotherhithe gangs like Tom's - also under attack. The sheer scale, the manpower, the resources, something like this took...

For the first time in a very long time, Arthur felt out of his depth. For twenty years, he'd ruled Shadwell from the shadows. Building the largest, most successful criminal enterprise the place had ever seen. And he'd done it with only a small amount of bloodshed, and a lot of cunning. He'd seen other bosses come and go, felt some trying to come after him and his, but he'd never been outmatched.

Even by the Ghost of Shadwell, the circle of vigilantes Viscount Egerton had created with an ex-sailor called Cal. At first, the two of them had roamed the streets of Shadwell, taking down those who preyed on its inhabitants and visitors, then, over the years, they had become an army. The viscount had formally stepped away from the Ghost's mantle when he married Meg Lowell, a lighterman's daughter, but before that, Egerton had tried to find St. Nick. He'd never succeeded, and as Arthur helped just as much to keep the peace, the Ghost had relented, and let him be.

This new threat however…

Was something completely new.

And Arthur had a feeling he might have to try something equally novel.

Ask for help.

Perhaps the time had come for an alliance.

Perhaps I should speak to some of those Ghosts…

But first, he had some tenants to visit. To reassure, to put at ease.

Later, he could go find a Ghost to talk to.

Right now, he had to be Arthur Dudley. Kind, good, landlord.

Because in the end, he really didn't have much else.

∞

'Lily,' Sarah exclaimed when she opened the door, wearing a bright smile. 'What a surprise,' she continued, bursting out to enfold Lily in her arms, hugging her tightly. Lily didn't hesitate to enjoy the demonstration of affection, holding on tightly in return, enjoying the comfort and warmth of her friend. It soothed her in a way nothing else these past days had, and she congratulated herself on thinking to come here.

'Came to see how those costumes were comin' along,' Lily mumbled into Sarah's bosom.

Sarah, like everyone else really, was so much taller than her. Often, it annoyed her; once, it had scared her, being a small, little thing in a world of big bad things, but today, being enveloped in her taller friend's embrace was absolute perfection.

'Good,' Sarah smiled, pulling away, giving Lily a quick, but sharp once-over. 'Tea?'

'Aye, please.'

They wandered in, Sarah closing the door then marching on ahead to get tea started.

Lily took a moment to soak in the place which had once been her home. Nearly a year she'd been in London by the time Sarah had found her. She'd tried different areas, Covent Garden, Whitechapel, until finally she'd come to Shadwell hoping to find cheaper lodgings, and more customers. Life hadn't been easy until then, it had been Hell really, and not any better when she'd come here.

But then she'd met Sarah one night, as she'd tried to get away from a drunken bunch that her gut had told her she *definitely should under no circumstances* go with, and Sarah had not only told them in poetically colourful foul language where they could go for the remainder of the evening, she'd taken Lily under her wing.

That meant, not only sharing the better spots with her, but a room, and a safe place to lay her head at night. There was no doubt in Lily's mind that Sarah had saved her life that night. And in the four years she'd lived here, they had shared so much. Happy times, sad times. As Sarah navigated her grief from losing her parents, and the joy of meeting her husband Jonah. Together, they had scrimped and saved to make this place the home it was now. Not just a room, but a warm, safe haven.

It was small, simple, with wood floors and white-washed walls, boasting two rooms off from a main living area and kitchen, with windows that looked over the rooftops and chimneys of the neighbouring houses. The sturdy and worn oak table and chairs were the same as they'd been when Lily first came, as was one of the armchairs, Sarah's father's, but they'd bought those other armchairs to set by the hearth. That chestnut table, they'd found when one of the better houses near where Art - *Mr. Dudley* - lived was emptied, and the rug Jonah had won from someone at cards one night at the Queen Anne's.

And all the little touches, the porcelain figures on the mantel, the white cotton curtains, the new range, all the kitchen ware, even the bedding in the other rooms that she couldn't see but knew remained, all of it, they'd chosen together.

Like a family.

It had felt so good to feel that again. Safety, belonging. After Kit had been taken, Lily hadn't ever thought she could find that again, not until she found Kit. But life had surprised her, as it was wont to do.

And she was grateful beyond words for that. Because she'd been in danger, of losing hope. Of becoming someone she wasn't. Of losing strength. Losing her will. But life here, with Sarah, friends throughout it all, had taught her one lesson: *never give up.*

And here is where you met him...

Shaking her head, Lily tore herself from her little reverie of nostalgia, and joined Sarah at the kitchen table, setting her hat, gloves, and coat on a chair as her friend began pouring them cups of tea from the cracked little set that had been Jonah's first gift to her.

So much love. In cracked and worn porcelain.

'How's Jonah?' Lily asked, forcing herself to remain focused as her mind and heart threatened to run away with her again.

'Busy, but good,' Sarah sighed, smiling into her tea. 'So's Renata,' she continued, mentioning the girl who had first come to Lily's for work, but that she'd instead sent to Sarah. The room that had been Lily's had needed filling, and Sarah needed more helpers at the Silver Bell refectory. Even if she hadn't, the refectory had been so successful that five other wharves had started one; so there was an abundance of that work going now. 'But then I think we've all been busy. 'Aven't seen you since you brought the fabric by.'

'Yes, the house has been busy,' Lily offered as an excuse. Which wasn't technically one, they *had* been busy, but then, if she had wanted to carve out time for her friend, she could've. Why she hadn't... Well. That wasn't worth examining just now. Needless to say it had something to do with living in her little bubble of hazy infatuation. 'Which is good.'

'Good, good.'

They both looked at each other, and smiled, before bursting out laughing.

God it feels good to laugh.

'I'm sorry for not coming by,' Lily said softly, gazing down at her tea, wishing her future was written at the bottom of it. 'Everything's changed so much, and I...'

'I understand.' Sarah reached out and lay her hand on Lily's with a gentle smile. 'Life changes things.'

'I miss our dinners together.'

'So do I,' Sarah said. 'You should come over some time. Perhaps I can even convince Meg to drop by quietly.'

'How is Meg?' Lily forced herself to ask with a bright smile and interest.

It wasn't that she had anything against Meg, *Viscountess Egerton, actually,* as she should be called. She'd liked her when they'd first met last year, still only a lighterman's daughter as she'd been. And she was happy for her, for all the love and joy, for the life she'd found with her mad viscount. But at the same time, she still had a pang of envy whenever she thought of the woman who had nearly become Mrs. Dudley.

When she thought of all Meg was, that she was not and could never be.

All that means I could never be his.

'Alright,' Sarah said, eyeing Lily with a question in her eyes. She forced herself to drink the tea rather than grip the cup and potentially smash it. 'Goin' off to Cornwall soon, when the foundling home is officially open, though she's right mad about it.' Ah yes. The foundling home. The Viscountess' pet project that she'd started with her grandmother in law, the little Fitzsimmons chit that was always coming round the house like some explorer of new worlds, and Mr. Dudley. *Always him.* 'Only she's been workin' herself too hard again, and I think his lordship is worried. It's still early, and a secret, but she's with child,' Sarah added conspiratorially.

Lily smiled, genuinely this time.

She was happy for the viscountess.

'Do pass on my congratulations. I doubt I'll see her before she leaves.'

'I will,' Sarah nodded. 'She asked about you.'

'That's nice.'

'What's troublin' you, Lily?'

'Hm?'

'You came to see your costumes, and you've not pestered me to see them.'

'Only a bit distracted, that's all,' Lily said dismissively with a less than convincing smile.

'By...?'

'By nothing,' she shrugged. 'By everything. Trying to prepare for that damned bill coming up.' The Vagrancy Act - set to be passed in the summer - was a well-known secret among those who would actually suffer for it. And people like Lily were scrambling to ensure they had protection when it came into effect. 'Trying to deal with lice,' she continued. 'And that worm Winston, and make plans for the future, and the mask, and -'

'And...?'

'What about you, Sarah?' she asked, changing tactics.

'Busy with the sewin', busy with the wharf. Nothin' new. Tell me. Ain't we friends?'

Yes, of course they were.

And it wasn't as if they hadn't talked about anything and everything when Lily lived here, their trade was sex - and so it had been a popular topic of discussion. But speaking of what had happened with Art - *Mr. Dudley dammit girl!* - was an entirely different beast altogether.

Sarah might've shared about Jonah - but that too was a different beast.

'We are,' Lily reassured her, hoping to get her off the scent. She should've known it was a bad idea coming here, even if they hadn't been friends for so long, Sarah had as sharp a gaze as she did when it came to people. 'But it's not even worth talkin' 'bout and wastin' me breath.'

'Your accent slips when you get emotional, Lily.'

'No point gettin' emotional, he's gone and that's good.'

Isn't that the damned truth of it?

'Mr. Dudley?' Sarah asked softly, and had Lily not been sitting she might've fallen to the floor in shock. As it was, it took everything she had to remain upright, staring at her friend, her mouth open and welcoming for any flies that might care to drop in. 'You know there ain't no secrets in this place. He's been visitin' every night for weeks.'

'Could've been visitin' one of the girls,' Lily offered weakly, recovering her voice.

'With the way you look at him?' Sarah asked, raising a brow. *Have I really been so transparent?* But then, yes, she supposed she had. When she'd lived here, and Mr. Dudley passed by to visit, or collect the rent, always himself, and always in person, she supposed even then her interest had shown. She'd called it fascination back then, interest in the mystery he was, but now she couldn't even fool herself. She'd been infatuated from the first. By his strength, and his kindness, and those damned eyes of his. 'So what happened?'

'Fell in love with him, didn't I, idiot that I am,' she admitted, defeated. No point in trying to hide it now, Sarah could probably read the words written all over her anyways. Proof: Sarah nodded understandingly. 'It's not like I had illusions,' she added, needing her friend to know for some reason that she wasn't the foolish country girl she hadn't been for a very long time but that many still saw her as, just because she dared, sometimes, to dream. 'But I did think... Don't know what I thought.'

'That you weren't a whore to him?'

And there it was.

The core truth that Mr. Dudley had speared her with - that she *was* - and always would be to him.

Nothing more.

Lily nodded weakly.

'Like I said,' she laughed bitterly. 'Foolish and not worth my breath.'

'Have you told him how you feel?'

'Pssshaw. Why would I do that?' Lily asked, staring at Sarah as though she too possessed three heads.

I was glowing and now I should confess my heart to a man that -
That nothing.

'Maybe there's somethin' for him,' Sarah said, shrugging slightly.

'No, why would I do that? What's the point?' she asked, clarifying. 'It's not like we'll get married someday and retire to the country together.'

'You never know. I found Jonah, and I was a whore.'

'It's not the same. Mr. Dudley is...'

'Better than Jonah? A gentleman?' Sarah offered, a cutting edge to her voice.

'That's not what I meant,' she sighed. She hadn't meant to hurt her friend's feelings, but it wasn't like she could lay out all that Mr. Dudley was. His life was built on secrecy, and no matter what he'd done, she wouldn't betray him, risk his life like that. 'It's complicated,' she continued, trying to explain without divulging the truth. 'There's things about him you don't know, and...'

'But you do know?' Sarah supplied, the hurt vanishing and making way for interest. 'Hm.'

'*Hm?* What does *hm* mean?'

Sarah and her annoyingly knowing *hms*.

'All anyone knows of Mr. Dudley is what we see,' Sarah said simply. 'If there's somethin' more, and you know it... Perhaps that means somethin'.'

'Perhaps... I should get a look at those costumes now.'

Sarah nodded, smiling a knowing smile at Lily's refusal to continue any further down the path of speculation.

And so they rose, and Sarah led Lily to her bedroom where the mask costumes waited. They were glorious, and beyond anything she'd ever dreamt, but even as the incredible creations enchanted her, she couldn't quite dismiss Sarah's words entirely.

They swirled around in her mind, in her heart, endlessly, reviving the flame of hope she had thought she'd killed.

'Perhaps that means somethin'.'

Perhaps...

VIII.

Oh bloody brilliant, Lily thought as she stepped out of Sarah's building and spotted the last man she ever wanted to see again across the street. Over the last hour she'd been with Sarah, looking at costumes and discussing more, along with all the other bells and whistles to match them, Lily had finally managed to put away the *perhaps* niggling her into the little box in her heart where she kept the dangerous dreams.

Dreams like finding Kit, and living a quiet, beautiful life, happily ever after; and where she now kept similar dreams regarding the man currently standing a few feet away.

But...

But nothin' ya daft moppet. Move along.

So she did, scurrying away down the street, not running away *per se*, simply moving along, back towards her *real life*. She thought for a moment she might escape, he was speaking to one of his tenants, back to her, but just as she turned to take the long way back to the house, through the dark labyrinth of covered streets and alleys, he turned towards her, touching the brim of his hat in farewell to the woman he'd been speaking to.

Damn.

His eyes widened when he saw her, then narrowed with determination.

Damn, damn, damn.

'Mr. Dudley,' she said curtly, nodding her head, still scurrying.

There.

She had acknowledged his presence.

Been polite.

She would not stop.

She would not look at him.

She would keep her head high, and get back to the house, and that was it.

Anything else...

She wasn't quite ready for.

It wasn't like he should even want to engage more than that, on the street. Their connection, though apparently spoken about, was delineated by certain rules. *Whore. Client.* And whores and clients met at certain times, in certain places, and really, that's all she was to him, so here, in the daylight, with him as the kind businessman Mr. Dudley, well, they really had nothing to say to each other after all.

Quite so.

'Lily,' he called, hastening after her as she continued on her way. 'Please, wait.'

She didn't care that he sounded contrite, and desperate. She didn't care that apparently *he* had forgotten the rules, or that he was changing them. She didn't care, not one bit, about any of it.

No sir-ee.

'Terribly busy I'm afraid,' she said in clipped tones over her shoulder.

Those elocution lessons she'd taken really had paid off handsomely.

'You cannot avoid me forever,' he warned, ducking behind her as she turned into a brick-tunnelled alley, which would take even longer to get her home, but which was nice, and narrow.

'I can avoid you for a while,' she retorted.

She didn't care that he knew she was doing it.

She didn't care that they were supposed to be *business associates* yet again and that *business associates* could talk to each other without venom, without resentment, without bloody heartbreak in the middle of the day.

The mortification, the shame, the disappointment, she couldn't keep it all in check when he was here, and the last thing she needed was for him to see it.

That would just make it infinitely worse.

Showing her hand, that she cared beyond the simple insult of it...

Not possible.

'Just give me a chance,' he pleaded.

'Why?' she exclaimed, her damned emotions getting the better of her. She rounded back on him, and immediately wished she hadn't when she spotted those bright silver eyes that looked as downcast as a puppy's even in the low light of the alley. 'To do what, Arthur?' she asked through the knot in her throat, hating herself for slipping and not saying *Mr. Dudley.* 'Apologise? You have nothing to apologise for,' she stated proudly. *Good girl. Look at you.* 'We had a simple misunderstanding, that is all.' *Ain't that the truth?* 'You got what you came for, now we can go back to business as usual, which is us rarely ever having to see each other.'

She turned back, and marched on through the maze that was this part of Shadwell.

Her heart twisted as she passed the old Lowell house, the reminder of Meg, and all Art - *Mr. Dudley* - had offered her a fresh sting.

'I don't want that, Lily.'

'Well, I'm afraid I'm not open for business,' she bit back, proud that she was managing to speak coherently, and push back the relentless flicker of hope that whispered for her to stop, and hear him out, and give him whatever he damn well wished. 'That was a one-time only happening for you, and now I am back to my retirement.'

'That's not what I want either,' he ground out. Lily stopped, and turned to raise an eyebrow at him. 'Fine, it's part of what I want,' he sighed, frustrated, and she might've laughed had she not been on the verge of... *Throwing myself at his feet again and imploring him for things he can't give.* 'But I don't just want that,' he pressed. *Things like those words suggest.* 'I want...'

'What, Arthur,' she said, as flatly as she could whilst also stamping out the hope that was flickering within, higher and higher; more powerful than she could tame into submission just now. *Not again...* 'What *do* you want?'

'You,' he said simply, and yet there was nothing simple about that proclamation. Her heart stopped; that one single word the one which had brought them to this place to begin with. Sighing, she closed her eyes for a moment and shook her head. 'I handled everything so poorly the other night,' he continued, taking the advantage her silence had given him. 'Because the truth is, it terrified me. You terrify me,' he said softly. Her heart beat again, but it skipped a few as it resumed pounding in her chest, the flame untameable, stealing her breath and reason, and she looked up to him, surprised. She couldn't believe it, and yet, the truth of it was there, in his eyes. In his uncertain manner. The unbelievable truth that *she* could scare the man she didn't think feared anything at all. Just as he terrified her. 'More than anything else I face,' he continued, taking a tentative step closer to her. 'I didn't... I couldn't let myself believe that you weren't...'

'Asking for payment?'

'Yes.'

'I thought... I couldn't say it,' she confessed, her voice weaker than she wished. The damned hope within her just wouldn't die, growing until it was an unquenchable inferno. She shouldn't be listening, shouldn't be speaking all she was about to, because even if the hope was right, this, whatever *this* was, it still wasn't right. It wouldn't end well. It would end with her shattered, and broken, and likely dead. 'You have no idea what it's like, to want what you can't have,' she sighed, her voice tight. She was dooming herself with her own words, but she didn't care. She couldn't live with them in her breast, clutched tightly anymore. 'I don't want to be one of those women who deludes themselves. Who asks for what can never be given. Who hopes. But it was only ever you I wanted.'

'I know, Lily,' he whispered, coming even closer now, so that there was barely an inch between them. And God help her, it didn't feel wrong, and dangerous, and stupid; yet again, it felt right. *He knew.* 'I cannot make promises. You know that.' She nodded, her hand moving of its own volition to land on his chest. 'And I... I do know what it feels like to want what you can't have,' he said, his hands coming to hold her face, his thumbs sliding across her cheeks, and yet again there was that awe in his eyes, that wonder, and God help her, but she was definitely lost. 'I wish I could offer you the world. I wish I could pretend to be anything other than who I am. But I can't. All I can offer you is time.'

The mercury-tinted eyes she adored held a resolve, and a promise, that broke everything and anything she could still hold on to, that would keep her heart as safe as it could be considering the circumstances.

The next hurt, the next time he left her, when the promised time was over, it might just kill her. Or at least, whatever was left of herself that could believe in beautiful dreams.

But even knowing that, she also knew there really was no choice.

There never had been when it came to him.

He was offering something incredible, a chance, *time*, and their time might not last for eternity, but her love would.

The memories would.

So she did all she could do, and nodded.

∞

At least two things were consistent when it came to Lily, and somehow the knowledge of that was reassuring. He lost his reason, and nothing went according to plan. Two of the things which had ensured his survival, his rise of the past twenty years. Two things which, if lost, could get him killed. But when it came to her...

All bets are off.

He hadn't meant to say all that he had. Admit, all he had.

He hadn't meant to promise anything, not even time.

But one glimpse... And it was like a part of himself he didn't know, or perhaps had known, once, sprang forth and took control. It was the only explanation really.

How else to explain today's events? Yes, he'd been thinking on her, incessantly, but he hadn't *done* anything about it. He'd said he would be the good kind landlord, and so he had been, right up until that second when he'd glimpsed her. And something had changed, in a split second, his body no longer accepting his mind's commands. Before he knew it, he'd bid his tenants good day, and followed her, pursued her, speaking in no hushed tones, caring not one bit for who saw him with her. *Pursuing* her. Wanting her; needing her.

Because one glimpse had been a shining moment of truth, a slap in the face telling him in no uncertain terms that there was no going back to being *business associates.* There was no going back to whatever it was they had been. There was only forward. The natural progression to what they'd truly been all along.

He'd known that he needed to make things right, to beg her forgiveness, to implore her for one last chance. He couldn't offer much, that was true, but even a second of her light, her comfort; a single moment in the world he discovered with her, and he could die a happy man. Something he'd never thought possible. And by some miracle, the words had just come out. Things he hadn't known until his mouth said them. That she terrified him. That he'd known all along that she truly only ever wanted *him*. It was...

Magical.

And what was even more magical, incredible, miraculous, was that she'd accepted him and his pittance of an offer. She, the wonder, had forgiven him, and accepted what little he had to offer, and now those amber eyes that tormented his dreams, waking and not, were gazing at him again, as if she was the lucky one.

And he knew all the rest - the fear, the resolve, the wonder, the surprise of what they'd stumbled upon, all that he felt - shone in them too. For the first time in a long time, he was embarking on an unknown voyage, but not alone.

Together, they could find somewhere beautiful, for a time.

To seal the pact, he slowly lowered his head, closing the final few inches of distance between them, and kissed her. He was trembling again, not with unrestrained need, but with excitement, and with fear, yes, a little. It was a slow, agonisingly sweet, gentle kiss, and it felt like returning home.

How had he survived five days without her, in his hands, her taste on his lips, sighing, soft beneath him? How had he survived this long life without her? God only knew.

And he... Really couldn't care. Because here, now, he had her. Breathing life and vitality into him again, her tongue and lips moulding and playing gently with his own, and that was enough.

On a breath, he pulled back, resting his forehead against hers, but not releasing her face, and slowly he opened his eyes to meet hers.

God she's beautiful. And mine. All mine.

For now...

'Can I come to you tonight?' he asked because even though he wanted her more than anything, right now, somehow he felt he needed to do things... Differently this time. In a bed, where he could properly worship her, with plenty of time to spare and no responsibility plaguing either of them, for a few hours at least. 'When the house closes?'

'I'll be waiting,' she smiled, and so did he, and wasn't that wondrous too?

'Three o'clock then,' he stated, bending down for one last, quick kiss, which was anything but simple.

Three o'clock, when the last of the house's customers were summarily dismissed.

'Three o'clock,' she repeated, and God help him, but she sounded as giddy as he felt.

It felt like there was more to say, so much more, but the words didn't come to him just then, and so he nodded, and turned to leave, before changing his mind, stealing one last kiss, and then, finally, leaving.

Three tomorrow morning can't come soon enough.

IX.

L ily hadn't been this nervous, this jittery, this... *Alive*, in well, ever. Because she'd never really had anything to be nervously excited about before. Sure, when she'd been a child, there had been Yuletide, and birthdays, that her parents had always seen fit to celebrate as much and well as they could. There had been fêtes, and fairs, and even the opening of this, her business. Her pride and joy.

But with all those things, there had been a sense of... *Knowledge.* That tamped down the excitement and wonder, just a tiny little bit. She knew what Christmas and birthdays contained. She knew the wonders of fairs and fêtes. At least, she couldn't remember the time before remembering. And when it came to opening *Miss Lily's*... She'd known, in her heart, that it would be a success. She'd known that when she'd marched up to Mr. Dudley's - *Arthur's* - door, and presented her idea. So when the time came to actualize it, well, she'd known. It would be good.

Tonight, however, she was leaping, feet first into an abyss she knew nothing of. It was exhilarating, but also, tiresome. The hours since he'd asked to come to her, had been tiresome. The routine of it all, the work, the waiting, staring endlessly at the clock ticking away, had been exhausting. Because she was on edge, and excited, and giddy, and it felt like something incredible was waiting, just beyond a door she'd never known existed, but she didn't have the key yet, and was instead forced to stare at it, wondering.

Which in fact, was precisely what she was actually doing.

Staring at a door.

The door to her private room.

She'd finally finished all her work, informed Bill of tonight's visitor, and instructed him to tell Arthur the way to her room. If he had any thoughts on the matter, which he certainly did, considering the face he made, *surprise, a little bit of amusement, some reserve*, well, he said nothing. Which was for the best. The last thing she needed was to hear that she was glowing again or something. She was nervous enough already, and the thing was, she needed...

She needed to not get caught up in all this. It was wonderful what was happening, but there were limits to what would happen. And getting caught up in her own happiness risked... Well, it risked tipping Arthur off as to her true feelings, and she'd said she didn't want to be the woman who asked for more, and him knowing she actually *loved* him felt like making demands. Which she wouldn't do. She wouldn't ruin this chance at something, *anything*, before it even began. Blossomed.

Breathe.

She did, glancing at herself again in the mirror above the mantel as she paced before the hearth for perhaps the thousandth time in the past ten minutes. She looked...

Like you're glowing.

It was just the candlelight. And the slight blush in her cheeks. And the light in her eyes. And the gold satin nightdress and robe she'd donned for him after washing. That's all -

A knock interrupted her thoughts again, *thankfully*, and she managed to force out a semi-strangled *come in* as she turned to it.

The bells of St. Paul's Shadwell rang out three as he stepped into the room, looking more handsome than she'd ever thought possible. Her heart, traitorous little thing it was, leapt straight out to greet him, landing in his hands, for safe keeping, not that he would ever know.

He had dressed for this occasion too, and she didn't really care what Bill might say right now - *that I'm definitely glowing* - because it showed... Something she didn't want to name. The fact that he'd dressed in a finer suit than he wore on the street, that he'd washed, and tidied his beard, it meant so much to her.

It means he cares.

'Hello,' she smiled weakly, and he strode to her, producing a posy of violets from somewhere unknown.

Her eyes widened and she gazed up at him, completely lost now.

'Hello,' he smiled back, his eyes flitting across her face.

∞

Here she was again, throwing him off balance, and surprising him. With the care she'd taken, with herself, with this room, to make this night something special. He'd done so too, because *she* was special, and important, vital to him somehow, and he'd needed to demonstrate that in any small way he could, *bathing, dressing, flowers*, but he'd never expected this.

If he was honest, the truth of it was that he'd never expected *her*. He'd never expected, never believed it possible, that someone like her, *young, smart, beautiful, a wonder, really*, could want him. *Care* for him. Because try as he might to deny it, he could feel it. In every gesture, every glance of those now dark amber eyes, every tentative smile, every blush. He'd turned away from it, ignored it, even as he'd relished in it, sought it out, but tonight, he couldn't turn away any longer. Her beauty at the very least demanded he not look away.

It demanded that he worship her.

His mother had been catholic. His father had been a fisherman. His love, his obsession, fascination with saints had come from them. From the stories, and the prayers still whispered. He remembered seeing icons in his youth, relics of an old world that had kept him spellbound. Gilded in gold, and the deepest shades of purple, blue, or green, the images had shone brightly, as if illuminated by Heaven's light itself. They had been seared into his memories, illuminated the darkness of cold nights and terrible times. Fed him, kept watch over him, given him hope that there was more. Given him a way out. Because that is what saints did. His faith in the Almighty was generally questionable, but he'd believed in them all, his companions through thick and thin.

And now, before him, stood the brightest of them all.

It might be blasphemy. He didn't rightly care.

Swathed in gold, her hair shining in the candlelight, her skin glowing, it was as if her soul itself was shining through, unable to be contained any longer.

Arthur didn't know when he'd become a man who thought that way, of souls shining through skin, of earthly women becoming something more. He swallowed hard, thinking for a moment to push it back, to push it all away, to *walk* away, because surely whatever it was, *Lily, her and only her*, transforming him, it couldn't be good. Especially not right now, with so much at stake.

The now, demanded the cold, vicious beast he'd been for twenty years.

Not, whoever this new man was.

But when she slid her fingers against his, taking the posy with a shy smile, he knew he couldn't do it. He had been strong his entire life, but now, with one simple touch, all his strength had left. He had promised her time.

And by God, if he stood by at least one thing, it was his word. *Only...*

'I feel at a loss of how to begin,' he admitted softly, and she grinned, amusement, and agreement mingling in her gaze. He found himself following suit, and then more words tumbled from his mouth without forethought. 'I don't... I don't know how to do this. I want it to be... Right.'

'Just, be with me, Arthur,' she whispered with a shrug, stepping closer, so that it felt like they were in each other's arms, without even touching. The same spell she cast over him that first time, was cast again, the world beyond the bubble they were in, disappearing. 'If anything isn't, *right*, trust that I will tell you.'

'I trust you, more than anyone I ever have, I think,' he said, wonder, and confusion dawning within him all at once. His fingers rose without conscious command, and his knuckles traced the line of her cheek. She leaned into the touch, and he marvelled at the exquisiteness of that simple connection. 'How is that possible? How is any of this possible?' he asked.

How is it that you want me?

He didn't voice that question, and still it seemed she heard it, for she shrugged lightly again, as if she had asked herself the same, and decided it best not to question what life had given them.

The convergence of their paths, for whatever purpose, for whatever time they had.

And then, she lifted up on her toes, and slid one hand behind his neck, and pressed her lips gently to his, and the time for questions was over. Because this, *this* touch, this connection, this thrill, and settling all at once, it was the reason he allowed irrationality to take over.

The posy still in her hand, he felt her slip off his hat and toss it somewhere, as he wrapped his own arms around her waist, one hand resting on the small of her back, the other higher, so he could bring her close again. Lily took his bottom lip between her own, swiping her tongue gently across it, asking him to open to her. And it felt… Like she wanted more than his physical opening, and in that split second as he granted her wish, he realised he wanted to grant it to her entirely. He couldn't, but the pang in his chest told him he wished to with everything he was.

Instead, he simply gripped her tighter, the gold silk under his fingertips nothing compared to the velvet he knew was hidden beneath it, and she feasted on him, slowly, achingly slow, her tongue stroking and dancing with his own, as if *she* was taking from him. Claiming him. He found he didn't mind that either, he let her do as pleased, surrendering control and lead as he had never before.

With her hips pressing against his own, his desire mounting between them, her fingers sliding from his neck to caress his beard, the last semi-rational thought he had was that somehow, he'd found what he'd never been looking for.

A match.

∞

It should have been terrifying. This feeling, of another being having such power over you that you forgot reason, that you forgot the potential of hurt; that everything that was the world, and time, and anything but the present moment, the present sensations, and feelings, was quietened. But it wasn't. It was liberating, and drugging.

Just like Arthur's kisses.

This was so different to what they'd shared before. Before...

It could all be chalked up to desperation, to need, to a search for something to numb the grief, even if it hadn't felt like that to her. It had felt like discovery. But this... This was a choice. On both their parts. And she could feel him, giving something, pieces of himself, and control. It wasn't that there wasn't need, and desire, she felt it as surely as she felt his own, but that same care he'd put into himself, his appearance, his gift, it was there, in his taste, in the way his fingers trailed and gripped against her back.

It was in every stroke of his tongue, every nip of her lips, every nudge of his nose against her cheek. The way he breathed her in, as she did. As if they were both memorising, taking in, feeding off the other to survive.

Out of breath, she finally broke the kiss, her head spinning, but her mind somehow clear of concern, of despair, of anything but him. Unable to break her gaze from his, she slowly faded back down to her feet, and for a moment, he leaned over, resting his forehead on hers, studying her as if seeking answers. She longed to scream that *this*, what they had somehow found, was the answer, at least to her, but she couldn't. She had to keep reminding herself, that time was all he could give. All she could have.

And that was...

Just fine. Enough to survive on.

Yet the bittersweet edge of that thought pricked something inside her, spurring her on to find more of the drug she'd just consumed, and so she let the fingers already resting on the lapels of his coat begin their work. Slowly, meticulously, she divested him of his coats, laying them once she had neatly folded on the very handy chest at the foot of her bed, along with the posy she would carefully dry tomorrow. Not a vase for these flowers, no. She wanted to cherish them, always. It might be the only proof, other than memories, which could fade so easily, she knew that well enough.

He followed her those few steps, and when she turned to continue her work, he was already there, within reach. So she did, her fingers nimbly undoing the buttons of his waistcoat, and then his shirt. She took both from him again, laying them neatly on the chest, and then finally, she allowed herself to look, to see, what she'd uncovered. His form had been apparent well enough through his clothes, but now she saw the true strength, the life, woven into the lines of his chest, his arms, his abdomen. Muscles and scars, and a bold smattering of grey hairs told of all he'd lived, all he'd done to become who he was.

His wasn't a body like those statues women fawned over in the galleries, of young pups and pretty dandies. Arthur's body was of a fighter, a man who had fought life itself to thrive. And it was beautiful. And awe-inspiring, and she didn't really care that it shone on her face. She let her fingers trace him gently, revelling in the little shivers, and contractions as she explored the dips and hollows with more fascination that she'd ever discovered anyone before.

And as she did, she was somehow drawn in closer, as if he was exuding some sort of power that forced her closer, until she was close enough for his cheek to gently nudge against her own. He stole a kiss when she turned to him, a swift meeting, before he nodded, and then her fingers were finishing what they'd begun, and he was bared to her, in his entirety, quite literally stealing her breath.

Everything about him was power, and strength, and he was hers, and the way he was gazing at her now, it was with that tenderness and awe again, and she thanked the stars silently, for giving her this man.

'Will you show me yourself, Lily?' he asked after a moment, in that voice that had enchanted her from the first. Just like him, so much quiet power. 'Unwrap yourself for me?'

Anything, Arthur.

∞

That expression, *don't look a gift horse in the mouth*, kept coming to the forefront of Arthur's mind. It was odd really, what came to one's mind in the most defining moments of one's life. And he knew without a doubt, this night was one of them. Just like the day Lily had marched to his door, and knocked on it as if her life depended on it.

Because she was a gift. He hadn't used the word *unwrap* lightly. She was a gift, given to him, why, and how, well God only knew; if indeed such a power existed.

The way she had taken his clothes, the way she had looked at him... Again, the same awe he felt deep inside shone brightly in her eyes. Not that he knew what to do with it or about it, other than what the lady commanded.

Be here.

And surrender to her spell. As much as he wanted to unwrap his gift himself, he somehow wanted more to give her tangible proof of his relinquishment of power. That was *his* gift.

She took it, not lightly, but with a seriousness he wasn't sure he'd ever witnessed in her. The same dogged determination that had first persuaded him to give her what she'd asked for; this house. As slowly and precisely as she'd divested him, she removed the few layers of gold she bore like a second skin, until she too, was entirely bared to him.

He'd had glimpses before, he'd imagined what lay beneath more times than he cared to admit... But this, the reality of her, changed something within him so profoundly he could almost hear pieces of himself clawing, rising from the depths they'd been cast to out of necessity, to take a place in the forefront of his being. He'd admitted she terrified him before, but now...

He didn't think he'd ever understood the meaning of the word *terrified*. There was no going back to who he was after this, no matter how he might wish to; even if this new thing emerging from the darkness he'd dwelled in forever could ruin him, he knew he couldn't go back. And that was beyond terrifying. It was a monumental mistake, but yet again, he recognized there was no going back.

Arthur took in everything she was, his eyes greedily feeding off her, feeding those demons of light clawing up within him. From the tiny little feet, to the strong, thick thighs his hands remembered all too well were soft and welcoming. From the swell of her belly to those generous peaked globes whose taste he couldn't forget as long as he lived, to the freckles on her shoulder, like golden stars in the firelight, and the thatch of dark blond hair he knew hid a treasure no words could describe.

He took it all in, every detail, best he could, though he promised that in the time they had together, he would memorise every freckle, every line, every dip, and curve thoroughly, so that when whatever this fit of madness was, was over, he would have something. Another icon to keep him warm in the darkest night.

The incongruity of them both standing a few feet apart, completely naked, struck him suddenly. It was something else he'd never done before; been alone, *like this*, with a woman. There had been a few to satisfy needs over the years, and it wasn't as if he'd remained completely clothed when he was with them, but this...

It felt, *natural*.

It had that *rightness* about it he just couldn't shake when he was with Lily.

She licked her lips, or rather, not really licked, but rolled her lips into her mouth, one by one, and he was gone. His body was moving again, to her, and without hesitation, without faltering, he lifted her up, as one lifted up a bride, not that he'd think about that comparison too hard, and his lips found her own again, and this was Heaven indeed.

He rounded to the side of her bed, and laid her down gently, before tucking himself alongside her, peppering her with quick, deep, but swift little kisses. Her hands roved over his chest, fingers tangling in the hairs thereupon, and down his side, his ribs, then his hip and thigh, and it struck him too, that no one had ever touched him there. No one had feathered their fingers over his ribs, as if counting each one, tracing the valleys between.

His eyes opened as she scooted closer, tucking herself nearly under him, and she broke the last kiss they'd been sharing, and instead bestowed him a blinding smile. So relaxed, so open, so free, and full... His fingers set about tracing her brows, her jaw, her cheekbones, her lips, as the other cradled her head, gently massaging her scalp, the tresses of downy silk curling warmth around every nerve.

Everything about her, her scent, her warmth, her breath, it curled around him, like plumes of smoke, ensnaring him, binding him into a sweet prison he'd never want to leave. One last taste of her lips, and he shifted, moving down, careful to avoid her neck, lavishing affection instead on everything past that. Her collarbone, those wonderful breasts, first the tops, then the tips, mindful to enjoy some time suckling each one, and then he moved to their sides, and then beneath them, watching how she moved, how she arched, or pulled back, when the breathy sighs turned a little bit tighter, or she writhed a little bit closer, her skin gliding against his like molten fire.

A sheen of sweat blossomed on them both, and a flush on her, particularly in those spots he visited with his mouth, his beard abrading the perfection of her skin ever so slightly. The air filled with the scents and smells of their togetherness, and they seeped into him, driving his desire, his need higher, even as it seemed a balm to his troubled and angry soul. And then there was the deeper scent of her musk, as he travelled lower, he could smell it, its tang heavy on the air; so much so he could nearly taste it.

Not yet, but soon, I shall.

First, he wanted to visit more of the landscape of Lily. The little mole, there, where her waist ended, and her hip began. The tiny wisp of hair beneath her belly button, and the small creases above her thigh. As he did, her own fingers continued to seek him out, drifting through his hair, whispering over his shoulders, as her own whispers joined the music of the moment.

Arthur... Arthur... Arthur...

She chanted it like a litany, and so her name was to him, underscored by the rhythmic breaths and moans. And when he reached his destination, he need not even ask, already her legs opened to him as he settled between them, softly rubbing his beard along the nearly translucent skin of her inner thighs. One of her feet curved around, tracing little patterns on his back, and he smiled, inhaling deeply before parting her lips even wider, and beginning his feast.

Lily was already glistening wet, her desire smeared on her thighs, and that vision of her, petals open, and waiting, it changed him too. It was like witnessing something elemental. *She* was elemental. And he needed her, needed her essence to seep into him like the rest of her had, to revive and restore him.

So he swiped his tongue against her, first where her desire had slipped onto her thighs, then along the creases where they met her sex, and then, the sample driving him nearly wild already, he ran his tongue from the entrance of her core to that bright, swollen tip. She bucked, hips high off the bed, and his mouth followed.

Her essence was so potent it made him feral, unleashed the part of him he'd never let roam free, except with her. He licked and suckled, and drove his tongue into her, drinking this ambrosia that he was quite sure would in fact make him immortal. Again he listened, and watched, following the shifts in her body, her sounds, telling him the way to her highest pleasure. And so he followed, until he felt the curling of her foot against his back, and against his hip, and the tautness of her entire body, and that strangled cry that caught in her throat, and he raised his eyes just enough so he could glimpse her face in ecstasy.

This is Heaven.

∞

Lily was still riding a crashing wave of satiation, pure, incandescent ecstasy, and utter calm, when she felt Arthur settle over her, his own body a shield around her, his arms beside her head, his fingers toying in her hair, and smoothing it from her sweaty brow.

So this is what it feels like to be adored...

There had been men who took pleasure in her own pleasure before; who seemed to worship her. But never had it been like this. Raw, and sticky, and yet, intangible all at once. As Arthur came between her legs, his own desire pressing into her still tingling, and sensitive folds, she looked up at him, her hands idly sliding up to his, their arms tangling together somehow until she could slide her fingers along his. There was a glint of pride in his eyes, and a glint of her inner self on his beard, and she grinned, raising her head so that she could clean it off him. And off his lips, off his tongue, and the groan that rumbled through him, echoing through her own bones, it was energising and thrilling.

Sliding one hand down to where they met, she gripped him tight, stroking the silky strength for a moment before positioning him where he belonged. He waited, until her hand had found his own again, and when she met those mercurial eyes, there was something else in them that made her heart feel as if that tear he'd made then stitched back up, had been gently soothed with a balm of silver light. Her breath hitched, and as if he knew, his eyes drooped closed, and he kissed her again as he drove into her, her own hips rising to meet his, her legs locking at the small of his back.

The kiss they shared then, as with all others that came before, was different. It was filled with strength, and grit, and a frantic desire to be united. Or so it felt, so each stroke as he filled her, and left her, and filled her again, felt. It felt, for those few precious moments when time stopped and they simply existed, together, slowly reaching for ecstasy together, that he was giving more than time. That he was giving himself, much against his own volition, and though it was the last thing she wished, she felt tears escape her tightly shut eyes, their salt mingling with the salt already on her skin.

He drove her to a height she'd never reached before, nearly painful pleasure tightening her inner self from her belly button to her sensitive lower lips, searing in its intensity, opening her in a manner she'd never felt herself open before.

Open to receive, and to give.

A moment later he followed her over the edge, the tips of his fingers desperately seeking to grasp hers even as he forced himself to remain strong on his arms, until finally he collapsed, rolling as he did so that she covered his chest like some strange primal sort of blanket.

And in the midst of their panting breaths, and thrumming hearts, she heard two little whispered words floating in the air.

Arthur... Lily...

X.

September 1823

*A*n incessant, loud, and obnoxious pounding made him frown, and set down the paper he'd been reading. He'd heard the steady, sure steps of his butler, one of only two household staff he kept. He didn't need them, but the world expected him to have some, and so he'd hired a butler-cum-valet and a cook-cum-housekeeper. He didn't need to risk anyone else witnessing something they shouldn't - not that he ever conducted that sort of business here.

Better safe than sorry.

Raised voices had caught his attention as he tried to focus again on the paper, and then a door closing violently, and the steps of Watkins, his butler, before a light knock sounded at the door. Watkins had begun scratching - though he'd forbidden that immediately.

'Come in,' he'd said, wondering who it was causing this racket, and why at six in the morning his butler who could handle anything was coming to him.

A thousand thoughts and a sliver of concern had crossed his mind as he'd waited for Watkins. Turning in his chair, he'd found the man looking as if he'd just been asked to deep clean the streets by the tanneries.

'There's a... Young woman,' Watkins had said, his diplomacy

contradicted by the wrinkling of his nose. 'Who wishes to speak with you.'

'What?' His mind had searched for who it could possibly be - Watkins knew better than to judge or make faces about any of his tenants. 'Who? Where did you put her?'

'Nowhere, sir. The young lady refused to enter.'

Frowning again, Arthur had risen.

'I'll take care of this.'

He'd gone downstairs, and opened the door, and been greeted by the sight of a Lily with tear-swollen eyes; mud-soaked, and red-faced. He remembered the worry he'd felt for a second magnifying, into concern, he'd taken a step forward as if to...

Take her into his arms? Had he really?

Yes, he had.

But she had shaken her head, and gulped in a large breath before he'd even been able to ask what was wrong and who he could kill to make it better.

'I ain't here to see Mr. Dudley,' she'd said, quietly, so dangerously so, he'd known, right then, everything was about to change. 'That's why I ain't comin' in. I came to talk to Saint Nick.'

And there it was.

He'd felt as if he were tumbling, headlong down a bumpy hill, his entire life and world topsy turvy.

No one knew. No one could know.

But somehow, this girl, this woman, did.

How...?

'I got a proposal for Saint Nick,' she'd continued, before he could deny everything, shut her up, pay her to leave and never come back. 'And he's gonna hear me out.'

'Very well,' he'd said, his voice not his own. 'The park, just there,' he'd added, nodding to the green before his building, not caring one whit for who saw what for the first time in a very long time.

She'd nodded, and he'd grabbed her a coat, and his own, to brace against the chilly autumn wind, and together they'd walked across to the green, where the trees were just beginning to turn.

And they'd sat on the bench, and she'd made her proposal, and

they'd struck a deal.
   He'd been right.
   From then on, everything had changed.

∞

The bells of St. Paul's rang five thirty, but even their hollow echo through the quiet, slowly waking world outside couldn't break the cocoon they were wrapped in, Lily's magic weaving far past his own body, all the way into the tiny world contained in this room.

After that shattering first time, they'd lain there, her rising and falling on his chest with every breath, until he'd needed to have her again, and so he had, her settling onto him, riding him like a goddess, reviving *herself* with all he could give. And there was no denying now, that he had given parts of himself he'd never wanted to, and never thought possible. But her body, her eyes, had demanded it, a price for her own gifts, and so he'd given.

There had been something between them, when he was inside her; he'd glimpsed it in her eyes that first time. She'd tried to hide it away, he'd tried to ignore it, ignore the moisture on her cheeks, ignore a piercing pain in his own chest, but it was all in vain. The reminder of it, burned at the back of his mind, like an unquenchable flame.

Now, as they simply lay side by side, gazing at each other, both washed and Lily's necessary steps to ensure no babe would come of this coupling, completed, he knew he should go, but it felt wrong.

And, it was still early.

A little longer...

There were things... Well, truth was, he wanted, *more.* Of her. Not in the physical sense, but more of her mind, her soul, everything that composed her into this beautiful prism of light.

And there was one question he'd longed to ask forever it seemed.

'How did you know?' he asked, his fingertips tracing the line of her brows, then her cheek, then every line and dimple and mark on her face, committing them to memory, as he'd resolved to, wondering if perhaps they held the key, the answers to his many questions. *What is this feeling? What is this connection? What is this miracle?* 'How did you see what I was when no one else could?'

'I know men, Arthur,' she said quietly, a faint smile turning up the corners of her lips. 'If there is one thing I know, it is men.' She closed her eyes for a moment as his fingers traced her lips, then looked back at him when they moved further along down her neck. 'Everyone spoke of the Ghost. He was, *is*, an avenging shadow in the darkness. But Saint Nick... He wasn't a shade, or a spirit, he was barely a whisper. A clever man, a careful man, who knew this place intimately. A fierce, generous man, who no one knew. And then there was you,' she sighed, studying him as intently as he did her. 'An intelligent, careful, generous, fierce man, who no one really knew anything of. Who everyone saw, but no one really looked at. And every time I looked in your eyes, I saw something. I just... Felt it.'

'Still, you couldn't know I wouldn't kill you,' he said, his fingers now tracing the curves of her belly. 'You couldn't know what I would do to protect my secret.'

'I couldn't be certain,' she admitted, and though it felt like the faint slash of a dagger across his breast to know she hadn't known instinctively he would never lay a hand on her, even to protect himself; even then, he appreciated her honesty. 'It was a gamble. But I also had a feeling you wouldn't. And if I had been wrong... The reward was worth the potential cost.'

Power, safety, privilege; a fair reward indeed.

The reminder was what he needed, though the twinge he experienced hurt more than he'd expected.

And he knew, what she'd sought from him, what he provided her with, it wasn't only for herself. Lily wasn't like that. He knew that much at least.

His fingers travelled upward again, to her own, which he

took, entwining them with his, and staring at the design they made. The contrast, and the similarity of the strength they both seemed to hold.

'You care about them,' he said, referring to all those under her protection here.

He'd thought so, suspected it before, but then he'd tried so hard not to give her much thought. He'd tried to limit their discussions, to business; consciously and unconsciously.

'Of course,' she frowned.

'I didn't mean offence, Lily,' he said soothingly. 'I just... I didn't realise.'

'And you never asked.'

'I never did.' He could tell her why, *I didn't want to think on you, think any better of you than I already did, acknowledge that you are a generous and caring soul*; but a glance at those bright eyes told him he didn't have to. 'I'm asking now. That day you came to me, what happened?'

A shadow crossed her face, and her jaw tightened, so he ran his thumb along her own, hoping to chase it away.

'A friend died,' she said simply, pushing the emotion of it away, as if she could, the tightness impossible to conceal. 'Her name was Marigold. Found her in the refuse pile outside the Lion,' she spat. 'I couldn't do it anymore. Couldn't watch them have the life snuffed out of them, quick or slow, not if I could do something, for some, at least.'

'I'm sorry,' he said, meaning it, not only for the loss of her friend, but for everything she and all others endured in the world, that he truly had no concept of.

She nodded, a wan smile moving her lips for a brief moment as her eyes travelled to their connected hands, and she twisted and played, her fingers twirling and curling and caressing all at once.

'Some people, they try to make you believe it's you against the world,' she said pensively after a moment. 'It isn't. If you have the power to help another, even one life, for one tiny moment, that's what you have to do.'

'Why?'

'You tell me.' He frowned, and she raised a brow, meeting his eyes again. 'Everything you have, you've shared. Power, money, protection. You've done so much for the people here. I don't believe it's guilt, or some twisted sense of debt.'

'No?'

'No,' she breathed seriously, sidling in a little closer. 'I think you are as your namesake was. A man who believes in more. Honour. Truth. Defence of the weak.'

Her words slashed him again, digging deeper, and he rebelled against the truth of them, the warmth of them.

Because...

Both my names are taken - not truly mine.

'Don't make me a hero, Lily,' he warned her, willing his eyes to show the ruthlessness, the fierceness that had helped him survive. That had drawn her to him, he was sure, and that meant no matter the wonder of what they shared; some things were not to be. 'I'm not.'

'Don't have to be a hero to have a good heart,' she whispered, attempting to silence any further protests by kissing him.

But he couldn't have it, couldn't have her believing that, making him into something he wasn't.

In a flash, he had her under him again, and with his free hand, he gently cupped her jaw, and forced her to look at him.

'I'm not *good*, Lily,' he seethed, trying to make her understand. 'None of me is. You, more than anyone knows that. There is no magic heart inside me that is what you think it is. Don't make me, don't make *this* into something it's not.'

A flash of what looked like hurt shone in her eyes, and that tore through him like a sword. He pushed through it, determined to make himself clear. He had to, because if he didn't

-

'Told you once, Arthur,' she said, her tone as brittle and yet fearsomely warning as his own had been. 'Ain't got no illusions. But you got a good heart, and deny it though you may, don't make it untrue.'

If he didn't, and she said things like that, it made him believe.

That maybe he did have a heart.

That maybe there was good in him.

That maybe, just maybe, there was more to be had.

But just because she had somehow become... *Important*, to him, it didn't mean...

He should, could, would, become anything more than a man who shared her bed, and body, for a time.

Another question rose to his lips as she settled more comfortably beneath him, slinking her body along his like a snake.

'What are you doing with me, Lily? You're so young, and beautiful, and smart, and you have your whole future ahead of you,' he said softly, his breath sending wisps of hair flying from beside her face, still, always, searching her eyes for those answers they contained but that he couldn't seem to decipher. 'I'm not fooling here; I have nothing to give you. I'm old, and broken by this world. What I am now... There isn't more.'

'Maybe that's enough for me,' she said weakly, that little shrug of hers reappearing.

And as he felt himself growl, and claim her lips, he forced himself to push away the thought that he could be.

That what little he was, would be enough for someone like her.

That maybe, she'd been made, just for him.

Instead, his body took hers again, more wildly passionate than before, as if it too needed to prove that there wasn't any goodness, anything but pleasure to be given.

Or taken.

Liar.

XI.

The days following their first night together, or at least, what Lily liked to think of as their first *proper* night together, were busy, and most of all, thrilling. Business was booming, and though there were the usual problems - rowdy customers, a late-winter fever that took out some of her workers - Lily felt invigorated each day as she tackled it all. The promise of the upcoming mask helped with her renewed verve, but she knew very well the main reason for her renewed appetite for every aspect of her life.

Arthur.

He came to her every night as the clock tolled three, and stayed until the first rays of sunshine crept over the horizon, chasing the inky night away, transforming it into pale grey. They brought each other to the heights of pleasure relentlessly, as if each was aware of the fact that they only had a short time together. Every morning, when he disappeared, until such time as he reappeared at her door, Lily couldn't help but wonder if she was dreaming. If perhaps, she'd conjured him; that she'd wanted him so desperately her mind had made him real. But the warmth on her sheets for those precious few moments after he left reassured her that he wasn't just a fantasy.

Only, she couldn't quite grasp that she'd been lucky enough to be granted her wish. Lucky enough to find him, to have him, to hold him each night, and kiss him, and be with him. The wonder of it all, was thrilling, and set fire to her blood.

For a time, at least.

As the days passed, slowly, perniciously, the thrill started to fade. The passion remained, but it grew increasingly bittersweet. It began one night when she lay in Arthur's embrace after a first tangle in the sheets, and she told him about the feathers and beads she had gotten for an exciting price to add to the mask costumes. How she'd brought them round to Sarah's, and seen the nearly finished wardrobe for her workers, so beautiful and promising. He'd commented on how nice that all was. And that had been it.

At first, Lily had dismissed it on account of their being tired, after all she was accustomed to being up all night, albeit not *exercising* quite so much, but Arthur worked during the day. If he slept at all after he left her every night, it couldn't be much, he was always out on the streets, speaking to his tenants, collecting rents, more so now than ever with the continuing threat against them all. There had been a few new instances of harassment, and threatening notes, and she understood well the toll that took on him, because he wasn't alone in his worry. She was concerned for all those under his care, and also for him.

Not only did he have all of that responsibility, he was still grieving.

In any case she realised, he was likely tired, and overwhelmed, and had little time for her silly little thoughts on silly little dresses. Only, that prompted her to try and get him to speak of all that weighed on him, that clouded those normally crystalline eyes she loved so much. Each time she tried over the following days, he made it clear he didn't want to speak of any of it.

And as days turned into a fortnight, Lily realised that after that first night, they hadn't spoken at all. Bittersweet had turned bitter; and she was lonely. She had a passionate man in her bed, who made her feel things she never had before, but the connection she was sure they had shared for a time, when he'd first begun coming after his sister's passing, even that first night, had disappeared. She still felt *everything* for him, but he had closed himself off.

She tried to reason with herself. She'd known accepting his proposal that there would be limits to what they could share. He had promised time. He'd made it clear there couldn't be anything *more*. And because she loved him, she had accepted those terms. She'd seized the opportunity for fear of getting nothing. Scraps were better than no food at all, right? She should be ecstatic that she had gotten what she'd wanted, just as she had been days ago.

The problem was, she had thought she had *him*, only she didn't. She wasn't asking for promises of marriage and forever, she wasn't asking for him to be anything more than present, only he wasn't. They satisfied a need together, just as her clients did with her workers. Just as others had done with her for years.

That realisation struck her as she rose the morning of the mask, and the brush she'd been untangling her curls with stuck in them as she stared out of the window onto the roofs of the surrounding buildings, the morning's rays brightening the grey with deep oranges and pinks.

Pain cut through her chest, as she realised something more.

You can't love him.

Not truly.

Because you don't know him.

What a bloody fool she'd been.

Foolish, foolish girl!

Swiping away angry, burning tears, she redoubled her efforts at untangling the knots in her hair, wishing she could brush Arthur out of herself as easily. Wishing she wasn't standing here crying, because she'd only just now been woken from her idiotic little dream of love. She'd envied people like Sarah, even Meg Lowell, for so long. People who found love, and *kept* it. She'd thought herself lucky because she'd at least found it, even though she'd known she could never *keep* it. Even confess it. But now...

The shimmering vision of wonder concealing the hard truth vanished, swept away with the last of the night. She'd thought what she had with Arthur was so different from anything else, that it was *love*, but in the end, she'd simply become what *he* needed and wanted, just as she had with everyone else in her life. And she had deluded herself into thinking that version of herself was enough; was true, and good, and *enough*. Deluded herself into thinking the passion and pleasure would be enough.

If she was honest with herself, she was also guilty of letting herself become hypnotised by the image of Arthur she'd created in her mind. The blanks her imagination had filled in. Not only had she offered up another version of herself, one that would be satisfied by what he had to offer, and what he thought of her, but she had let herself believe he was more than what he said. Despite her promises, to herself, and to him, she'd let her mind conjure up *more*, even as he swore there wasn't any to be had.

Dreams were good. Dreams had kept her warm for so long. Dreams of Kit, dreams of a safe place for people like her, dreams of Arthur. But in a split second, their beauty, their power, the hope they brought, was snatched away. She felt as if she'd just woken from a dream herself; been transported to the real world.

Grown up.

She'd thought she'd done that long, long ago, but apparently not.

Sucking in a breath, forcing air to rush past the twisting tightness in her throat, she told herself to just get through the day. Weeks she'd been planning this mask, countless hours they'd all spent preparing for it, and she wouldn't let her stupid little heart, or a *man*, ruin it all. She had work to do, and she would bloody well get to it.

And there'll be no cryin' either.

No, there wouldn't be, she promised herself, tapping her cheeks lightly after setting down the brush and tying up her hair.

No cryin' over that man again.

∞

'Let the festivities begin,' Lily exclaimed with forced alacrity, raising her glass to the packed room. Those gathered therein joined her, raising the glasses of bubbling golden liquid high in the air, some cheering, all smiling, and drank greedily as the musicians began the slow, tantalising music that would underscore the evening's events.

Not normally one to drink whilst working, Lily nonetheless took a large swallow of the champagne in her glass, hoping it would help settle her nerves, and help her keep the bright smile affixed on her face for as long as she would have to wear it.

Tonight, she should've been able to smile brightly without any aid, or even thought for it. She should've been able to be her seductive, welcoming, gregarious self. Though there were always small issues with any endeavour, tonight should have lived up to her expectation of it being *perfect*, or as close to it as it could be. Everything today had suggested it would.

All the whiskey, champagne, wine, and food they had ordered, was in the house and being chilled, cut, decanted. Delicious smells had filled the house from the early hours while in every public, and private room, lanterns, candelabra, boughs of laurel, vines, twists and threads of beads and tiny shards of glass had been hung to make the entire place seem like spring, and enchanting light were overflowing in it. Dusting, polishing, new candles, final beatings of rugs, fluffing of pillows, all of it, had happened, and transformed her already sumptuously seductive house into a clean, sparkling, lush, Roman-inspired dreamworld, with plenty of hidden coves for frolicking.

Sarah and Renata had delivered the costumes, and the evening dress suits for those serving or working security had come back from the laundress, pristine and neatly starched. It was about that time that the day took a turn.

Renata had come to Lily asking the whereabouts of three of her workers who couldn't be found for their final fittings. Mary, Jack, and Winnie were not in the house. After asking the others, Lily had discovered they'd gone to the apothecary for some last-minute necessaries; two hours prior. A sick feeling had washed over her then, and without delay, she'd sent Bill and twenty others to find them.

They had.

In one piece; but barely.

They'd been attacked, on their way back to the house, in broad daylight, but in one of the dark alleys that meant there were no witnesses. Not that many would bear witness, particularly not when it concerned their *kind.* They'd been taken to Guy's, beaten to within an inch of their lives, and the familiar mix of white-hot rage, and helplessness, had taken hold of Lily.

They were meant to be safe. Here, under her protection, and that of St. Nick. That is what she'd fought for, the reason she'd built this place. To keep as many as she could, *safe.* It wasn't a mystery as to why, after losing Kit... She couldn't lose anyone else she cared for. Only she'd failed, *again,* and it had nearly cost them their lives. When Bill had told her...

She'd broken anything there was to break in her office. She'd wanted to get out there, and find whoever was responsible, *somehow,* she didn't care how, and it had taken a lot of effort from Bill to keep her inside, and calm her down. Not that he was any less angry about it, only he had the luxury of reason by then.

'*We have to keep on, Miss Lily,*' he'd said, and even as it wrenched her heart, she'd known it was true.

Tonight, wasn't just about success. It was about becoming successful *enough,* with the right crowd, that safety, would be possible for more. For longer. With men from Mayfair and the West coming; men who made policy, and controlled the law, she could ensure a future for herself and those in her care. So as much as she wished to cancel it all and march out on the streets demanding blood, she knew she couldn't.

Bill and his men had been tasked with reinforcing security for the evening, and he'd called in favours with some of his old fighting friends to have extra hands. St. Nick's men had been tasked with ensuring Mary, Jack, and Winnie's safety, and eventual return to the house. Not to work, simply, to be... Safe. *Safer.* They'd also been charged with finding those responsible, though Lily had little hope regarding that. St. Nick - *Arthur* -

himself would likely be informed, but she couldn't do it. She knew she should, but putting words to paper, so coldly, callously, when all she truly wanted was for him to be there, holding her...

It simply wasn't something she could do.

Instead, she'd gathered the household, informed them of the happenings, told them to be extra careful this evening, and report anything odd. Reassured them that all was well, even as she doubted it down to her very core. And then she'd stood there in the main hall, welcoming, greeting each guest personally, ushering them into the Grand Salon to relax until the night truly began.

Now, here she stood, in the midst of the growing revelry, emperors and gods and vestals laughing gaily with powerful men in immaculate evening wear and intricate masks, trying her best to do something she'd been good at, once.

Keeping emotion out of her work.

It was something she learned early on to do - it was one of her great talents. Her work was one thing. Emotion didn't factor into it. Only tonight...

Tonight she couldn't quite manage it.

She had wanted this responsibility, and most days, she did enjoy it, only when people got hurt because she wasn't smart enough, or strong enough...

That was a completely different beast altogether.

Is this how Arthur feels - oh stop it!

'A goddess should not be hiding in corners,' a deep voice murmured in her ear, and Lily forced that seductive smile back on her face. She was actually glad for the distraction, the reminder that she had work to do this evening. 'A goddess should be worshipped. She should be in the midst of it all.'

'Viscount Rasenhurst,' she grinned, swaying a little, fanning the silken, nearly transparent, white and golden swaths woven with peacock feathers that served as her dress this evening, so that they flowed around her. She had thought of making her costume a bit more martial as was Juno's tradition, but in the end, she'd opted for a more subtle, and seductive reference to the ancient deity. 'I am in the midst of it all. I enjoy watching my devotees find their own pleasure.'

The viscount shifted so that he was beside her, and she looked up at the quite literally, tall, dark, broodingly handsome specimen, whose dark eyes were glittering in the shadows of the simple black velvet mask he wore.

A notorious rake, he was nonetheless heir to one of the most powerful earldoms in the kingdom, and had been known to champion the causes of whores and hell owners; if only because he enjoyed them too much to lose his favourites.

Though typically he frequented houses like *The Emporium*, Lily had managed to draw him here tonight.

'I'm sure you do,' he drawled, his eyes travelling up and down her body, in what surely should have felt like an intimate caress, but that Lily merely noticed. 'Why is it that the most glorious women are in charge of houses such as this, and off-limits to those of us with most excellent taste?'

'As you so aptly remarked, my lord,' Lily breathed, leaning in a little closer, careful not to touch lest the wrong message be sent. 'I am a goddess. It is not for us to cavort with mere mortals.'

'Ah, but I think you have forgotten quite a lot of your mythology,' he laughed, not in the least put out. 'Though you cannot blame me for attempting the impossible.'

'No, my lord,' she agreed. 'You would not be yourself, I think, if you did not.'

'I like this place of yours,' he said, more seriously, the flirtation in his voice disappeared like smoke.

'I cannot tell you what that means to me.'

Bill's shadow appeared in the door across the room, and she nodded imperceptibly, before her eyes travelled across the Bacchanalian happenings before her.

Not even midnight and already things are well underway...

Which was undoubtedly good. She caught Amelia's eye, and luckily the woman was only one of three currently entertaining Baron Redmond.

Within seconds, Amelia was before them.

'I do hope the rest of your evening convinces you to become a regular patron of our little house. This is Amelia,' Lily added, waving her hand like a good goddess at the half-naked Venus, covered in tulle made to look like waves. She didn't miss the flash of interest in Rasenhurst's eyes, and smiled. 'Perhaps she can help you explore our enchanted land.'

'With pleasure,' he said, dipping his head and taking Amelia's outstretched hand.

Lily took a deep breath, ensured she wouldn't be missed, and slid to Bill's side.

Together, they walked in silence to her office, and she turned to him once the door was closed.

'Please tell me there's no more bad news,' she sighed.

'No, Miss Lily,' he said, and the snakes wrestling in her belly she hadn't even noticed, calmed. 'Just wanted to tell you all is well, and quiet, and there ain't no news.'

'That's good,' she said, more to herself than him, heading to her desk.

'Yes, Miss Lily.'

'Well, keep a sharp eye. I think I'll retire for now, go down again later. Tomorrow, I'll go see them all at Guy's, and -'

Lily froze, her eyes catching on a perfect little white card propped up on her desk.

The handwriting on it was neat, and clean, and it chilled her to the bone.

Change is coming. Saints cannot protect you anymore.

'Miss Lily?'

Unable to form a single word, she simply stepped aside, and let him see.

A thousand thoughts passed through her head at once. A thousand decisions to be made, orders to be given, things to do. Bill was voicing them too - she could hear him, as if from a distance, telling her all he would do, quietly, discreetly - but she couldn't even nod to acknowledge him.

Because fear was creeping into her veins, numbing her whilst making her feel nauseated, and weak.

Not fear for herself.

Fear for others. For all those under her protection, and fear for a man she loved.

Even if he was a mere illusion.

Saints can offer protection, and I ask you all now, protect us. Protect him tonight.

XII.

Inhaling a deep lungful of nippingly cold air, Arthur left the chandler's, the tinkling of the bell on the door following him out into the cool, freshly spring, evening. One of his many tenants, the chandler had, like so many others, heard of what had been happening recently to those who paid rent to a certain Mr. Arthur Dudley, and was concerned for his own welfare, that of his family, and that of his business.

Arthur had just spent the past hour as he had so many these past days, weeks, really, reassuring him that all was well, that things were in hand, and that the authorities were dealing with it all appropriately.

If only it were the truth.

The *actual* truth was, nothing was *in hand*. Nothing was being dealt with because Arthur had no damned clue who was after him, and his. For the first time in nearly thirty years, Arthur was powerless. More attacks, small, but enough. On his tenants, on St. Nick's business. More harassment, more threats. And no clues. No whispers, nothing.

He'd finally heard from the Ghosts, and the messages they'd exchanged through Arthur's usual labyrinthine methods had brought nothing. The band of vigilantes had certainly heard the same rumours of assaults on St. Nick's business, Barrowman Bill's business, The Hook's business, and Waterman Tom's business. The assaults on tenants, and buildings, from

Rotherhithe to Shadwell. They too knew something gigantic and well-organised was happening, but neither did they know what. They found the same as Arthur did.

Bodies.

Bodies of men they now guessed had betrayed Barrowman Bill, The Hook, Waterman Tom, St. Nick, and others. Bodies of men no one had seen, nor knew; likely called in from somewhere else.

And the Ghosts came to the same conclusion as he had.

Someone had a hankering for control of Shadwell, Rotherhithe, and Wapping.

But why?

The relentless question that had had him on edge for weeks. That had him restless, and *nervous.* Another thing Arthur Dudley, or more aptly, St. Nick, or whoever the Hell he actually was beneath it all, was not. Along with questioning, which was something he had been too.

Popping up the collar of his coat, lowering the brim of his hat, Arthur decided a walk would be good to expend some of his restless energy, and help him think. He walked these streets every day, but with purpose. With somewhere to go. Not to simply... *Think.* But dire circumstances called for dire measures.

The High Street was still teeming with activity, which was good. It distracted him a little from his own turbulent thoughts, watching people bustling in and out of the shops, bustling along the street, bustling in and out of the inns, and pubs. Traders, workers, dockers, sailors, children, whores, lightermen... Anyone who lived from or near the river. In the pale pink glow of sunset, with the nip of a chill in the air, it all felt... Cosy.

A couple passed by him, arm in arm, a posy in the woman's hand of faded violets, and Arthur quickened his step. That image, of the laughing, smiling, simple couple, he a stevedore by the look, she a kiln-worker, looking as fresh as the air felt, even though their life was likely nothing but hardship on the best of days... It irked him. It made him feel...

Envious.

That whatever bond they shared, could make the rest of it fade away, even if for a second.

He'd been envious of that idea for a long time; he'd thought for a time last year he might've found a way to something *comfortable*, but then he'd lost that, and it had been for the better. But these past couple weeks, with Lily...

These past couple weeks with her had changed him in a way that wasn't *good*. When he was with her... It felt like the rest melted away. For a few precious hours, when they lost themselves together, it felt like what he'd seen on that couple's faces. But that wasn't good, because it made him forget his responsibilities, his duties. It made him lose his edge.

He tried to keep it all in check. He limited the time they had together. He made sure he wasn't tempted to give or ask for *more* by limiting what they shared. That first night, he'd wanted more, and they'd talked, and he'd gotten more, of *her*, and he'd loved every bit of it. He'd treasured every facet she'd shown, but her words about him, the way he was with her... It was a stark reminder of what he could, more importantly, *couldn't* have.

He couldn't have her.

He couldn't have a *relationship*.

He couldn't have her thinking of him as some good-natured hero.

He couldn't start believing it.

He couldn't get attached.

He couldn't start imagining there was something more.

Though a pernicious little voice whispered it was far too late; for any of that.

He ignored it, as he often had these past weeks. He ignored it every time it tempted him to ask her how her day was, or tempted him to answer her questions. Every time it tempted him to invite her outside, for a stroll in the park, or tea in some little shop he'd passed in Fleet Street the other day and that had made him think of her. Because that wasn't who they were.

It wasn't someone he could be.

And keep her safe.

Which was something he needed to do. More than he needed *more* with her. He needed to keep her out of whatever was going on, and that was all there was to it. She, and so many others, relied on his strength, his power, to survive. This wasn't the time to start being selfish. Or...

Stupid.

Nodding to himself, he turned down an alley cutting back north, having realised this little walk idea to clear his head had done nothing of the sort. He'd be of better use getting back to St. Nick's, to see if there was anything new. He'd look at some maps, put a timeline together, try and decipher all -

Something smooth, and very heavy hit him across the side of head, making his ear ring and his mind jumble. Arthur stumbled, hitting the damp bricks beside him roughly, though it was a good thing as the pain radiating in his shoulder cleared a bit of the fog of his mind.

Not a second too soon either, as his eyes processed the glint of a long knife just as it came towards his gut. He caught the wrist holding it, and raised his eyes to find a typically broad, rough, and big bruiser dressed about as foully as he smelt. Out of the corner of his eye he caught more movement - another one of the same coming from either side.

His head was still spinning, and he could feel blood trickling down his ear, but his instincts kicked in. It had been a long time since St. Nick himself had graced the streets of Shadwell like this, but that didn't mean Arthur had lost *that* particular edge.

With a kick to the knee of the brute before him, he twisted the blade away and shoved him against the opposing wall with all his might. The man to his left was that little bit closer, a similarly viscous looking blade in his hand, so Arthur stomped on the foot of his friend still in hand, spun so the arm holding the blade was before him, then slammed backwards against him, delivering a sharp blow to his face with his elbow. Sure the man was at least dazed enough to be moveable, he then spun away, throwing him against the approaching ruffian.

He kept the blade that had come for him though, and

managed to throw it just in time so that it met the man at his back, right in the chest. The hired would-be-killer dropped his own blade, and clenched the one embedded in his heart, looking utterly shocked. He tore it from his own chest with a grunt, and within seconds, the gush of his blood from the wound saw to it that he would never draw breath again.

But Arthur didn't have time to enjoy his victory - there were still two left breathing, and though one was currently trying to scrape himself from the disgusting ground, the other was coming, and quickly. With no time to grab another blade, cursing himself for not carrying weapons anymore, Arthur grounded himself, and then bobbed left as the bruiser still standing came for him. Left, right, left, he bobbed, the blade sailing past his head and body with barely an inch to spare, until he could drive his fist upwards into the man's face. Only as he did, the man's arm came slashing down, and the blade took a fair slice out of his left arm.

Keep moving.

He wouldn't die here. Not like this. Taken down by some hired help. Taken down before he could... Do more. Protect *her.*

Wrapping his bleeding and slowly failing arm around the other man's, he managed to hold him still enough to deliver more blows to his face, before finally kicking him in the sternum, and then for good measure, between the legs. The brute stumbled back to the ground, only to be replaced with the first, now recovered.

But they'd been foolish attacking here, there was only room for one at a time to come after him head-on like this. And he had just enough time as the man now standing stepped over his partner and lunged at him, to turn, throw himself to the ground, and pick up the bloody blade the dead man had left for him. He lunged up, as the other lunged down, and firmly lodged the blade between the man's ribs. A gurgling, enraged sound bubbled from his assailant's lips, before he began to slump over, Arthur following the movement to rise to his feet, and extract the blade.

One left.

He could do this. He was tiring, and the cut on his arm was nasty, he could feel it, soaking through to his coat, but he was angry. And skilled. He was St. Nick for God's sake.

And these men would not be his end.

With a growl, he went for the final brute come for him, and the man never knew what happened. He too stared in shock, blood trickling through his fingers as he held the wound on his throat. Too late, as he stood there, watching the life trickle out of this man too, did Arthur realise, he should've kept one alive. Asked some questions, and *maybe*, just maybe, got some answers for a goddamn change.

Idiot, he thought, as he dropped the blade in his hand after determining it had no particular significance to be of use. *Bloody distracted fool*, he cursed, checking his surroundings to ensure no one had seen; and no one else was coming for him, before rifling through the pockets of the dead men, to absolutely no avail.

The echo of rowdy shouts caught his attention, and he listened for a moment, determining which direction they were coming from, before heading the opposite way, leaving the trail of dead bodies behind him.

Bloody distracted fool.

∞

Two hours later, Arthur was still cursing himself. The rage and bloodlust that had fuelled him through the fight, had simmered down as he slowly made his way back to St. Nick's, more careful than ever not to be followed. It had lessened with every minute, as he stripped, cleaned, and tended to his injuries best he could, and redressed with the clothes he kept here for such cases; though he'd hoped to never have to use them.

Only now, hours later, he was still angry.

Not with those who had come for his life; but with himself.

People coming after him, was nothing new. At least, people coming for St. Nick. Though the men this evening he was convinced had come for Arthur Dudley, which *was* new. And good, in a way, since it meant firstly, that whoever was attacking the area was getting desperate, and secondly, that whatever they wanted could be achieved with his death.

Grim, but reassuring. And helpful.

Not helpful enough to dispel the frustration he felt at himself though. He'd been too damn distracted with thoughts of Lily to even hear the brutes coming for him. He should've smelt them for God's sake, let alone seen or heard them. He was slipping. And it had nearly cost him his life. It could have cost him so much more than that.

And what more could you lose than your life, the devil on his shoulder asked. He swatted it away quite literally as he strode towards the desk, messages for St. Nick in hand to go through. He threw them on the already messy desk, and lit the lamp before settling in his chair, and picking up both the messages and his spectacles.

He sifted through them quickly, most reports on how bad, or good as was the case downriver, business was. Rumours from London had affected every aspect of his concerns, particularly after that debacle and his losses to the west, but things, for now, were holding steady, and it seemed anything outside London was faring well enough.

His fingers stopped as his eyes processed the words before him.

A representative of the Ghost of Shadwell would like to meet to discuss potential solutions to our mutual problem.

'Not likely,' Arthur grumbled, tossing it aside.

Desperate times may call for desperate measures, but secrecy was all he had.

Was this what came of asking for help? People asking for more?

Goddammit.

And then, as he tossed that note aside, to be dealt with later, and his eyes read the next, fear speared through him. It was ice to the fire that up until now had been flowing through him -

keeping him going.

Three of Miss Lily's attacked and taken to Guy's. Men searching for guilty, no news.

Fuck.

Fuck, fuck, fuck.

'Fuck,' Arthur screamed, rising with enough force to knock the chair back onto the floor with a mighty fracas. 'Fuck,' he raged again, the note, along with everything else, save for, miraculously, the lamp, went flying to the floor as he swept it all away.

This, *this*, was precisely why he couldn't get distracted.

Why he needed to concentrate, and solve this damned problem as he had all the others over the years.

If anything happened to anyone in her care, beyond what already had... She would be devastated. She likely already was. And if anything happened to her... He would be...

Devastated.

There, he'd admitted it.

Just like he admitted to himself that he needed to see her. He needed to speak to her about this, all of this, end whatever it was happening between them. Now. Tonight.

The mask.

'Damn it all to Hell,' he grumbled.

Glancing over at the clock on the mantel, he realised it was too early for him to barge in there.

As much as he needed to know how she was *right this instant*, he also knew how important tonight was for her. And he knew that no matter what had happened, tonight's mask would still happen. It meant so much for the future of *Miss Lily's*, and she'd worked so hard for it; all of them had. He wouldn't just barge in there and ruin it.

Smarter than that.

Yes. It was about him being smart. Nothing else.

So he would wait, clean up this mess he'd made, and do what he'd said he would before.

Find answers.

At least, that's what he told himself as he began his task.

Whether or not he'd achieve it, with his heart beating as if keen to leave his chest, and ice still flooding his veins, his heart, every nerve of his body, well.

That was a question he'd neither ask nor answer.

XIII.

It was only coincidental that Lily was in her room at the usual hour of three tonight. It was only because she couldn't stand to be in her office just now, where it felt, once Bill had left, *unsettling*. Unsettling, and unsafe, and as if whoever had come in and set that card on her desk had touched her. Riffled through her underthings, and got too close, and soiled every single item in the room which had once made her feel powerful, and now felt tainted.

She was only in here because there really wasn't anywhere else she could just pace, wearing down the floorboards as if treading her own personal widow's walk. The party was still going, excellently in fact, and was likely to continue on until well after sunrise.

Which was good.

Which was what someone wanted from a party such as this.

Only she couldn't very well go pacing around, not even in front of her staff, looking, and feeling, so...

Scared.

It was hard to admit, but it was the truth. She'd hoped never to feel this again, not in this house, with her own band of men, under the protection of St. Nick, of *Arthur*... But her little world had been invaded, and she had to make it right, she knew that, just not right now.

Right now she couldn't even bloody well think straight, let

alone plan, let alone -

The door slammed open and an already skittish and on edge Lily jumped, catching her foot on the rug before the hearth. She tumbled to the floor but scrambled away from the door, ready to scream until she caught sight of the man standing there.

'Arthur,' she breathed, panic dissolving into relief, not just for herself, but for him. 'Arthur...'

A tiny sob caught her throat as she said it, and tears pricked her eyes, but she swatted them away.

It didn't matter what conclusions she'd come to - *was it only this morning?* - she couldn't endure losing him, and truth be told, she wanted nothing more than him to be with her, right now.

She scrambled to her feet as he shut the door and rushed to her, concern darkening his eyes.

'Lily,' he said, and the relief she heard in his voice made her heart soar.

Because...

Because it means he cares.

He gathered her in his arms as she launched herself at him, and she held him as close as she could, not hesitating one second before kissing him. She let all she had pour into that kiss; relief, joy, hope, fear, even.

Arthur returned her ferocity tenfold, and she grabbed hold of his arms to steady herself, but with a hiss of pain he pulled away. Lily let go of him, staring down at his arm. Where she'd been holding him, or rather clutching to him for dear life, a bright red stain was now marring the wool.

And growing, quickly.

'What happened,' she asked, her heart skipping a beat at the thought of whatever danger he'd encountered tonight. Her eyes flew back to his face, and only then did she notice the bruises and cuts. 'Arthur?'

This, *this*, was precisely what she'd been afraid of.

They were all under attack, and whatever was happening was big enough that a man who'd enjoyed secrecy and safety for decades was now bleeding in her arms.

'Nothing,' he growled, quickly placing his own hand on the injury. *Nothing?* 'Damn.'

'Let me clean that up.'

'I already did.'

'Well, obviously not well enough,' she bit back, and he stopped and stared at her for a moment before nodding. She led him over to the wash basin, and pulled a box from the cabinet beneath it whilst he stripped off his clothes. 'It's quite deep,' she noted when she had unrolled the blood-soaked bandages from around his arm. The gash was at least an inch wide, and four long, all down his upper arm. *Nothing? This is not nothing, Arthur, why won't you tell me what happened?* 'I'll clean it again, best I can, but we should put a poultice on it,' she told him, concern filling her heart for what might've happened. What could still happen. She glanced up at him, and his gaze was affixed on the wall beside them. 'What happened,' she repeated, gentler this time.

'Nothing,' he said flatly. 'Just a spot of trouble. Nothing I can't handle. I came here -'

'I don't doubt that you can handle it, Arthur,' she sighed, placing an alcohol-soaked linen over the cut. He hissed in a breath and winced, and she reached over to take his other hand in his. Gently, he rubbed his thumb across the back of it, and closed his eyes. 'Why won't you tell me what happened?'

His eyes opened slowly, and studied her closely for a long moment.

'It's not important,' he said finally. 'What's important is what happened here. I heard about your workers.'

The proof of his concern on her behalf, though heartening, had lost some of its power.

His complete refusal to open up had been heart-wrenching before, but now...

Now that things were coming to a head, it was just, pointless. *Enraging.*

'They will be fine, in time,' she said, trying to give, so that he might realise what that looked like and do the same. 'Your men, and mine, are handling it. I should tell you...' Taking a breath,

Lily released his hand, and went back to her ministrations, carefully padding and wrapping his arm, though it would all need to be undone when she had a poultice ready. Which she would, as soon as they finished this conversation. 'There was a note, in my office. It said: "*Change is coming. Saints cannot protect you anymore.*"' Arthur's jaw ticked, and a flash of pure bloodlust flashed through his eyes. 'Do they know who you are? Did they come after St. Nick tonight, or Mr. Dudley?' Silence. *Damn him.* 'Arthur, please, speak to me. *Tell me,*' she begged. 'Tell me what happened. It's important to me.'

'I don't want to involve you, Lily,' he said, sensing her frustration. 'I'll take care of this. But that part of my life... It is dark, and dank, and full of things I won't poison you with.'

Oh for fuck's sake.

He did care - but just as she didn't know him - he didn't know her. Worse, *he* hadn't even tried, he'd simply created some image of her, and cared for that. That image, blinded him to everything else. And God help her, she'd let him do it.

Everything you thought this morning...

Was true.

For a second tonight, she'd thought he'd kept his distance because he was trying to protect her, though she wasn't sure how not learning more about him was protecting her. But now, she understood. He was preserving an innocent, simple vision of her.

That is what he was afraid of *tainting.*

Idiot.

'I'm already involved, Arthur.'

'I said I'll take care of it,' he snapped.

'I can't do this anymore,' she breathed, tying the knot on his bandage, and stepping back.

It broke her, to fully accept it, to admit it, to decree it, but it was the truth.

And for too long, she had been something, anything but herself, to please others.

No more.

'What are you talking about,' Arthur asked, frowning, a hint of fear in his voice.

'This,' she said, gesturing to them both. 'Whatever *this* is between us. I can't.'

'Because I won't tell you about what happened tonight? I'd have thought it obvious.'

'Because you won't share anything with me,' she exclaimed, the pure hurt of it tearing through her, compounding with all else she'd felt today. 'You won't trust me, and share yourself with me.'

'I told you, warned you I couldn't promise you anything,' Arthur growled angrily, as if she were asking too much, whipping his shirt back on and wincing with the pain of it. 'Give you that kind of relationship.'

'You mean one where two people share a *little* more than just a bed,' she asked, rounding back on him. 'I'm not even your whore, Arthur, because men tend to share *something* with their whores.'

'You know me better than anyone, we do share more,' he protested, coming towards her as if he meant to sweep her into his arms.

But she wouldn't have it.

She couldn't go on like this.

'No, we don't,' she cried, and the pain in her must've shown because he stopped. 'I know something about you, I don't know *you*.' Taking a deep breath, she steadied herself. 'I am not one of your saints, Arthur. You cannot worship me, and set me high up on a pedestal like some holy effigy. I am a living, breathing creature of flesh and bone, and blood,' she said, tapping her chest with her hand as if she could make him see it, realise it. 'I have seen, and done terrible things,' she told him. 'I want to trust you with those parts of myself, with all that I am, and I want you to trust me with all that you are. It may feel wondrous to be worshipped but I don't want that. I shouldn't have let it happen. I want to be seen. I don't want to be kept and taken care of; I want...'

'What?' he asked after a moment.

'Something you cannot give,' she said, the words making the truth tangible, and in the process stealing her breath and nearly felling her.

'Tell me.'

'You're right,' she breathed with a shrug, and a bitter smile. She should never have given in to begin with. All this, this was on her. 'I knew the deal when we started this. And I told you, I won't be this woman,' she declared, straightening her back and refusing to be broken. *Never let anyone break you. Don't let this man break you again.* 'The woman who asks for what cannot be offered.'

'Lily, for the love of God,' Arthur growled, and she liked to think he cared, that this hurt him as much as her, but she couldn't see anymore. She couldn't read him anymore. 'Tell me.'

'I want to be your equal,' she said simply, the pain so terrible she was numbed by it. Removed from it, if only for these final moments. And she was grateful for that. 'I want to be your partner. In all things. So you see,' she shrugged. 'I cannot be... *This*, anymore. I am sorry. It's my own fault for believing I could be satisfied with what you offered. That it would be enough.'

Arthur opened his mouth as if to protest, or promise, or beg, perhaps, but then, he stopped.

He frowned as he studied her, and then finally, nodded.

Then, without a word, he took his clothes, and hat, and left.

Lily didn't crumple this time. She didn't fall to the floor and cry her heart out like some fool. Because she was past that now.

In the days after they'd taken Kit, after she'd pounded on doors, demanded, begged, screamed, for answers, for help, she'd cried. But then, she'd realised, there was no hope. At least not where she was.

It had felt like this.

And just like then, the pain would help. It would make her stronger, give her the push to get things done. Give her the ability to do *anything* to make things right again.

So she would.

She didn't need a saint's protection to do it either. She just needed her wits, her grit, and the help of some good men and women.

I protect my own.

∞

'She tell you about the note?' a deep voice grumbled as he closed the door behind him. He tried not to think of it as closing the door on Lily, as closing the chapter on, as she so aptly put it, *whatever it was that they shared*, even though that's precisely what it felt like.

Which should be a good thing.

He'd come here, intending to check on her yes, but also intending to end *whatever it was they shared* because he needed to get her out of his life. He couldn't protect her from what was coming. Unless she was far enough from him not to be entangled by it.

She already is entangled in it.

Arthur shook his head, shook away the thought along with the more frustrating one: *she wants to be entangled in it with me.*

Pushing all the frustration, at her, at himself, at everything, away, he brought himself back to his surroundings and focused on the burly brute leaning against the wall a few steps away.

Bill, Lily's right hand.

Who, from what Arthur could tell, didn't like him all that much.

'She did,' he heard himself saying, walking towards the man then continuing past him.

He needed to get out of here, put his mind back in order, and get down to business.

He needed not to have a conversation with this man who he suddenly felt angry towards, for not protecting Lily well enough. And most of all, he needed Lily's words not to continue repeating themselves in his head, torturing him, beckoning him towards...

Something far more dangerous than anything else.

'Really rattled her, ye know,' Bill said, following, apparently undeterred by Arthur's *fuck off* glance. 'Someone comin' into her house, her office like that.'

'I can imagine.'

He could.

It was...

A violation.

Terrifying.

He hated that it had happened, he hated that he wasn't back in that room, making it better; that any of this had happened at all.

'Ye should take her away,' Bill said, and the inanity of that statement had him whirling around, the shock, he was sure, written all over his face.

Master of disguise, indeed.

'What?'

Eloquent, as well.

Still, it was all he could manage, and it conveyed the appropriate intention.

'Ye should take her far from here,' Bill repeated. 'She's scared. And not for herself, for everyone here. I can take care of 'em. But someone's after her, because of who owns this house.' Arthur was careful not to show any emotion this time; the last thing he needed was more people learning his greatest secret. 'Ye've got means, and I think... I think ye care for her. She cares for ye.'

Arthur's jaw clenched and he shook his head.

He did - that was precisely the problem.

But he couldn't just, run away.

And Lily...

'She'd never agree,' he said, though why he was explaining and indulging the man, Hell knew.

'Ye could make her, take her, and keep her, she'd hate ye for a while, sure, but...'

'What's your interest in this?' Arthur asked, stepping forth to look Bill in the eye.

Was he too part of this infernal scheme? Trying to get rid of a problem?

No...

When he looked in his eyes, he saw the same concern he felt in them.

'You care for her.'

'Aye. Miss Lily... She gave me a chance to be a man I'd thought long dead,' Bill admitted proudly. Not for the first time, he wondered how the two had found each other. From the beginning, Lily had been adamant on having her own men inside the house - on having Bill lead them. Even if he'd wanted to ask, to *know more*, somehow he got the feeling neither would answer. And for once, he'd let it lie, not looked into it himself. He'd trusted her. 'Whatever it takes, I'll see that debt paid.'

Arthur nodded, and sighed, his eyes glancing off the corridor's walls as he tried to find the words to say what he had to.

'I wish I could do it,' he said finally, meeting the man's eyes again. 'I truly wish I could. But I won't take her power, her choice from her. It would kill her.' Bill frowned, but then, after a long moment, nodded. When he did, Arthur realised it was the truth, and only that. There were a thousand other reasons why he couldn't, but in the end, he wouldn't, because he wouldn't hurt Lily like that. He'd hurt her already, and that, he would surely burn in Hell for, if not the rest. 'Keep her safe, Bill. She will need you, soon enough.'

'Aye.'

On that, Arthur turned on his heels, and left the house.

But as the cold early morning air hit him, so Lily's words did again too.

'I'm not one of your saints. I want to be your partner.'

Somehow, they cut deeper than any blade ever had.

Impossible, was not a word he'd ever allowed into his vocabulary.

Yet he would need to, because that's precisely what Lily's temptation was.

Impossible.

XIV.

It had been over a week. A quiet time, not in terms of the business, but in terms of everything else. Which was unsettling, and worsened the acid burn of the feeling that now seemed to permanently reside in Lily's gut. There had been no more notes, no more attacks, *anywhere*, at least from what Lily had heard, and she'd made it quite clear that she didn't care if a brawl at the Queen Anne looked suspicious, she wanted to hear about it.

But there had been nothing.

As if whoever had been terrorising Shadwell had suddenly, disappeared. Lily knew better, knew better than to hope it had all been some miscalculated power grab, or that whoever had orchestrated it all had simply dropped dead. They were lying in wait, regrouping, planning, preparing for something far, far worse, and all she could do, was gird her loins, and carry on with a damned smile.

Which was all one could do generally. It was how one survived. You prepared, and smiled, until whatever inevitable terrible thing was going to happen, happened, and then, you faced it, and hopefully survived it, and so forth, onward, and onward. Once, she'd seen the beauty in that. The reassuring simplicity of the pattern. Now, it felt like torturous drudgery; her impotence at being able to fully ensure those who depended on her survived, like salt in a gaping wound.

At least she wasn't constantly thinking about Arthur, or moping and crying like a useless forlorn chit. Which was good, because she'd already wasted far too much time and focus *thinking* about that man, dreaming of things... That she'd known could never be. Quite as she'd said to Sarah, she knew there would never be a quiet retirement to the country for the both of them. Neither of them were that person. He'd promised her time, and they'd had that, and it had been good, and now it was over, and she was moving on.

It wasn't that she *wasn't* thinking about him at all, she did, regularly, at least, once, or twice, very well, much more than that every hour; but that was natural. Especially since his name was on many people's lips with the opening of the foundling home he'd invested in at the request of Meg Lowell, even as ensconced as she was in her office most of the time.

It would take a while to stop thinking of him if she glanced over at that chair by the hearth, or when she went to bed, swearing she could still smell him on her sheets even though they'd been laundered at least five times now. She had been... *Enamoured.* So it would take time for things to go back to normal. His being completely absent from her life, was helpful in that.

As was the success of the business. The mask had not only garnered her more clients from the upper and middle echelons of Society, it had also marked her house as one that mattered. One that was worth every penny. Every night since they'd been busting at the seams, and she couldn't have been happier. Or busier. Already she was thinking of making *soirées* like the mask a regular thing, perhaps one in the summer. Definitely one next winter, for Saturnalia.

Winnie, Jack, and Mary, had returned to the house to convalesce, and everyone was taking good care of them. Their recovery would take time, and they offered to get lodgings elsewhere to make room for newcomers, but Lily wouldn't hear of it. Even if they didn't return to work, ever, which would be understandable after what they all had suffered, they were still her *people*. She wouldn't abandon them, wouldn't allow them to go on alone. It was a promise she'd made to all those in her care, silently; that none of them would ever be alone again.

What had happened to them had also reminded her of her plans to yet again copy the divine Madam E. *The Emporium's* boss had started buying homes in the country, to which she sent her workers if they retired, were in need of rest, or *isolation*, and provided them with work, such as cooking, or laundry, or a stipend until they returned to her. Lily had wanted to do something just like that as soon as she'd started *Miss Lily's*, but until profits were secure and steady, she didn't have the capital to do so without asking Arthur for more - which even then she hadn't wanted to do. Something to get her started, that had been the deal. From there, she was on her own. But now with the business' success, it was beginning to look like the plan might be feasible, perhaps towards the end of the year.

If it stays quiet.

A giant, taunting, *if*.

There were still no answers as to who had attacked her people, not that truly, she'd expected any. Her men and St. Nick's had done the best they could, but there was nothing to be found. Security had tightened at the house, and no one left without a big hulking bruiser by their side. So far, everyone was safe. There hadn't even been any peeps from Winston, who was still being watched. Bill had floated the idea he might have had a hand in the attack, but Lily doubted it. It didn't *feel* right.

And to top it all off, for the first time in what felt like forever, but had only been a couple months, the runner she'd hired to find Kit had contacted her, only to say that he was still working on it, but things weren't looking good. Apparently he'd lost her trail somewhere in the vicinity of Norwich, and he wasn't sure if he would be able to pick it up again. Lily tried to not be disheartened by it, because she couldn't afford to be; because that hope, was the one she couldn't ever let go of, and because he hadn't said he *couldn't* find her, or that he had, and something was wrong. So she had to see that as *good* news, and keep hoping.

Like always.

We'll be a family again, someday.

I promise.

'Come in,' she sighed, tearing herself from dreams of lost futures when Bill's knock sounded.

'You comin' down tonight?' he asked, as he came to stand before her desk.

She blinked all the thoughts swirling in her mind away, and realised darkness had fallen over her office.

She hadn't even noticed.

Rising, she lit the lamp on her desk, and went to light the fire.

'I always do,' she answered finally, as the kindling caught. She remained there, crouching, staring at the growing flames. 'I lost track of the hour, Bill. I'll get dressed shortly and come down.'

'You don't have to, ye know.'

No, technically not, but she always did.

It was part of her ritual, and it was, after all, *Miss Lily's.* It was good for her to be seen, and also to see, to feel, the atmosphere, the clients, to check on her workers.

And it keeps my mind away from things it shouldn't be on.

'I know,' she said instead, rising with a smile. 'I like to, you know that Bill.'

It faded when she caught Bill's shadowed face, the same look in his eyes that had been lurking in the depths for days, now front and centre. It irked her for some reason, the wariness, the concern. Though she couldn't quite say why. Maybe it was because she feared he saw her the same way Arthur did. Weak, useless. To be protected.

No...

It's because there is a smidgen of guilt there too...

'Bill, what's this about,' she asked bluntly.

He started, as if she'd physically shaken him, then sighed, rubbing his brows.

Finally, he met her gaze again, and nodded, as if agreeing with himself to say whatever he was about to. His hesitation, it worried her. Bill was not a man to hesitate.

Only once had he, and though that had been for the better, his steeliness, his steadiness, were what had gotten her through so very much.

'Bill?'

'I asked him to take ye away,' he admitted quietly, and Lily's mind whirled, trying to make sense of the words, until finally, she understood, and then shock hit her like a damp cloth to the face. 'He said no,' he continued quickly, as if needing her to know that, and God help her, but she did. 'Said it would kill ye to take yer choice from ye.' The realisation that Arthur had, after all, known *something* about her, unknotted something in her heart, though she tied it back up just as quickly. *Arthur knows people well. That's part of the key to his success.* 'But I'll ask ye now, Miss Lily,' he forged on, steel in his voice as he took a step closer. 'Leave. We both know, whatever's happenin' here, it ain't good. I know ye won't leave 'em, so take the others, ye have enough, we'll all help, or ye can ask him to find ye a house elsewhere. Go, before it's too late.'

'Runnin' ain't who I am, Bill,' she said, helplessly, willing him to see that, acknowledge that. 'I can't just leave everythin' I built here. I won't.'

'When we met, ye told me anyone can change,' he pleaded, coming closer than he'd been in years. 'No matter how far down a path we are. I feel it in my bones, and I know ye do too. This ain't gonna end well. I swore to protect ye -'

'Bill. Stop,' she breathed, taking the final step to him, so that they were toe to toe. She let the idea flit through her mind, the idea of packing up, taking everyone, and starting afresh, somewhere new. They could make it. They could make it work. But what was to say there wouldn't be trouble there? They couldn't run from fights forever. 'I ain't gonna lie. I'm scared. For all of us. But life, it don't stop comin' at you, no matter where you go, how much you try to avoid problems. I don't want anyone gettin' hurt, but whatever's comin', I believe we're better off makin' a stand here. Where we got people, and we got this house. I ain't bein' stubborn,' she said, a wan smile lifting the corners of her lips. 'For once. I'm tryin' to be smart.'

Bill sighed, and nodded, defeated.

Lily raised a hand, and smoothed it across his weathered cheek.

'I'm scared too, Miss Lily.'

The confession tore through her heart, and she dropped her hand, only to embrace him fully. After a long moment, he finally wrapped his arms around her, and she smiled, thinking how strange it was, that they had arrived here, after how they'd met.

'We'll make it through, Bill,' she said, her words seemingly echoing through his chest, to bounce back at her, doubly reassuring. 'Lookin' back, no one knowin' the two of us before we met woulda guessed we'd end up here. So that's some right good odds in our favour, don't you think?'

She released him, leaning back to smile, and he offered her a small one in return.

'Ye make yer own odds, Miss Lily,' he nodded. 'Always have, always will.'

'We both do.'

'I'll see ye downstairs,' he said, heading for the door.

'Bill,' she called before he reached it. 'Thank you,' she said, her tone as serious as death. 'For everything.'

He nodded, and left.

Here's to hoping I've made the right choice.

∞

December 1819

The night was bitter cold, frost and ice making the streets tricky to navigate. Lily was glad to have earned enough already to be able to get back home before midnight, because nights like these weren't only Hell to stand around in, most of the time, they were Hell to get clients, who didn't like the cold any more than whores did.

They did like the warmth of a whore, but too often they'd beg to come back to her bed, and that was something she never allowed. Not only because it was a rule of Sarah's house. But because that's why

God had created dark alleys, and back rooms of pubs. So that clients would never be a part of her private world, meagre and threadbare, and miserable though it might be. The blessedly comfortable though simple room in Sarah's home was her safe place, her refuge, and no one could ever know where it was because then it would be no longer.

If she could do without paying for a room at all, she would do it. Every penny went to saving for a runner to find Kit someday. To making a future together possible. So if she could've done without food, or shelter, she would've, but sadly she knew to have a future, she needed to live, so that was that.

Lily quickened her step as much as she could whilst still remaining vigilant of her surroundings, rubbing her fingers together before interlocking them and blowing on them, just like her papa had shown her once. She smiled, the memory warming her more than the gesture, or her worn excuse for a coat ever could.

Stopping at a corner to let a cart pass before crossing the street, Lily didn't even register the footfalls her ears heard mingling with the hooves of the horse ambling away until it was too late.

Rough, strong, meaty hands grabbed her as the scent of warm sweat and stale ale enveloped her. Hands grabbed her arms, and covered her mouth, and she scraped, and tore at them, trying to bite, trying to get purchase on her feet, but they too were swept away, and so was she, into the dark recess of an alley so like those where she made her living.

Desperately she tried to take some breaths, her heart beating out of her chest. This wasn't the first time men tried to take what they hadn't paid for, and it wouldn't be the last. The key was not to panic. To be smart.

Everyone thought whores were stupid. Because selling your body apparently meant you hadn't enough brains to do anything else. But really it was good, because when people thought you were some stupid little country girl who could only open her legs they underestimated you. They made mistakes. And those mistakes more often than not saved your life.

Two men, Lily thought, as they brought her back to a semi-illuminated little square where several alleys met. The moonlight shone brighter off the glittering cobbles, and it was quite beautiful, really, she thought, calming her heart that little bit more.

'Scream and yer dead,' a rough voice said in her ear, before she was summarily tossed to the hard ground, rolling until finally she could scramble to her feet with the aid of a long-abandoned crate, and face the men.

Two big hulking masses, barely visible in the darkness with their hats tipped low and their holey coats tucked up high.

What she didn't miss was the glint of their eyes, or that of the blade the one standing closer drew.

'No need for this, gentlemen,' she said as calmly, and sweetly, and enticingly as she could. 'Can give ye a right fair price for me services.'

She added a smile for good measure, but it froze, then faded, as the man with the blade took a step closer, and it wasn't lust in his eyes, but bloodlust.

'We ain't 'ere to be warmed by yer cunt, bitch,' he said, and dread invaded her once again. 'We're 'ere to teach ye no one says no to Gordy.'

Fuck, she thought.

And it must've shown, because the man's smile widened.

Gordy had been a client back in the Garden, a man who dabbled in everything from smuggling to murder, and who fancied himself a boss, but was far from it. He was dangerous, and despicable, and Lily had known that, which is why she'd refused to be his regular girl, and fled from the Garden when he'd become insistent.

She'd never dreamt he would come after her, but that had been her miscalculation.

But I won't die here tonight, she promised herself silently. Too many like her had died like this, and she wouldn't be the next. She could do this, survive this, and she would find Kit, and they would be a family, and then she could die.

But not tonight.

She glanced over the shoulder of the approaching brute, but the other remained in shadow, simply watching. Which was good, it would make her fight easier, facing them one at a time.

'Be a good girlie now,' the armed one said, coming ever closer,

which really was good, because she needed him close. 'And stay still while I make ye prettier. Then we'll take ye back to Gordy and he can have some proper fun with ye. Yer his, and always will be till he's done with ya.'

And then he was upon her, shoving her against the wall at her back, and cupping her jaw, his blade sliding across her cheek, his smile wide and reeking of rot.

It remained that way until the light had faded in his eyes.

He didn't even know what had happened, no dawning came to him, as he simply fell to his knees before her, his blade rattling as it tumbled to the cobbles, the only other sound the gurgling in his throat, the thick rasp of a blood-coated attempt to draw breath. But he couldn't, as her own blade went straight through his throat, right and true above his Adam's apple.

'I ain't no man's,' she spat, and warmth spread over her nearly numb fingers when she quickly pulled her knife out, kicking him away as she did, and bending as quickly as a striking snake to retrieve his own blade before facing the second man. 'Well come on then, ye try me too,' she barked at him ferociously. 'I ain't afraid of ye. Fuckin' cowards, comin' after a woman, two of ye, for little ol' me, and yer boss, not havin' the bollocks to do it 'imself. That ye even work for a cowardly fuckin' worm like 'im tells me you ain't no better.'

He didn't move.

Why wasn't he moving?

'Come on!' she screamed, but all he did was quirk his head.

'Ye're right,' a deep, gravelly voice said after a long moment, and she blinked, completely thrown off by the strange sincerity, and gentleness of it. 'Never meant for it to come to this,' he continued pensively, and Lily stood there, staring, her blades thrust out and ready, even though it didn't feel like she would have to use them. 'I'm a fighter, Miss Lily. Was real good too. But then I couldn't get no fights no more, and Gordy had work goin', so 'ere I am.'

This was definitely not what she was expecting, and still she stood ready, because it could be a trick, but her gut told her it wasn't, and that bitch was never wrong.

'Just because ye made a choice, don't mean it's the only one you got,' she offered, with a shrug. It's all she could think of to say; all she could think of to do, was talk to him. 'Ye can change the path ye take, no matter how far down ye are.'

'Hm.'

He pondered that for a long moment, then he took a step forward, and Lily stood strong and didn't flinch, but then he removed his hat, uncovering a bald head, and laid it over his chest.

'Name's Bill.'

'Evenin' Bill. Ye know me name.'

'Aye, Miss Lily.'

'So. Ye ain't gonna hurt me, and I ain't gonna kill you like I did 'im, right?'

'Right.'

'Hm.'

Slowly, she lowered her arms, and took a deep breath.

Whatever was happening, it was incredible, and unbelievable, and like one of those miracles people talked about, but she knew it was real, and life surprised you with good things every so often.

'Thank ye,' she said, looking back at him, a little closer now. She could see the tell-tale signs of a fighter - the broken nose, the scars - and a genuine gentleness in dark depths she couldn't quite make out the colour of. 'Think I could use a drink, Bill. Ye?'

'No thank ye, Miss Lily,' he said, putting his hat back on. 'I have some business to attend to.'

'I'll see ye then, Bill.'

'Ye will, Miss Lily. Ye will. Now get 'ome, I'll clean up 'ere.'

'Thank ye,' she said again, before doing just that.

She'd arrived home before Sarah, stunned, grateful, and completely unsettled, not by Bill, but by the terror that had threaded through her veins and was now slowly, dissipating. As it always did.

She'd made a cup of tea, and settled herself best she could, thanking the Lord she was still breathing, and reminding herself there was nothing to do but pick herself up, and keep moving.

As she always did.

As they all did whenever something like this happened.

There was no time to feel anything other than relief. No time to think about anything but the next night.

Days later, she'd heard that Gordy's body had been found in a rather disturbing manner in the middle of the Garden. She'd realised then that she'd not been afraid of him coming after her again, because deep down, she'd known that was Bill's business. And after that, she'd seen Bill hanging about Shadwell. They'd never spoken, but she'd always felt him, around, watching her, keeping an eye on her.

When it had come time to open the house, she'd known, there was no other man she'd trust to keep it safe. They had saved each other's lives that night, in very different ways.

And bonds such as that, could never be broken.

XV.

Arthur stared at the map on the desk before him, the ink circles he'd marked on it gleaming brightly in the low light of the single lamp he kept in here. They seemed to taunt him, mocking him for not seeing the pattern sooner. For being distracted, by Morgana's death, then by Lily.

For becoming so blinded, like all those fools over the years that he'd raised a critical brow at; even as their nights with whores, at the hells' tables, or indulging in whatever vice they did, made him who he was.

Allowed him to slip in quietly, and do what he had to to become St. Nick.

But he saw it now, the pattern. Understood it. Saw the enemy's plan as clearly as his own he'd made over the years. Saw the brilliance, admired it even, saw the next steps clearly, as if they too had been marked on the paper before him which represented so much more.

It had taken days, every minute of every hour since he'd left Lily, to solve it. To re-focus, to concentrate and gather all the information like pieces of a puzzle, and then, to assemble it all into one coherent image. It had taken much of what he had left in him, to make each inky mark, to go out and assemble all the papers at this office, or that, discreetly, of course, and to follow each trail. Every bit of strength he had to not think about Lily, the hurt in her eyes, the pleading in her voice. The temptation.

But he had, and it had paid off.

The problem was, he was still struggling to make a plan.

Because the truth was, the trails only led so far. So far into a world he didn't know, couldn't navigate, no matter his means and inside men. It led to more questions, which meant his usual plan of *bring down the enemy* wouldn't work. He knew what type of enemy he faced, but he had no names. And he wouldn't find any. They were much too good. Even if he had all the time in the world, which he didn't. He had days, weeks, at best. Now it was quiet, but soon...

They'll look to finish it.

There was one from that world he could ask. One, among all those he knew, that he knew he could trust. The rest... The rest were acquaintances, people who came here for pleasure and sin, or money. Some could potentially be pressured into finding some answers, but if they didn't wind up dead, they would likely betray him instead. One, among them all, he could trust.

Egerton.

But involving him... Something inside him tugged against it. He'd thought about it; the opening of the foundling home Arthur had helped finance at the request of the viscountess, would have been an ideal occasion to reconnect. To *talk*. Only, when the morning came, he couldn't do it. Couldn't go; couldn't even step out the door.

The viscount had stepped away from his vigilante days. He was married to Meg, and if rumours were true, they were expecting a child. He had a family. And though he may be a dangerous man, with a past that spoke of helping others, even at a cost to his own reputation... The viscount was settled now. A few years ago, Arthur wouldn't have hesitated to make use of him. To involve him. But now, he couldn't do it. Couldn't pull him into the darkness and ask him to risk what he'd found. Couldn't risk doing anything to harm the Lowells.

Becoming sentimental in your own age.

Yes. He would blame it on old age. His code even.

Not, on Lily.

Regardless of where the blame lay for his sentimentality, it was still a fact, just like all the rest. Which meant, that for the first time in his life, Arthur had to admit, that in this fight, he was outmatched.

Leaning back with a sigh in his chair, he removed his spectacles, tossed them onto the map, and rubbed his eyes.

Perhaps he'd always known this day would come. The day when he met an enemy he couldn't fight. Not with his wits, and not with his fists. It was inevitable, really. It was how they all ended. Met their match, and were vanquished by it. Once upon his time he'd thought his match, the unbeatable enemy, would come from the shadows, as he himself had. That it would be one of those great evils he knew dwelled far below even he; that he'd heard whispered about, but been careful to stay very far from. To even imagine. And maybe, his enemy was just that; only emerging from a world he hadn't expected. Regardless, they would be his end. There was no doubt in his mind about that, and it wasn't about giving up the fight.

It was about knowing when you couldn't fight, and make it out alive. Every man had to know the limits of their capabilities. It was how you played your strengths, worked on your weaknesses, and grew stronger. But there would always be someone stronger, and recognizing that, was also part of it. Knowing your own mortality; knowing that one day it would be time to pay the piper.

There is no way out of this for me.

He'd had a good run, after all. Years of life, of a good life, for his mother, his sister; for him. Twenty-five years of ruling in the shadows, with more power and wealth than any one man should ever have; but then he'd given a good life to many people in Shadwell too.

All in all, he'd spent over thirty years of his life fighting, not only for himself, and his own survival, but for others'.

Just because this is the last fight doesn't mean I will stop fighting.

Arthur nodded slowly to himself, accepting the truth of the matter.

There was no great plan to get him out of this. He *could* run, but he also couldn't. It wasn't who he was. He would fight until his last breath; it was the kind of death he'd wanted after a lifetime of fighting. And he could ensure his demise worked in favour of others. He could craft a plan to make his end *worth* something.

It came to him slowly, swirling in his mind like wisps of smoke curling around themselves until they met to form something more solid.

It could work.

It's the best outcome.

It will require help.

So he would ask for some.

Just because he wouldn't involve the viscount, didn't mean he couldn't make use of the next best thing.

Arthur chuckled to himself as he scribbled a note to the Ghosts, the irony of his change in resolve somehow amusing. Vaguely, he blamed it on Lily. Had she been here, she would've told him asking for help showed strength, or some such nonsense.

Not that it was nonsense, because she was right.

About everything.

So long he'd laboured alone; he'd liked it that way. But now he saw, admitted, that he couldn't do it alone. Didn't want to. And most of all, it wasn't him alone these decisions would affect. So those it would, should have a say.

He didn't push the thought of Lily away this time. He kept it close, like those memories of saints that had kept him warm as a child. He thought of her bright smile, the twinkling of her whiskey eyes, the sounds she made when she came, and how it felt to simply hold her. Flesh to flesh, heart to heart, skin to skin. It had all meant something.

He'd tried hard to fight that too, first by dismissing the notion she could ever care for him, then by dismissing his own capacity to do so. He'd found excuse upon excuse to explain how she was with him, how he was with her, when the simple fucking truth was that she saw him, and cared for him, and he'd tried to blind himself, *she was right again*; tried to paint a picture of her that was easier to make sense of, to control in a way. If she was as he painted her, she was simple to understand, and to let go, and to keep hidden in his heart for as long as he needed. It was easier to explain away emotions that way. But in the end, he did *see* her. All that she was. All that she'd shown him.

And he wanted to see the rest. To know her, as much as he could, in the time given to him. He wanted to *love* her, even if he had only a vague notion of what that meant. What it could mean. He knew what it meant to love family, but a partner...

I want to know.

Really, he wanted to do as Bill suggested, tie Lily up and send her far, far away until this was all over. He wanted to stay away, to protect her, but that wasn't love. Maybe love was realising, and accepting, that what *she* wanted was to be a part of it, regardless of the danger, because whatever they had together, it was worth it.

Right about that too.

And about the fact that she was already involved.

He couldn't tell her of course, the truth of what he'd uncovered, because she wouldn't accept his plan, she'd want him to fight, and that, he couldn't do. Not when he was certain of the equation laid before him. But he could still protect her. Put a plan in motion to keep her and hers safe. Just like the others.

This is madness.

It was. Pure, unfettered, madness. But even a condemned man was allowed a last meal, wasn't he? This would be it. A feast of love. He would do what he'd never thought himself capable of. He'd give into his heart, follow it, and indulge on the gift of love. For the first time in his life, he would be selfish. He would savour every single second, and that would be good; it would be the final gift to send him smiling off to the Devil.

If she'll have you.

Yes. First, he would have to beg forgiveness.

And then? Give her what she wanted.

Me.

That would perhaps be the greatest fight of his life.
But first, make sure everything is in place.
Then, you can rest until the end.

∞

'I believe we have an appointment,' Arthur said as he clicked the door of the Fleet Street pub's private room shut behind him, and raised his head to meet the man's gaze. Surprise flickered in Lionel Harrow's eyes, but then it was gone in an instant, and a smile of understanding lit his face as he nodded, rose, and offered Arthur a hand. They shook, and Arthur knew he'd made the right choice. 'Mr. Harrow.'

'Mr. Dudley,' the ex-runner, now security for Silver Bell wharf, and Ghost, said. 'I'll admit I was surprised. But it makes sense.'

Arthur nodded, and they took seats across from each other at the small, simple table set by the blazing hearth.

It was a good enough pub, quiet, and nowhere Arthur had been before, hence why he'd suggested it when he'd set the meeting with the Ghost. That, and the availability of a private room in this quiet hour of mid-afternoon.

Harrow poured them each an ale from a pewter jug as Arthur removed his coat and hat, laying them on another of the nearby chairs.

'I'll admit I was a bit hesitant to keep this meetin' from his lordship,' Harrow said, cradling his tankard and leaning back, deceptively relaxed, although both men knew neither would do the other harm. 'No matter that he's stepped away from the Ghosts. In fact I was all set to let him know Saint Nick had decided to make himself known. But when I arrived to see him, he'd just received news of his father's death.'

'I'm sorry to hear that.'

'Just thought I should be honest with you,' Harrow shrugged, then leaned forward, elbows on the table, seriousness in his eyes Arthur appreciated. 'See, I'm guessin' you know what's goin' on in Shadwell, and that's what this is all about. And I'll admit, if you're comin' out of the shadows, I'm a bit worried to hear what it is. So, I didn't think it was right, bringin' this to him, considerin'.'

'It isn't good,' Arthur agreed. 'And you'll understand, why I had asked he not be involved. Though I am grateful for your honesty.'

A deep breath, and a large sip from his tankard, and Arthur told him.

When he finished, Harrow's brows raised, and he sighed, before downing his drink, and leaning back in the chair, his gaze flicking to the fire over Arthur's shoulder.

'He'll have my head for it,' Harrow said finally, his gaze swinging back to Arthur's. 'But you're right. His lordship cannot be involved. So... What are you thinkin'?'

'We can't win,' Arthur admitted, the admission ringing as clearly as the last trumpets would someday in the silence of the room. 'Not all of us at least.' Harrow raised a brow, suspecting the line of Arthur's plan, and so he continued to unveil it. 'It's important to recognize when we've been bested. But that doesn't mean we can't prepare to fight another day. My men... I cannot promise their loyalty once I am unseated. Over the years, it is retribution, and a strong hand which has kept them in line, but without that... I cannot truly say for certain who will remain. Not that I blame them for that. I chose many for ruthlessness, and intelligence. It would be unwise to not bow down to new kings. I'll reach out to the leaders in Rotherhithe, and Wapping. Who knows if they'll listen to my warnings, but I can try. You should muster the Ghosts, make sure that when the time comes, they keep quiet, and out of the way. The next time the enemy strikes, it will be a final blow. Swift, and true. All we can do, is prepare for it. And ensure as many lives as possible are spared in the transition. Someday, perhaps, you can take it back.'

'Any idea when this final attack will happen?'

'I will,' Arthur promised. He would, because he would choose the time himself. As many variables as he could, he would control. 'When the time is right, when I've settled all that needs to be, ensured they can never get what they want, then, I'll set the rest into motion.'

'Why are you doin' this?' Harrow asked, his curiosity unconcealable. 'You could just run. Instead, you came to us for help.'

'I've tried my best over the years to protect the people of Shadwell,' Arthur said slowly, trying to put it all into words. 'They've been good to me. As good as family. These men who are coming for us... They are the kind of men I've despised my whole life. Men whose greed drives them, who will stop at nothing to achieve what they want.'

'Regardless of your name, I'll point out you ain't no saint.'

'I don't pretend to be,' Arthur said coldly, but truthfully, and Harrow conceded. He'd taken the moniker as a shield, to protect himself but also to give those around him hope. *Protector of whores and sailors.* 'I've been at this a long time. The world has changed so much... And now, my time is over. These men are a different breed, and I think you know that. If I could take them down, I would. But they are from a world I don't know. A world I cannot even begin to learn how to navigate. And they are coming for our world. All I can do, is ensure as many as possible live to see another day. You ask why I come to you? Well, it was my understanding the Ghosts were created to protect people. That's all I'm asking you to do now.'

'We'll do as you say,' Harrow said after a moment, leaning back on the table, and pouring himself another drink. He raised the jug, a question in his eyes, and Arthur nodded. 'It's as good a plan as any. Still, I have to wonder...' Taking a sip, he surveyed Arthur for a moment, before finally voicing his question. 'You could've said all this in one of those notes you're so fond of. Didn't have to meet, Hell when I wrote the invitation, I never thought you'd take me up on it.'

'Neither did I,' Arthur admitted with a wry smile. 'Neither did I... But I realised, we all have to come out of the shadows sometime. Even if only for one final sunrise.'

'Lily,' Harrow smiled, as if all the explanation lay in those two syllables.

It does.

'How did *you* know?'

'Everyone knows you been visitin',' Harrow shrugged.

Arthur nodded; he should've guessed Mr. Dudley's nocturnal habits would garner attention.

That they *would*, if Lily took him back.

Which made this next part evermore essential.

'I need to ask you a personal favour, Mr. Harrow,' he said quietly after a moment, and the man's smile faded, as he understood the seriousness of what was coming. 'When the time comes, I need you to get her out. She will fight you, but I need you to do it. She is the most precious being to me, and I need to know that she will live.'

'Why would you trust me with this?' Harrow asked seriously.

'I know you, Mr. Harrow,' Arthur said with a smile. 'I've watched you, over the years. I know your past. Even today. You told me the truth when it might've cost you. You're a good man, and a loyal one. Your word means something.'

'It does. And I give it to you,' Harrow said, offering his hand again. 'I'll take care of Lily.'

Arthur took it, and a weight seemed to lift from his shoulders.

'Thank you.'

'Of course.'

They fell into a thick, pensive, silence, and without consulting each other, they slowly finished the jug of ale, before both leaving, separately.

When Arthur was yet again on the street, he took in a deep breath, and enjoyed the wonder of it filling his lungs for a moment, before setting out for Shadwell.

It was done.

Now…

Now for the most important part.

Winning back my love.

XVI.

Another busy night. More success. Lily should be pleased. Ecstatic. But somehow, she just couldn't quite muster those emotions. And well, she didn't have to. Which was a relief, in a way. Didn't even have to fake them, now that the evening was well underway, and she could escape to her office, to put a dent in the work waiting for her there.

Huzzah, she thought grimly, taking the final stair, and turning into the corridor leading to just that.

She stopped short as she raised her eyes, and found something else waiting for her.

Arthur.

His own eyes met hers, the silver as bright as the moon itself in the dusky corridor, and he straightened from where he'd been leaning against the wall beside her office door. Despite her best efforts at ordering it not to, at telling herself it meant nothing at all, her heart skidded right out of her chest, and landed back at his feet for him to trample on.

Treacherous beast.

Somehow she managed to conceal her heart's betrayal, raised her head, and continued on, a mask of polite indifference painted on yet again.

'Mr. Dudley,' she said, stopping before him.

There were a thousand questions in there, all underscoring the most important of them all: *what are you doing here?*

'Bill let me in,' he said, almost sheepishly, though that was impossible because that wasn't something he could be. Even if he was twirling his hat in his hands, and looking as hesitant as a schoolboy about to confess all his pranks to the headmaster. 'I thought about waiting in your office, but... It didn't seem right.'

The little gesture was a knock on that defensive wall she'd managed to build, nicking it in just the right place to weaken it entirely.

But he's not here for anything other than business ya daft lump, so don't even think it.

'Thank you,' she said nonetheless, because it was appreciated, and he should know that. 'But why are you here?' she asked, voicing the question he hadn't answered yet.

Only, she needed to know, right now, before her mind followed the path of her heart, and completely betrayed her, and went off to imagine things.

He glanced at the office door, then, when she didn't make a move to invite him in, no matter that it wasn't professional in the least, this was her house, and she needed to do this right here, and that was that, he looked back at her, resigned to say his piece here.

'I came to ask you to come with me somewhere,' he said, as if that bloody well explained everything.

Try again.

'Mr. Dudley, I'm quite busy, and I -'

'Please, Lily,' he said, in that soft voice that truly was magic for it had the power to undo everything she was. 'I know, I hurt you. I know, I'm asking a lot, asking you to trust me again, even for a moment. But I am asking.'

'I can't keep doing this, Arthur,' she said softly, not bothering to try and dissimulate the pain in her voice. He needed to hear it, to know that she had the strength for much; just not this endless torment. 'Coming together, breaking apart. I can't.'

'Come with me tonight,' he said, as if that was the simple answer to preventing her further heartbreak. 'I have something important to show you. And after that, if you want me to step out of your life completely, you can say so, and I will disappear. I swear it.'

Don't do it, her mind screamed.

Lily studied him, stared into his eyes, hoping to find some clue as to what awaited her with either choice, but all she found was a light she'd never seen before, and her own hope, reflected back at her.

Do it, her gut whispered.

'Very well,' she breathed.

And when Arthur smiled, a beautiful, heart-stopping, incredible smile that seemed to light the night with its intensity, chasing the cobwebs from untouched corners of her heart, she knew, as always, her gut was right.

∞

After changing into an actual dress, wrapping up in a coat, and informing Bill she would be gone for the evening, they made their way to a row of tiny, cramped houses in the Hamlets. They made their way in silence, and, Lily noticed, in the shadows. Arthur was more watchful than she'd ever seen him, taking more twists and turns than were necessary, making the journey which should've been half an hour, three times that. But with her hand in his, his presence beside her all the while, she never felt afraid. Merely...

Apprehensive.

It felt as if they were marching towards some great event, some monumental happening that would change their lives. Even as they stood before the houses, half stone, half wood, some with many windows boarded up, all looking very much like any other in the East End - worn, and rather unextraordinary - she couldn't shake the feeling.

A key in hand, Arthur led her into the dim confines of the second to last house, but rather than stop, he continued through it until they arrived at a cellar door. She followed, unable to see anything in the darkness, but her footsteps sure as she focused on the warmth of Arthur's touch. At the door, he squeezed her hand gently before unlocking it, then slowly led her down stairs which creaked only a little, though the sound seemed to echo like shots in the dark. Lily shivered once they reached the cellar, the damp, mouldy air seeping through and tickling her bones. Still, they didn't stop, Arthur leading her to what she could only imagine was the wall adjoining the next house.

There was a sound of wood scraping against brick, a click, and then on they went. Her mind whirled with questions, *where, how, why*, but she focused on breathing, and walking steadily onwards in the dark.

The answers would come, she knew that in her heart.

'There are steps again, Lily,' Arthur said, stopping. 'Up this time.'

She nodded, realising too late he couldn't see her.

Though perhaps he could, perhaps that was one of his magical abilities, for the next moment he was leading her slowly forward, until she felt him rise, and then her toes butted up against the first step. Painstakingly, they made their way up, until another door was unlocked and opened, and they stood in yet another dark corridor.

The scratch of tinder, and a candle reared to life.

Shadows flitted across Arthur's face before her, his eyes searching hers, but for what, she didn't know. Whatever it was, he seemed to find it, for then they were moving again, until they reached a tiny square room, bare of anything except whitewashed walls, and a window closed off by thick velvet curtains.

This was what he wanted to show her? An empty room?

She turned to him, searching his eyes this time, wanting to understand the importance of wherever this was.

'What is this place?' she finally asked quietly, afraid to even disturb a speck of dust.

'This... This is the last place my sister, and my mother, called home. The last place we were a family,' Arthur said evenly, though she felt as if the confession had been ripped from his soul.

She sucked in a breath, her mind whirling, her heart thumping.

Across from her, in the gloom, he stood tall, and strong, though there was hesitation in his eyes. Whether it was from bringing her here, or what he was about to say, she didn't know. All she could feel, was that hope springing to life again; the hope that perhaps they could be together.

That this gesture, meant what she truly wished it did.

'I was born and raised in Rochester. My father was a fisherman. When I was six, he took his own life after accumulating more debts than anyone could repay in three lifetimes,' Arthur said, so calmly, so evenly, as if he spoke another man's tale. She longed to reach out, to hold him, touch him, help him through this, but still, she was afraid that if she moved, he might come to his senses. Send her away, or simply leave again, and never return. So instead, she waited, for the rest. 'My mother took us, and we fled, disappeared in the middle of the night. Changed our name, came to London. For six years we all worked ourselves to the bone to make our living, to afford this place. My mother, then sister when she was old enough worked the looms, while I worked the kilns. When mother passed of the bloody flux, we couldn't make ends meet, and we were thrown to the streets.' Arthur took a breath, set the candle down in the middle of the room, and began wandering the empty room, studying it as if he could still see all it had been in his youth. The flickering of the candle against the uneven walls nearly made her able to see it all too; his shadow playing out the tale of those years. 'I started working the streets we lived on. I was a bulk, a snakesman, a bob, a cracksman, for any of the bosses that would have me. We saved enough to get a place of our own, a hovel really, but I knew, it would all happen again if I didn't find a way. That my sister would be forced to do things...' Arthur glanced at her, as if to apologise for not wanting the life she had led for his sister. But she smiled a tiny reassuring smile; she understood all too well. 'So watched, and I learned, and I listened, careful not to work my way into anyone's sights. And slowly, I built my empire as I built a life as Arthur Dudley, for myself and Morgana.'

'Did...' Lily paused, wondering why after all he had told her, this would be her question. After all he'd given, somehow this is what she needed to know. 'Is Arthur your true name?'

'No,' he smiled, pleasure flitting across his eyes, as if he liked that she'd guessed. 'Mother chose them when we moved. She was rather a romantic, you see, even despite it all. I was Lawrence before, but I haven't thought of myself as anything other than Arthur for, well, ever.'

'Why this house?'

'It reminds me of happier times,' Arthur sighed, resuming his tour of the room. 'Despite the hardships, for a short time, there was love in this house.' He paused, running his finger along the dusty curtains. 'And I suppose, it reminds me of all that can change in a single night.' Arthur turned back to face her then, his eyes alight with intent, and fire that burnt through her. 'Not even my sister knew I had bought it again. It's from here that I built it all. In the study, across the corridor,' he said, gesturing to the door behind her. 'There is a safe. With all the keys to Saint Nick's organisation. This is the epicentre, the heart of all that I have. Of all that I am.'

And he was trusting her with it all.

Sharing it all.

She had asked for his trust, his partnership, and here he was, giving her all she had wished for, but never truly dared to dream.

Tears burned her eyes and spilled without warning onto her cheeks.

'I have a sister,' she breathed as he made to come for her, and he stopped, his eyes wide in surprise. But she had to... Say this, share this, share something. A demonstration of her own, that they would be together, equals. 'My family tended a farm, in Sussex. We too were happy for a time. Until the winter of 1814. A fever took my parents, and nearly took my sister too. After that, I was left to care for her, and we did well enough for a time, with the sale of what little we had, and charity. But soon...

I had to find another way to provide for us.' Arthur nodded his understanding, and it gave her strength to see there was no judgement in his eyes. She realised then, there never had been, and her heart clenched. 'I went to work at an inn nearby. I was Lily the tart then. And soon, the people of my village, the wives of the men who came to me, even the men themselves, they took offence with my ways. They didn't want a whore in the village. So they took my sister from me. Christian charity they called it. Saving her soul,' she scoffed, the pain still unbearably fresh after all these years. The shame, the anger, the fear. 'They chased me out of town, and sent her away to a good place. I tried,' she told him, wanting him to know that she had, that she hadn't been as capable as he, but by God had she tried. 'To stay, to find her... But I lost her. I came to London to find her. Maybe even offer her a life someday. *Something.* First thing I did when I saved enough, I hired a runner. He's been searching for her ever since.'

'What's her name,' Arthur asked gently, closer now, though she couldn't recall him moving.

Close enough that she could feel the reassuring heat of him; smell the reassuring scent.

'Elizabeth,' she breathed. 'I called her Kit, because she reminded me of a little fox.' Arthur smiled, and she knew she had to continue. She had asked for this; she couldn't be the one to baulk now. Not when everything was right here, within her grasp. 'I'm not... I'm not just some simple farm girl who fell on hard times, Arthur. I need you to know that. I've killed,' she confessed, waiting for him to step away, to judge and condemn her, but he didn't. 'And I would again if I had to. I've hurt people,' she pressed, challenging him to leave her again. 'I've done things to survive that would even make you blush. I don't want to be saved, and I can't save you. I can't be your light in the darkness because I live in it as much as you. I like it, as much as you do.'

'I know,' he said simply, that smile not fading from his lips. 'I don't... I never thought I could trust someone,' he said softly, taking her cheek into his palm, lightly sweeping his thumb across it. She couldn't help but lean into it, into him, to drink up the comfort and care he offered. '*Enough.* I never wanted to ask someone to share the kind of life I lead. Not entirely. But the truth is, I understand now... I love you, Lily,' he said, and the thrill of those words shot through her like a current. She searched his eyes for anything to believe the truth of it, it was so unbelievable to her, but there was only light. 'I have for a very long time. And as much as you saw... I couldn't ask. I couldn't allow you to be part of this. I'm scared to love you. Scared you'll get hurt, or hate the man I am. I have always protected, shouldered the burdens, lived the life I have so those I loved didn't have to. I can't say I am happy that you want to share this life with me, if in fact, you still do. I can't say I will do so easily, without fear. But I can promise you now, that I want to. I want to share a full life with you. And if that means giving you the keys to the kingdom... I'll do it. I'll do anything for you.'

'You love me?' Lily asked quietly, still unable to believe it.

Unable to believe she was being offered most of all she had ever wanted.

A life with Arthur; his heart.

'I'd thought it quite obvious by now,' he grinned, before leaning down to kiss her.

And that kiss felt different than all the rest they had shared, because there was no more doubt that they felt the same.

No more secrets, or at least, the promise of utter openness and truth.

'I love you, Arthur,' she breathed when he finally broke the kiss. 'Though not nearly enough, I think a lifetime sounds perfect.'

XVII.

All his life, or at least, for the greatest portion of it, Arthur had straddled two worlds. Like a shade, a ghost, a revenant, he'd been split between the world of the living, of those that dwelled in the light, and the world of darkness, and death. Split, unable to fully *belong* to either, unable to truly touch either, only to witness, to observe.

Yes, there were times when he was technically able to touch either world. When he spilt blood or even allowed a tenant to remain with rent well past due. Tiny, infinitesimal moments where he seemed to take shape, a vengeful shadow or benevolent spirit. Moments with his sister, had kept him tethered to himself, to Arthur Dudley, preventing him from slipping entirely into the world of night.

And when he'd first touched Lily, it had felt as if she was opening the door to another world. A terrifying one with an unknown landscape and horizon. But when Lily's lips met his own again now, her hands slipping to grasp his waist, her love seeping into him like some strange, golden ambrosia, her soul embracing his own, *all* that he was, it wasn't another world he saw.

For perhaps the first time in his life, it was *this* one.

Opening himself to her love, refusing to deny his own any longer, it brought him clarity as the two parts of himself, the two worlds he dwelled in, seemed to reconcile. Like a wave beginning at his feet, grounding him in a way he'd never felt before. As if, he could finally feel the weight of himself against the floorboards.

From there, it was as if the wave of a gentle, but brisk and cleansing wind swirled around him, sharpening his already heightened senses. He held on tight to Lily, the scent of blackberries and summer sunshine mingling with the warm musk of her skin, the damp wool of her coat, and the old dust of the room. Deepening the kiss, he sought more, because with every scented note, every new flavour, the dusky veil separating each world from the other disappeared a little more. Everything was clearer, sharper, and intoxicating.

And the sounds… God the sounds…

Lily's sharp inhales through her nose, the tiny little moany gasps that travelled from the back of her throat to her chest. He could feel them echoing into his own chest, their vibrations lending power to the sweeping wind tearing him from the world of the half-living, back into the world she dwelled in. It was as if she were a great sorceress capable of resurrection, awakening him from the slumber of death which had left him covered in cobwebs and dust.

His heart beat so fast, faster than it ever had, resolute in its desire to pump his dormant blood through every vein, every nerve, until every inch of his skin could feel as it never had before.

And he understood, finally; reconciled himself with that concept of the heart as more.

More.

He needed more, as before, of her, of this, of *everything*.

But before he could lift her into his arms and take her across the corridor to the chaise in St. Nick's office, Lily's hands were moving from his waist, dancing over his chest to slide over his shoulders, and with a determined sweep she rid him of his coat. It fell to the floor, and his eyes flew open. He could've sworn he saw a cloud of dust puff up from the floor in the half-light, surrounding them in a haze.

Though Lily herself, had never been sharper. Truer. More real, than this moment.

Her eyes shone like a sunrise, bright, and warming parts of himself he'd never known existed. She herself glowed, and he could see every tiny hair on her face. Every mark, every freckle. He could see himself glistening on her swollen lips, and the shadowed lines on her neck that waxed and waned with every breath as her skin rose to meet the collar of her coat and dress.

And then she smiled, slowly, as his eyes met hers again, all doubt, all hesitation, all reserve, gone. She'd said she couldn't be his light in the darkness, but she'd been wrong. She was his sun, illuminating the world around him so he could see, truly, for the first time in his life. She was the centre of his universe, and that blinding smile so sure, and loving, filled him with a deeper sense of peace than he'd ever dreamt he could feel.

Peace, in the knowledge that if he died tomorrow, everything he had been, and done, up until then, would've been worth it, because he had this moment.

His own smile grew, crinkling the lines by his eyes, he could feel that too, and even though he wanted to take his time, and savour every second of this feast of the senses, his need, and her own, took hold.

Between fierce, deep, searching kisses, garments were stripped, and thrown to the floor. Hands roamed across wool, linen, and skin in their quest to rip every last stitch of cloth from the other's body, and when both of them had finally managed to relieve themselves of their boots, crouching near the floor, tongues and teeth clashing best they could as fingers fumbled with laces and shoes and stockings, Lily helped Arthur finish the descent with a final gentle shove to his breast.

He assisted her too, his hands encircling her upper arms and taking her with him, and a laugh escaped him as he landed on his discarded coat, and some other garments, Lily above him. It broke the rushed passion, but not the need, nor the connection. If anything, it strengthened it.

He brushed his thumb across her cheek, and then slid his hand into her hair, until pins tinkled on the floorboards, and her curls of sunlight were loose, curtaining her face, and tickling his temples, and then his ears, as she leaned down, brushing her lips against his briefly. She didn't linger, choosing instead to pepper kisses across his face, each touch like the highest, purest note of music anyone had ever heard.

She continued her work, discovering him as he had her; but as he'd never let anyone before. As no one had ever cared to; not with this intention, and care. She readjusted herself so that she was properly straddling his stomach, and silky flesh was like satin across the top of his hips, whilst the wetness of her sex against his belly was like a shot of pure vitality.

Desire raced through him, and he grew hard against her as she continued exploring him with her mouth, travelling down his own neck, across his ears, into the hollow of his shoulder, and then his own nipples.

Sucking in a breath, his eyes closed of their own volition, whilst his hands grasped the flesh of her hips. It was dizzying, and intoxicating, but even those were not descriptive enough words to describe what it was like to feel everything for the first time and all at once.

The hardness of the wood beneath him.

The rough and bunched cloth there too, warming him until he could feel sweat pooling at his lower back.

The whisper of feathery delight as Lily's hair brushed across his skin.

The delight of his flesh between her lips, her teeth.

The swirl of her tongue over the coarse hairs across his chest.

And that was only a minuscule portion of what his body felt.

The scents of their desire mingling, the sounds of their flesh meeting; all of it overwhelmed him. It felt as though he could grasp reality itself.

But none was so powerful as the tightening in his chest.

It wasn't bad, quite the contrary, but that didn't mean it didn't hurt. That it didn't feel as if that wisp of wind that had swept away the veil was now tearing through him, ripping muscle from bone, to make something new in his chest. A new heart, which beat for Lily, and which was born of the two halves of himself. There was light, and darkness within, swirling until it was vespertine.

The pain of being reborn anew was building, but it eased when Lily grasped his manhood, swirling her thumb across the tip, spreading the proof of his desire before guiding him into herself where he now understood he belonged. He'd known it before, but refused to give into *more*.

Now, he dove headfirst into *everything*.

He forced his eyes open and watched greedily as she raised up upon him, her fingers trailing down his chest until they rested beneath his navel, still dancing, gently, caressing the flesh there as her hips moved, taking him, then releasing him. His own fingers still holding tight to her, he helped guide her, and keep her steady, but he relinquished everything else to her.

Control, power.

Things he'd never given up once he'd finally had them within his grasp, because that was death, and destruction, and ruin, but not now. Now, it was love, and trust, and he wouldn't want it any other way.

So Arthur let himself go, let himself solely be present; see, hear, smell, touch, taste.

He let himself watch, and feel every emotion course through him.

He let Lily drive them both to a new height of passion; one which was ultimate pleasure yes, but also connection, and tangible truth.

And when they were both spent, and she collapsed back onto his chest, holding him as tightly as he did her, he felt whole.

∞

Outside, the city was waking, tiny dim slivers of light peeking in through any place it could, replacing the long burn-out candle. Though now covered in a blanket made up of her coat, and dress, they still lay where they had come together. *Made love.* Trite though the words may be, they felt like the only ones to describe what she and Arthur had shared.

Their nakedness had not only been physical, but philosophical as well.

They'd bared parts of themselves they never had with another, and when they looked at each other, it wasn't some version, some image of the other they saw, but their truest selves. They accepted each other, and loved each other.

And that was that.

Sharing such an experience, was beyond mind-shattering. It was earthly, and yet unearthly. Primally human and yet heavenly. Brutally real, and yet dreamlike. Her torn and shredded little heart had been sewn together once again, with threads of light, and she'd become herself, truly.

Lily.

The beauty of it, it didn't chase the darkness, the pain or fear she felt, away, but it soothed it. Put it all into perspective. Made it seem smaller, less...

Consuming.

Laying here with him, every breath lulling her like a babe, his heartbeat in her ear, his slick skin against her, felt so right. So natural, and essential. As if this is what she'd been made for, to love, and be loved by Arthur. Feeling like this, she could do anything. Conquer the world if she had to.

She smiled against his chest as her fingers skimmed along his ribs, and his own trailed down her spine. She wished they could stay here forever, live in this haven, always.

But the world beyond pierced into her mind, as thoughts of her house, of Kit, of the troubles, all of it, returned to the forefront. Their intensity, tamped down, but still, omnipresent.

And despite all they had said, despite all they'd shared, self-doubt in the form of a single question, appeared, as unbidden as the rest. It was a question that had haunted her from the beginning; the subject something they'd never before discussed, but which ate at her, like the little green monster it was. Resolved that if they were to continue on, sharing and completely open, as she had wished, she had to admit that strangely, in this moment as they lay in the remnants of his past, a flicker of doubt still remained.

A flicker of jealousy. Of what if.

'Arthur,' she said quietly, pushing back the fear of what he might think of her ruining their night like this. 'There's something... I must ask.'

'Anything,' he breathed, a smile in his voice as he lifted his head and laid a kiss on the top of hers. 'Ask me anything.'

'Would you... Would you have told Meg about Saint Nick? If you'd married her?'

A relieved huff escaped him, as if he'd been expecting anything but that; however the short bark of laughter was anything but mocking.

Lily had to wonder, if the relief in it meant that there were things he truly feared she would ask, and what they were.

Why that is.

'No,' he said, with a finality, and certainty as swift and true as St. Michael's blade, slaying her own emerald dragon. 'She would have been Arthur Dudley's wife, not Saint Nick's. She would have ever only known half of me. And there could never truly have been love between us for that same reason.'

'But I thought... You cared for her, you were to be married,' Lily said, unable to voice the rest.

Everyone in Shadwell had known, whispered about Mr. Dudley's partiality towards the Lowell family.

When the announcement had been made he was to marry Meg, it hadn't really come as a surprise to anyone. Though born in Shadwell, Meg Lowell was a proper governess, and would've made anyone like Arthur Dudley a good wife. She was beautiful, and smart, and -

So much I am not.

Hell she made a viscount – now earl - a good wife.

'Not many remember this,' Arthur said gently, his hand resuming its exploration of her back. 'But Meg's mother was good to me, as was her father. They were some of my first tenants, and for years, every time I would go collect the rent, they would insist I had a meal with them. They knew I was alone; I'd sent Morgana to live in the country by then, and they shared their family with me. Meg was maybe... Five then? I was barely twenty. You're right,' he continued. 'I did, I do care for her. For Jim too, and Charlotte, and Louisa. Their friendship, it helped me... Remain myself. When I first gained power, and wealth, as Saint Nick, I admit, I was... Corrupted by it. But their friendship, their family, helped me fight the corruption. You should know, however that I never... My thoughts were never other than chaste for Meg. I put distance between the Lowells and I slowly, as the business grew, though I was proud of her accomplishments as the years passed, and I grieved for her mother when she passed. But it was never anything more.'

Arthur took a deep breath, and she held him tighter, realising he was approaching something she needed to hear, or rather, that he needed to say, which perhaps was the reason behind her forcing herself to ask this question.

'In all my years after my mother's death,' he began again after a moment, his other hand trailing up to hold her thigh, as if every part of him needed to touch her. 'I only ever loved my sister. I protected her, kept her safe, and provided for her. That was enough for me. My life, as Mr. Dudley, and Saint Nick, as it grew, was enough for me. Until Sarah was married, I think. I was getting old by then -'

'You are not old,' Lily protested, lifting her head to scowl at him, but he merely smiled, and raised a brow.

'Lily, I may not be an old man,' he grinned. 'But I am old.'

'Not in spirit,' she countered, and his smile grew again.

'Well,' he said, somewhat conceding as he continued with his tale, and she set her head back on his chest. 'I was getting older. And the love I saw in Sarah, and Jonah, it, sparked something I suppose. A desire for more than what I had. Companionship, perhaps. I knew I could never share *all* of my life with anyone, but I thought perhaps, that I could have a warm home. Filled with something more than emptiness. And then Meg returned, and I wondered, perhaps, if it could be. It was odd, and fleeting, thinking of her in that way, I'll admit, and I resolved it wasn't to be. Until she came to me, and asked me to marry her.'

'She asked you?'

'Yes,' he told her, and somehow, that knowledge, slayed and burnt to ash the last remnants of self-doubt within. 'Her father was ill, as you know, and things with her viscount, well, the earl, had ended. She offered what I had found myself longing for. Friendship, companionship, care, in exchange for security, and a future for her family. I accepted, because yes, she offered what I thought I craved, but also in repayment, for what her family had done for me. Not that I think she even remembered, which was for the best. I told her, I did not want her gratitude if I accepted her offer. She should never have known mine played a part in taking her up on it.'

He fell silent for a moment, and Lily let his words, his tale, seep into her soul.

It seemed to add to the portrait she had painted of him with all the knowledge he'd unveiled, in the past months, years, but especially in the past hours.

He'd never dreamt of what they shared, he'd confessed as much before, and neither was he pleased with having her share his life, but still, he would let it happen. For so long now, it seemed as if she had dreamt of that, of *this*, of them, but she'd never understood truly, what love like theirs meant. What it meant, to choose a path you didn't want, solely because it was the only way to happiness. She'd wished for this, but never known the reality she was asking for.

It was both sobering, and so much more than she could've imagined.

'Do you want a family someday, Arthur,' she asked quietly, and he sucked in a deep breath.

'You mean, do I want children?' She nodded. 'I don't think so. I... Don't think I am quite built for that. Do you?'

The tension that had built inside her as she asked and waited for his response uncoiled, and she let out a breath as deep as the one he'd taken in.

The strange idea that perhaps they shared breath now crossed her mind.

How strange and wonderful that would be.

'No,' she said, and it felt as if he too was releasing some worry that she might ask for something he could not give. Again. 'I've been as careful as I know how to be over the years, and I've had my share of scares. Each time, I wondered, what it would be like. But I don't think I'm quite built for it either. The only family I ever wanted was Kit. Along the way, I've found others to care for too, but...'

'You still miss her.' Lily nodded. 'We'll find her,' Arthur promised, and when he did, she believed him.

'And then what,' she asked, the doubt that had always been there with that question returning a hundred-fold. Before, the answer had always been, *give Kit a good life*. But now, with Arthur in that picture, she had to wonder what it might look like. 'Shall we all go live in the country? Shall you retire from your empire, and I relinquish my house?'

'I doubt that would suit either of us,' he laughed, and she had to agree. 'But that does not mean we cannot build a home for ourselves.' With that final sentence, a cold swept over Lily, and she shivered. But it came not from the chill of the room, but the regret tingeing his voice, that she did not understand, only felt, to the marrow of her bones. 'We should get dressed,' Arthur said, rubbing her back more vigorously, to warm her. 'We will not have the shadows to hide us this morning, so we will need be even more vigilant. And I need you to pay close attention. I need to know, that after we have returned you home, should the need ever arise, you could return here, with your eyes closed.'

Lily raised her head again, and stared into the now dark grey of his eyes.

He had offered her so much, yet now she saw so much still he held back.

'Why should I ever have to return here without you?'

'In case there ever was trouble,' he said, deceptively lightly, something flashing across his eyes she wanted to ask him about. But he did not give her a chance. 'That is all. Now, let us get back. Besides, I am famished,' he grinned. 'I think I should buy you breakfast.'

And so he did, after they'd dressed, and slowly returned to Shadwell.

But that flicker of concern remained in her heart, and not even his love could erase it.

XVIII.

That flicker of concern refused to fade over the days that followed. It was like a candle left burning in the dark, something left behind and forgotten but for a whisper of memory. She tried to chase it away, and Lord knew Arthur seemed to as well, as if he sensed the question burning on the tip of her tongue.

What are you keeping from me?

Pushing the ledger into its place on the shelf, Lily turned away from it, and gazed at her office. So much was the same as it had been that night everything had changed between Arthur and she, when she'd spoken the truth of what she saw in his eyes, in *him*. And yet, so much was different.

For one, the accounts got finished rather quickly now, she thought, a wry smile growing. Because he would come, at his appointed hour, and remain, the night through, and she wanted no distractions.

For another, they *shared* now. So far, though granted it had only been a couple of days, he'd kept the promise he made at St. Nick's, and they talked, of everything, and anything. Even the business, hers, and his. He told her of how he'd kept his identity a secret all these years, and she told him of Mary, Jack, and Winnie's recovery. Nothing was too small or too big for them to discuss, and their intimacy only grew thanks to that.

Which is why this doubt in your heart is likely foolishness.

Yes. Perhaps it was her own mind simply being unable to accept that she'd well and truly gotten what she'd wanted. Apart from Kit, but that was a work in progress. The quiet in Shadwell, even Winston now apparently blessedly subdued and silent, it was still grating on her; she was waiting for what came next, because she knew something was, so likely it was that.

Only that.

Only that slightly marring her happiness, her fulfilment.

Hell, she'd even gotten back the feeling of ownership, dominion, and power over her office, tainted since that note, which she'd since burned. Her space had been invaded, certes, but she was now at peace with it. Which was good, because business was booming still, more clients from the West coming every evening, and her plans for a house outside the city for her workers to rest and retire in, progressing nicely.

Therefore, any and all imaginary candles left to burn without supervision, were...

Nothing at all.

'Come in,' she said when a knock sounded on her door.

She wondered vaguely when she'd become one to get so lost in her thoughts, as she did nowadays.

Before, she'd dreamt, yes, but she'd lived too. Met the days as they came, and moved on. Now, she fretted, and thought, and pondered, and yes, loved, she reminded herself, her lips tipping into a smile again.

Love should create certainty not doubt.

'Apologies, mistress,' Bob said, ducking into the office. 'There's a girl downstairs, dressed as a lad. Said she knows ye, and needs to talk to ye.'

'No name?'

'Wouldn't give it, mistress.'

'Very well,' she said, heading over to him. 'Let us go see who it is.'

Well, this should certainly be interesting.

∞

Lily's half amused interest died the moment she spotted the girl waiting for her at the back entrance, dressed, as Bob noted, in loose fitting men's clothing. Not that anything but a boy's clothing would be anything but big on the small frame of the little society miss.

Angelique Fitzsimmons was a friend to the earl, a free-spirited hellion if he were to be believed. She herself had met Miss Fitzsimmons through Meg Lowell, and when *Miss Lily's* had opened, the chit had insisted on coming to visit, and explore. Lily had been wary, she knew of all those *good* society girls and matrons who spent half their lives trying to convert whores and sinners back to the righteous path, but quickly, she'd learned that Angelique was different.

The girl had only wanted to talk, to learn, to understand this world so foreign from her own. And so, Lily had indulged her the few times she'd come, though usually she was accompanied by a fierce looking *footman*, who was actually a man paid to protect her, if she knew anything at all.

But tonight, Will the footman was not here, and there was a chilling fear and desperation in Angelique's chartreuse eyes that told Lily something terrible had happened.

'Come,' she said without preamble, her eyes still affixed on the girl who was so like herself, in age, in looks somewhat, and yet, so very different. 'Bob, watch the door. You never saw her.'

She felt Bob nod, then he passed them and resumed his post.

Angelique nodded to him, then came towards her, and Lily gave no thought to what she did next.

She took the girl in her arms, and held her tight, making a silent promise that if she could do anything to help her, chase that fear from her eyes, she bloody would.

For Kit, and the others I could not help.

Within seconds, tears were soaking the purple and burgundy silk she wore tonight, and Lily stroked Angelique's head for a moment, murmuring incomprehensible reassurances, holding her tight, before slowly disengaging.

'Let's to my office,' she said gently, taking Angelique's hand and turning back towards the stairs. 'I feel we've a lot to discuss, and not much time to do so.'

Willing whatever strength she had to pass to the girl, she led her up to the office.

There, she poured them both a measure of gin, gesturing for Angelique to sit.

'So,' Lily sighed, settling behind her desk as Angelique dropped into one of the armchairs before it. 'What brings you here in the middle of the night, *alone*, Miss Fitzsimmons?'

'Angelique, please.'

Though normally she addressed the girl only that way in her mind, careful to retain boundaries of propriety, for *both* their sakes, she decided tonight she would concede.

Because tonight she wasn't a madam, and this wasn't a miss.

They were women, bound together by, if not friendship, then understanding.

Nodding, she took a healthy gulp of her own gin.

'Angelique. What the Devil are you doing here?'

'I need to disappear,' the girl said, utter desperation in her voice. 'Quickly. I have money, I've been hiding bits of my pin money for years,' she stammered on, as if to explain something, that this wasn't a rash decision perhaps. Not that it truly mattered. Lily had already decided she would help her; though it would be a risk. For both of them. The earl, and the footman, would not take kindly to her offering aid, especially as it seemed they were part of what Angelique sought to run from. 'I thought I could do it on my own, I want to go to America, but the truth is, I have no idea how to... Be safe, and not found. I just, need to get where I'm going without anyone being able to track me. Without Will being able to track me.'

Lily grimaced with the utterance of that name, knowing it would be Hell to deal with him, and reached over to pour herself another gin.

'Why,' she asked flatly.

She might've made the decision already, still, she needed to know.

That this was the only way. That this girl's dreams of America, were the only escape.

The fleeting thought that perhaps she should be thinking of America, for herself, for Arthur, for her workers, passed through her mind, but she dismissed it.

Shadwell is home now. And it's in Arthur's soul.

'It's... Complicated,' Angelique said weakly.

'Are you in danger?' she asked, concern for the girl mounting with every second. What she wouldn't do if someone had laid hands on her... 'Has someone hurt you?'

'Yes. No. I don't know,' Angelique sighed, before downing her own gin and holding the glass out for more.

Slightly reassured, though not entirely, Lily complied with the request, as the girl gathered her thoughts.

'This isn't just a bored little miss off for an adventure,' Angelique said earnestly. 'I need you to know that. And there have been no... Direct threats, or misadventures. It's... I know, in my heart, that something is horrendously wrong,' she choked out. 'That if I don't disappear, tonight, something terrible will happen to me.'

Sipping her gin, Lily studied her carefully for a long moment, wondering if there was another way.

A smarter way.

Perhaps she *should* send word to the footman, or the earl, or even...

Arthur.

Doing this, without consulting him, it would be a blow. She'd asked for trust, for sharing, for partnership... She should at least tell him what she meant to do before the wrath of Brookton fell upon all their heads, only...

When she looked into Angelique's eyes, she knew there was no time.

Arthur wasn't due for another couple hours, and the girl would be gone within the next *one*, with her help or not.

Without, she would likely be dead by morning, and Lily had

sworn she wouldn't see any more die.

'I just want to find somewhere I can live my life,' she pleaded, not that she needed to.

'I will help you,' Lily said quietly, examining the bottom of her glass, praying that Arthur at least, would understand, and forgive. 'Tell you where and how to travel, give you clothes that'll make you invisible. From what I hear, you already know how to defend yourself, so that's good. You'll need to. And you'll need be patient. The Ghost'll be after you come morning, I'd bet my own life on that,' she laughed hollowly. No matter that he technically wasn't a Ghost any longer, or that he'd just lost his father. The man was not the sort to let those under his care simply disappear. 'And naturally that bloodhound you usually trail.' Angelique nodded grimly. 'It ain't about being quick, it's the opposite,' Lily warned, her emotions running high. So much could still happen to Angelique, she would face so many trials, and no one would be there for her. It broke her heart, and of course, reminded her of what Kit had likely faced. The best she could do was ensure Angelique was prepared. 'It's about runnin' them ragged and keepin' them guessin' as to where you're headed until it's too late for them to follow.'

'I understand. And thank you. I know what I am asking. As I said, I can pay -'

'Don't insult me,' she said, disappointed that Angelique would think she needed to be. True, they didn't know each other well, but still, the assumption. It stung. 'I know what you're asking. And what you're after. And I know you wouldn't come askin' here if you had another choice. So I'll help you,' she stated again. 'And I'll keep your secret if they come sniffin', which they're bound to. Every woman deserves a chance to make her own fate.'

'Thank you,' Angelique said softly, tears appearing in her eyes again.

Though she valiantly forced them back with the next gulp of gin she swallowed.

'Now,' Lily said with a mischievous grin and determined look as she rose, and came around the desk. 'Let's get you ready.

You've a long journey ahead.'

And God willing, you will survive it, and thrive in your New World.

God willing, none other than I will suffer for helping you.

XIX.

Arthur's heart sank, and his mind whirled in a million different directions when he spotted Lily waiting for him. It wasn't the fact that she was sitting by the hearth in her room, nor that she had a decanter of cognac and glasses, waiting for his arrival. Indeed, it had been much like this every night since they'd truly committed to each other, and somehow, the ritual, the routine of it, soothed him. The rest of his life, the world surrounding them, was chaos. But here, in this room, with her, they had the life he'd promised her.

So it wasn't her waiting, or the manner in which she awaited him. It was the look on her face, the grim determination mixed with sadness in her eyes that seemed liquid fire as she gazed into the flames, not even turning when he entered. He sensed it, in the air between them, as if her emotions had become his own. His instincts had always been good, his life necessitated that, but this was something completely beyond that.

Something is very wrong.

Heart pounding with fear and concern, he strode over and was kneeling before her in an instant, hands on her own knees, searching her face for any further clues as to what was chasing away the happiness they'd found briefly. Without his consent, his mind continued to explore the myriad of possibilities, discarding them, and moving to the next with lightning speed.

A problem with a worker - I would've heard.

Another attack - I would've heard.

She found her sister? Possible - that would mean the news was grim.

She learned the truth? Of my plan? Of theirs? Improbable-

'Lily, please,' he begged, without any shame in doing so, wanting to pull her face towards him, force her to look at him, but resisting the urge to force her into anything. 'I can see something is troubling you, and if you don't say something soon... I'm already out of my mind, please...'

Finally, *finally*, she turned to him, contrition now mingling with the other emotions in her eyes, which flicked across his face as though she were trying to remember each detail of it. He knew it, because he did it often enough himself to know what it looked like.

It looks like someone preparing to say goodbye.

'Lily -'

'I have to tell you something, Arthur.'

Yes, please for the love of God, woman!

'Whatever it is, we can get through it, together,' he said instead.

The wan smiled that curled her lips for an instant almost looked like a wince.

'Angelique Fitzsimmons came here tonight,' she said, softly, but with a firmness that belied any more hesitation.

His mind screeched to a halt, all those thoughts tumbling through it coming together into a giant fracas.

Nowhere, in any of them, had there been a single thought of Angelique Fitzsimmons. He knew the girl, through her work on the foundling home, and he'd heard the girl had come here a time or two, to explore London's underbelly. Had she done so again? Had there been trouble? Beyond that, he couldn't quite think of anything that would put Lily in such a state - she didn't know the girl any better than he - but surely if there had been trouble she'd have sent for him immediately, or the earl. Or Harrow. Anyone really - and how could there even be trouble with that footman-cum-bodyguard the Fitzsimmons girl trailed anyway?

Arthur knew dangerous men, and he was certainly a very dangerous one.

'And?' Arthur asked, when Lily didn't fill the silence, didn't give him answers.

There was so much more he wanted to say, and ask, but he forced himself to be calm.

'I helped her disappear.'

That is when Arthur's mind went blank - though not blessedly so.

It was as if it had stopped working altogether, the insanity of that statement, the illogical nature of any questions and answers which should follow, breaking it.

He frowned, forcing it to work again, if only to help him spit out the obvious questions.

'What? How? *Why?*'

'She came here alone,' Lily said, calmly, emotionless, save for the sadness and resignation still in her eyes. 'Begged me to help her disappear. So I did.'

Arthur rose, his mind functioning again, telling him just how right he'd been when he'd walked in the door.

Something is definitely, certainly, terribly wrong.

He set about pacing a tiny line from her chair to the empty one before it, raking his fingers through his hair. This was bad. Beyond bad. It was the very last thing any of them needed right now, with everything else going on.

Fear coursed through him, and anger, for all Lily had endangered.

His tenuous peace with the Ghost of Shadwell, the one thing that would keep her, and so many here safe, was on the line. The earl was attached to the Fitzsimmons girl, as was Meg, and if Brookton thought Lily, or himself, had any part in her disappearance, their accord, made with Harrow though it might've been, would be over.

Of course, Lily didn't know that, and *that*, that was on him.

'Did she tell you why she was running? Where was that

blasted footman? The earl, why didn't you send for him?' he asked, the questions pouring out before he could stop them, his anger, he knew, dripping from them. 'I mean surely you didn't just help some bored little debutante just run away into the night because she *asked* you to?'

He stopped, and stared down at Lily, and the woman had the blasted nerve to shrug.

'She was in trouble, Arthur. Terrified. Whether I had helped her or not, she would've been gone. At least this way she has a chance.'

'You asked me for trust, for partnership, for equality, Lily!' he shouted, beyond caring who heard what. 'And now you make a unilateral decision that could endanger us all? That could endanger your house? What were you thinking?'

'You speak to me of unilateral thinking,' Lily exclaimed, rising to her own feet. 'Of partnership, when you're hiding something from me? And don't deny it, I see it in your eyes, every time I look into them!'

She didn't want him to deny it, so he wouldn't.

And he couldn't address that either, because then he would have to admit to it all, and that was something he couldn't do. His mind sought another way to make her see what she'd done, to turn the argument back to its origin, even though he knew *she* knew very well the magnitude of her actions.

But before it could, some instinct inside him pushed him to end that line of questioning another way.

'You can't save every girl just because you couldn't save your sister. You have no idea what you've done!'

And whose fault is that?

His own, he knew, it was himself he was angry at for that, but it was too late, he'd already spat out those horrendous words. He saw her flinch, and he wanted to dig his own grave right then for doing what he'd promised never to do again.

Hurt her.

'I helped a girl who had nowhere else to go,' Lily choked out.

'I didn't mean what I said, Lily,' he pleaded, going to her, brushing his thumbs across her cheeks, and kissing her head, as if that could make it any better. 'But you should've sent for, spoken to me -'

'You're right,' she whispered, and he froze, thrown off balance yet again. She knew he was hiding something, and yet, she was offering her own surrender. Being braver than he could ever be - compromising, and trusting. 'You're right,' she sighed, taking a step closer to him, sliding her own hands onto his that cradled her face. 'I told myself she wouldn't have waited, that I didn't have time, but the truth is... I was afraid you would say no. That you would send her back to Meg, or the earl, and... I didn't trust you, to trust me.' *Likely because I don't trust her with everything*, Arthur thought solemnly, but then again, that was a moot point. 'Whatever terrified her, I don't think anyone could help her, but herself.'

Arthur nodded, pulling her into his embrace and dropping a kiss to her hair.

'I would've sent her back to the earl,' he admitted quietly, and she tightened her hold around him. 'I am sorry, for what I said, Lily. It is a good thing that you helped her, whether I agree or not. If she was intent to run, then hopefully whatever you did will help her survive.'

'Which saint is it, to protect travellers?'

'Saint Christopher,' he chuckled lightly, the tension, fear, and anger, somehow less now.

Not only now that she was in his arms, but because, as he'd promised, they had, and would, get through this together.

Neither of them had ever had anything like what they shared before. There were bound to be problems. Especially so early on. He was lucky that they had found a way through this one, because...

I am running out of time.

Arthur clutched her tighter, rocking her a little as they stood there, both their tempers returning to a somewhat natural state.

'I'm sure he will keep watch over her,' Arthur breathed.

'Arthur...?'

Reluctantly, Arthur released her just enough to look down at her, and there was something in her eyes now, that he did not recognize.

Or rather, he did - it was a battle - of a million different things. 'What is it, Lily?'

'Nothing,' she whispered after a long moment, a dismissive smile belying the seriousness of her tone. 'Take me to bed.'

He did not need to be told twice.

They loved each other until dawn, and then they fell asleep, entwined as they were always meant to be. Somehow, their fight made the reunion all the sweeter, all the more freeing, and passionate.

Though as he did succumb to slumber, Arthur had a feeling he would regret not forcing Lily to finish her final thought. That he would regret, being a coward in this instance.

Because he knew she was going to ask him to tell her, *everything*, and the thing was, in that moment, he would've.

∞

The bells echoing on the wind, tolling the hour of seven, told Lily she hadn't actually managed to get more than perhaps an hour or two of sleep. Still, she felt surprisingly... Refreshed. As if the previous night's events had settled the disquiet within her, which was completely absurd. She'd helped a young woman from Society disappear, sent her off into the dark night with nothing but guidance and some clothes on her back, then fought with Arthur.

And yet.

Knowing she had helped Angelique, even as she feared for the girl, reassured her that come what may, she'd done something *good*. And the fight with Arthur... As harrowing as it had been to face him, admit what she'd done, to hear his anger, feel the hurt of those words he'd not meant, but still, stung, she felt as if they had passed a test.

Not their first test, but perhaps their first test since

becoming...

Something true, and real.

It gave her hope, that whatever they faced, even if it put them at odds, they could come out of it together. Perhaps it was why she'd not pressed him about whatever it was *he* was hiding. She'd wanted to, and somehow, she'd known when she'd looked up at him in that final moment, that if she had asked, he would tell her.

But she'd also known that he would regret it. Whatever he kept from her, she trusted him to reveal it when he was ready. If he did it before he was ready, however... It would be a festering wound that would only poison what they had further down the line.

So perhaps it was that. The blind leap into faith, the trusting overcoming her desire to be included, to *know*, that was helping her feel refreshed, and at peace in the dusky morning.

Or perhaps it was simply lying here, waking next to, the man she loved.

Possible...

Grinning, she stretched languorously, and turned over, expecting to catch a moment to watch Arthur sleep, but instead finding him already awake, staring at the ceiling, his hands behind his head. Snuggling up to his side, she still allowed herself to watch him, to take the entirety of him in, marvelling at the clearness of his eyes in the dawn light. Like crystal, or silver glass.

After a moment, one hand descended, curling around her as he turned slightly and dropped a kiss on her forehead. It was so simple, so natural, and yet exquisite in that very same respect.

It is what I dreamed of.

'Dare I ask what you're thinking about,' she sighed, sliding her hand across his waist.

'About Morgana,' he said solemnly, and she kissed his chest. It was the first time he'd spoken of her since that night at his old home. 'How I wish she could've met you. That you could've met her. I was thinking about Kit. How I wish... So very many things that cannot be.'

Lily's heart clenched.

She knew that feeling all too well.

Wishing couldn't make things so, even if dreams could be manifested by will.

One of his wishes, however, she could make true, in a strange way.

'I met her,' she told him, and they turned to look at each other. She smiled and nodded reassuringly at the surprise in his eyes. 'Once. When she was living with you, during your engagement last year. I met her at market. She was kind to me,' Lily said, not expecting the pricking of tears nor the tightening of her throat. It had been such a small thing, the woman's kindness. In the grand scheme of things. But not to Lily. 'She knew what I was. Still. She was kind to me. Asked my opinion on a shawl she was admiring. She valued what I said.'

'She knew *who* you were,' Arthur said gently, gratitude, and wonder in his voice. 'Not what. I think... I remember that shawl,' he said, a grin ticking up the corners of his mouth. 'Blue and ochre, crocheted in the shape of daffodils and bluebells.' Lily nodded, grinning. 'She said a nice young lady had helped her choose it. She was going to wear it to my wedding,' he laughed, and the word *lady* stuck with her. 'Thank you.'

'For what?'

'For -'

A knock sounded, interrupting the moment.

Both straightened in an instant, Lily leaning over and grabbing her chemise by the bed and slipping it on quickly.

'What is it?' she asked, none too happy for this early morning disturbance.

Because whatever it was, couldn't be good.

'Come in, Bill,' Arthur said, glancing at her, his eyes promising that whatever it was, they would face it together.

In other circumstances, she might've resented his order-giving in her house, but not today. Bill strode in, and if he was surprised at what he found, he said, nor showed nothing of it.

'That footman usually trailing after Miss Fitzsimmons. He's wantin' a word.'

'Where is he,' she asked.

'Kept him outside. Didn't think it best he be allowed in till ye said so.'

'Put him in my office, and make sure he stays there.'

'Aye, Miss Lily.'

He nodded, and left, leaving Lily to return her attention to Arthur.

'I will handle him,' she reassured him before he could say anything. 'I think it best I take care of this alone. Your name need be nowhere near this. It is enough that all of Shadwell thinks Mr. Dudley is a client. Any hint of your hand in my business...'

'I understand,' he said, with a sweet smile, and swift kiss. 'And I thank you. But if you have any trouble -'

'Bill will take care of it,' she smiled back, gifting him a kiss of her own before sliding out of bed, and slipping on a dressing gown.

'I should like to take you out, Miss Lily,' Arthur said as she did, and she froze, shooting him a shocked look. What they had, because of the danger of it, they'd never discussed taking it from the safe confines of the house. Here, they could always be client, and whore, but out there... 'Mr. Dudley, it seems, has a hankering to take his mistress out.'

'Well, Mr. Dudley is a very important man,' she said with mock seriousness, coming to stand at his side of the bed, trailing a lazy finger down his cheek. 'Can't very well refuse his whims.'

'Go,' Arthur said, kissing her palm, and nodding to the door. 'Handle what you must. I'll... Make some plans. Might not be tomorrow, but soon. I will take you out.'

'I will look forward to that,' she smiled, before doing as he bid. *Yes, that, I certainly will...*

∞

'Mr... Will,' Lily said, as jovially yet professionally as she could, as she entered her office. The footman, *bodyguard*, whatever he was, stopped his pacing before her desk, and faced her, his ice-cold grey eyes cutting through her. Where Arthur's eyes *could* be cold, and soft, his seemed to be perpetual ice. He was handsome, in a tall, fine-featured, way, but also very much like a cold marble statue. She'd never felt the full force of his threat until now, because there hadn't ever been a need. *Not the time to fear - play your part and get rid of him.* 'Is something amiss?' she asked, all innocence. 'The hour is very early -'

'Where is she,' he growled without preamble, striding across the distance separating them, and looming over her.

Another one who thought he could simply *loom*, and small, delicate females like her would cave.

Straightening, raising a brow, she took a moment before responding, careful to ensure he saw not one ounce of fear nor hesitation in her.

'Since I only ever see you trailing behind her, I can only assume you mean Miss Fitzsimmons. You will be sorely disappointed to know I have no idea where she is.'

First rule of lying: speak as much of the truth as you can.

'Do you take me for a fool, Miss Lily?' he sneered, inching ever closer. Still, she did not move, nor did she even blink. If anything, his desperate need, that seemed beyond that of a man in fear of his charge's safety, made her dig her heels in even more. 'She has no one else to go to for help. And I know she left the house only with the clothes on her back.'

'I am very sorry to hear Miss Fitzsimmons has... Disappeared, run, whatever it is that has occurred. However, I will say this once, and only once. She is not here. I do not know where she is. And before you seek to force your way further into this house, or threaten me, you should know, I have no compunction in relieving you of your manhood.'

If the steel in her tone, and the serious intent in her eyes hadn't been enough, the blade now positioned at the aforementioned body parts finished the job.

'If I don't find her in one piece,' he whispered, death in his voice. 'I will return, Miss Lily. And nothing will save you from my wrath then.'

'Will,' she said before he could leave through the door he'd strode to in a rush of air. 'If I were ever to hear of anything happening to Angelique, you can be sure, nothing would save *you* from my wrath. There are monsters far bigger than you lurking in the shadows here. Monsters I call friends.'

'You don't know the meaning of that word,' he said quizzically, before disappearing, leaving Lily frowning at the empty space before her.

A moment later, Bill appeared, and she shook away the questions swirling around in her mind.

'All good, Miss Lily?'

'For now. I want you to find us some new recruits,' she said after a long moment. 'Be quiet about it, but make sure we can't be outbid on their loyalty. Keep them away from the house, for now.'

'Ye worried he'll be back? Or the earl?' Lily raised a brow and he shrugged. 'Bob told me about the lass, I recognized the Fitzsimmons girl.'

'No, it's not him I'm worried about, Bill,' she sighed.

'That feelin' gettin' worse?'

'Aye. You too?'

'Aye.'

'I just want to make sure we're ready for whatever it is.'

'I'll take care of it, Miss Lily.'

'Thank you, Bill,' she said with a soft smile. 'For everything.'

He nodded, and disappeared too.

Leaving Lily alone to wonder what it was they were all waiting for.

Nothing good.

XX.

It was a strange thing, the loss of hope. Everything he'd ever heard, everything he'd ever read about it, purported that it was the most terrible thing that could happen to a person. That in losing hope, one lost everything. The will to live, to continue on; or perhaps simply their humanity. A person's willingness to fight against all odds, or to make their life if only a little bit better, was what made them *live*.

For Arthur, the loss of hope was freeing.

It gave him clarity, and made every second of every day, precious, and beautiful, in some holy, hallowed way. If you knew your time had come, and that nothing you did could prevent it, you could either despair, or you could find peace, and relish the last of everything you were given.

He chose the latter.

After ensuring his deal with Harrow and the Ghosts was still in place, and that there were no repercussions from Lily's aiding Miss Fitzsimmons - not that he admitted she had to anyone - he held up his end of the bargain, and sent word of warning to the other bosses in the docks. Well, as much of a warning as he could give so that preparations could be made; but not so much that it would set fire to an already volatile powder keg. Some sent back words of thanks, others of derision; some of scorn, and others, nothing at all.

He cemented all the plans and preparations for his holdings, legitimate, and illegitimate alike. He secured and put into place as many methods of protection for all as he could without alerting anyone to what he was preparing *for*. With the troubles he and others had suffered recently, anything that was noticed was likely put down to that.

He pressured as many contacts as he could, high and low, to get names, to find the identity of the men behind this whole scheme, but as he'd told Harrow, there wasn't enough time, and his connections weren't *that* good after all. He tried, thinking perhaps they could find something that would help others in the future fight, but nothing. He hadn't expected much in truth. They'd served their purpose, clearing customs, forging papers, keeping the River Police and other lawmen away, but they could not truly serve him now. Even if they could - it would have taken them more time than he had.

It had taken a little less than a month to accomplish all that. If he hadn't needed to be so quiet, so invisible with it all, he might've been able to get it done sooner. But if anyone had got wind of the preparations, they would have all been for naught. So he'd taken his time, readying himself for the time when the final move would be made.

Arthur knew he shouldn't have said, *promised*, all he had the night he'd taken Lily to St. Nick's - to *his* once home. He knew the future which awaited him, for he had decided it himself. Not many men could boast that. Not many could say they had chosen their exit from the world. It was a rare gift, and not one to be spat on with dreams and illusions there could ever be more.

Only, he wasn't spitting on it. He had been... Swept away that night. By all he'd found with Lily, beyond his wildest dreams, born when he'd made the decision to enjoy what time he had left with her. And he'd been swept away with the desire to make Lily happy - a constant desire he would always have he realised now. She couldn't ever know what he had planned, that the life he promised her would soon be cut short. He saw the irony, *hypocrisy really*, of that; of offering her honesty, and openness, but then keeping something so important from her, but it was the only way. Telling her, would mar what they had, and she would want to fight, and he simply couldn't.

Besides, it wasn't as if he wasn't fighting. He was merely doing it in a manner that would cost him in the end.

A price I will pay gladly.

And though he could not fulfil his promise to Lily of a life with her, during the past month, he'd made good on his promise to take her out. Every day, he had taken her on various excursions, to the Royal Academy, for ices in the park, the British Museum, to a fair on the Southbank. He'd ensured every excursion was not too close to home, and that every last one was planned for the hours she could easily step away from her business, even though all he wished was to spend each minute of each day he still had with her. But that...

That would require asking her to step away from what she'd built, and it would require him explaining why everything was changing... Which was all out of the question.

So he had contented himself with daytime excursions, with spoiling her, and seeing her laugh, and her eyes widen at this marvel or that. He'd contented himself with tasting the remnants of iced fruit on her lips, and holding her hand as they marched up and down Regent Street. He'd contented himself with those beautiful hours where it felt as if they lived another life, one which ended well.

And he'd contented himself with visiting her at his usual hour, and staying the rest of the night, or rather, morning, loving her as much as each of their bodies allowed. His desire had grown a hundredfold, as if every fibre in his body knew soon there would be no beauty, no sweet smell of Lily, no feel of her beneath his fingers, and was trying to experience as much of her as he could. Even if he knew, with more certainty than before, that even a lifetime, a *full* lifetime, would never be enough.

Arthur still felt at peace with his decision, even if every moment he spent with Lily forced him to ask again, if there was any other way. If there was perhaps a way, for them both to have the ending they wished for in their hearts. But every time he loved her, every time he woke to her in his arms, every time she laughed or shared some memory of her youth, or coaxed one from him of Morgana or his life, *lives*, he had his answer. There was no other way to ensure she and as many others as he could manage, would be safe.

So he relished those moments. He relished the connection, the love they'd found, and tried to squirrel it all away, as if it were savings, for when the dark days came again.

Like it or not, Lily, my love, you will be my light in the darkness.

So yes, he'd contented himself with all that, until tonight. Tonight, Lily had taken an evening off from the business, even though it was Saturday, because he'd asked, pleading it was for a most special occasion. Which it was.

My last night.

Not that she knew that, naturally. All she knew, was that he'd wanted to bring her to a new play in the West End. A silly little pastoral farce, of which he didn't even know the plot. He'd only known that she'd mentioned she'd never seen anything other than the plays in the streets, and always longed to see something when she'd first come to the city. All he'd known, was that he had to make it happen, if it was the last thing he did.

Which it might very well be.

The final act to seal his fate, had been done. It would take time for the wheels to turn, for everything to finish setting into motion - but not long. He had originally planned to wait until morning, but then, he'd known, he was simply bargaining for more time, when there was no more time to bargain with. It had been quiet this past month still, but there was something in the air... In the whispers. He'd known it wouldn't be long, and if he didn't act, with everything in place, all he'd done until now would be for nothing.

So he'd sent the message before he could talk himself out of it.

He wasn't sure how long he had left, definitely not another full night enveloping himself in Lily's soul, but he had this. A delightful dinner, an evening watching her enjoy the play of which he'd heard not one whit, entranced as he'd been by her, and a walk home, through the streets that had borne witness to most of his life. The streets that had made him who he was, and brought him his love.

He raised the hand he was holding and kissed the gloved knuckles.

'You're a terrible influence,' Lily said with a playful grin, dropping her hand from his to envelop his arm with hers instead. 'I feel like a naughty schoolgirl, leaving the house on our busiest night.'

'Told you once, Lily,' he smiled back. 'I am not a saint.'

'You've been quiet tonight, Arthur,' she said after a moment of silence, comfortable silence, save for the sounds of Shadwell, and the river. 'I would ask if you enjoyed the play, but I know you weren't paying attention. And I would ask what is troubling you, but you won't tell me, will you?'

There was a brittleness to her voice, a wistful sort of pain, that he had to soothe.

Not with answers, but with anything else he could.

Steering her so she was facing him, he stopped walking, clasped one of her hands, and trailed the fingers of his other hand down the lines of her face that he knew so well now.

'I am not troubled, Lily,' he said, meaning it. 'Simply enjoying our evening. It's something… I never imagined.'

'You're right,' she breathed, a frown marring her forehead as her eyes pierced his own in the tiny bit of light pouring from the homes and establishments still open. 'Your eyes… They are clear tonight.'

He might've laughed at the sheer incredible fact that she could read him so well, only he'd known this already.

From the first.

And there was nothing laughable about the seriousness of that.

He did smile though, because his heart, his soul, his eyes, all *were* clear. As clear as she was in the dark night, in the simple, but fashionable *lady-about-town* midnight blue silk gown Sarah had made for her.

Her eyes narrowed for a moment, but then she smiled too, bright as a moonbeam, and raised herself up to kiss him. He lost himself in that kiss, absolute perfection, and togetherness.

When they broke for air, he gathered her into his arms for a moment, unwilling to break the beauty of the moment.

Yet it did break, seconds later, when he saw the shadows in the distance, growing as they approached. They had been quicker than he'd expected. But then, they had a Hell of a prize waiting for them.

So, this is how it ends, then.

I couldn't have asked for more.

∞

It was a strange thing to have your dreams become reality. She'd known that, felt it before, when she and Arthur had first found their way to each other, but she hadn't truly grasped how extraordinary it was until this past month. Because the dreams which had been manifested, by life, the universe, God, who knew, had been dreams she'd barely known were in her heart.

Dreams of a different life, not so different that she wasn't herself anymore, but a life that had possibilities she'd never thought of. A life where she and Arthur dwelled not only in the twilight and crepuscule, but in the light of day. Where they were... A couple. Where they went to fairs, and museums, and inhabited the world everyone else did, *together.*

And those secret dreams had come true. Life, for a moment, had been a dream. She'd floated on air this past fortnight, half awake, half still dreaming, or so it seemed. All her troubles, her doubts, her fears, hadn't quite faded away, but they had become...

Less significant.

Their power had been diminished. She'd felt like herself again. The girl she'd been once, happy, and if not carefree, sure in the knowledge that everything would, *could*, be all right with a little work, and people she loved to stand beside her.

Inhaling deeply of Arthur's scent, letting his warmth seep into her, she smiled, thinking back on this evening. Everything about it, had been perfect. Something she'd always wished for, had been made possible, *by him*, simply because he loved her. And that experience, the glittering candelabra and gilded corniches of the theatre, the witty repartee and silly play, though hypnotising and transporting, the magic of the theatre, was nothing compared to the magic of love. She didn't care how that sounded. Didn't care that it potentially marked her as a silly little schoolgirl, or some romantic, starry-eyed ninny. It was the truth.

Love, in all its forms, was the most awe-inspiring, powerful thing.

Smiling again, she nuzzled into the warm wool of Arthur's coat, but the euphoria of the evening, of the past weeks, indeed, months, faded away in an instant. Lily felt it, the world crashing down, everything ending, when Arthur stiffened in her arms. All warmth between them disappeared, replaced by an icy, foreboding chill.

She didn't want to look up, into his eyes. She didn't want to look, or feel anything but what she had these past hours. Days, weeks, months. If she looked up, there would be no hope, no chance of capturing it all again. She knew it. It wouldn't be a dream that would be manifested, but a nightmare.

I don't want to wake up.

But she did.

She lifted her head, and gazed up at him, and her heart stopped beating.

No. No. No.

Her fingers tightened their hold, and her eyes burned, knowing that no matter how hard she grasped, it was over.

Arthur was a stone statue. A cold, cold thing, murder, and a twinkle of fear in his eyes. Along with something far, far worse.

Resignation.

No. No. NO.

'Arthur,' she breathed, trying to turn and follow his gaze so she could see whatever was coming, and together, they could devise a plan, and they could get out of this -

But he held fast, tighter than he ever had before, forcing her to keep her gaze on him.

'I need you to run, Lily,' he said quietly, in a voice that was so flat, and yet so full of the same emotions tearing through her.

'No,' she stated firmly, digging her hands into his waist. She didn't care if it hurt him, she didn't care so long as it meant something other than him leaving her would happen. 'I won't leave you.'

He released her, but only to grab hold of her face.

And then he gazed down at her, pleading.

'Run,' he repeated fiercely. 'You run, and you don't look back, or turn back, for anything. Don't go back to the house. You know where to go.' Tears dripped from her eyes, and she tried to shake her head, but he held fast. 'Run, my love.'

Arthur pressed a quick kiss to her lips, a brief, but heart wrenching kiss that screamed *farewell.*

And then he grabbed her, rougher than she'd ever thought him capable, threw her into the darkness of a nearby alley, where she stumbled and slipped until her knees and hands met the sludge covered cobbles. But she barely felt it, too numb, her heart, her soul, in far too much pain for anything else to be felt.

Lily did not run.

She scrambled up to her feet, wiped her runny nose and eyes roughly with the back of her sleeve so that she could see, and breathe, and keeping to the shadows, she peeked around the corner and watched, as Arthur marched forth, hands raised, to meet a band of heavily armed Thames officers, and runners.

She watched, clutching the brick wall until her nails were surely broken and bleeding, as they threw him to the ground, and shackled him, calling him *Arthur Dudley* and *St. Nick*, her heart tearing itself in two.

Run.

Only when she heard them shouting about going after her did she heed his words.

She tore through the labyrinth blindly, tears blurring her vision again.

Soon enough, she lost them, and then, only then, did she take a moment, leaning against a wall, hands on her knees, and heaving in deep breaths she forced herself to think clearly.

This isn't over.

They'd all known that whatever was coming to Shadwell was big. Terrible. The men who had come for him had known Arthur was St. Nick for Chrissake - *how?*

Later.

It wouldn't end with him. Something big and terrible was coming, and it would be soon, so very soon, she didn't have time...

Don't go back to the house.

Arthur wanted her to run. To hide. To wait until it was all over, to stay safe. She understood. She would've asked the same of him. But... He had to have known.

She wouldn't run. She wouldn't hide. She wouldn't leave her workers.

Whatever was happening, she wouldn't run from it. She would face it.

The power to separate her feelings from herself returned to her then. She thanked whatever God there was for that. Because right now, she couldn't deal with her broken heart. She couldn't face having lost someone she loved, *again.*

Right now, she needed to make sure she didn't lose anyone else.

XXI.

It took Lily ten minutes which felt like hours to return to the house once she found her bearings. She was careful, minding her surroundings more than usual, keeping to the shadows, listening to every sound that met her ears. Whoever had orchestrated this, come for Arthur, she knew they would be coming for everything that was his soon enough. And that included her.

But I can survive this. I can do this.

At the top of the alley which led to the back entrance of the house, she stopped, checked that it was one of hers on guard, and that no one else lurked, waiting for her to do what Arthur would likely have deemed the stupidest thing she'd ever done in her life.

Bob.

Exhaling a deep breath, she rushed forth.

'Miss Lily,' the man exclaimed when he spotted her, likely looking like worse than the gutter itself. 'What -'

'No time, Bob,' she said, her hand already reaching for the door. 'You get everyone one of ours rounded up, and if you see any of Saint Nick's, you tell them to hide. Every one of ours, inside. Grand Salon, five minutes.'

'Yes, Miss.'

'Where's Bill,' she asked, already striding down the corridor, Bob on her heels.

'Front door.'

'Go.'

She sensed Bob nod, and then he disappeared up the back stairs.

Smoothing what she could of her hair, discarding the dirty gloves, trying to make herself as composed as possible, Lily headed straight for the front entrance, careful to smile as politely as she could to any clients in the public areas.

Bill straightened as soon as he spotted her, concern for her, but also steely readiness in his eyes.

'Something is coming,' she said quietly, making sure they were tucked into a corner of the front entrance. 'Bob is rounding up our men. You round up our people. Get clients out, discreetly, and gently, but quickly. Reimburse them if you must, I don't care. I want all ours downstairs and dressed in their best clothes in five minutes.'

Bill nodded, and was off without another word.

Lily rushed up to her rooms and did as she had instructed the others - dressed in her best, most enticing clothes, and made herself as presentable as she could. She tried not to look in the mirror, though she had to, afraid to meet her own eyes.

Afraid to see what she knew she would there.

Unbearable pain.

But she did, and she forced herself to stare into her own eyes for as long a moment as she could spare.

No one else can see it.

'No one else will see it,' she whispered to herself.

And it seemed to fade away, enough.

Satisfied, she gave a quick glance around, then moved to her office, where she set some added security measures into place.

Always have another way out.

Five minutes later, she stood before her workers in the Grand Salon. To their credit, though she could see the fear in many of their eyes, they all stood there silently and stoically, straight-backed, and ready.

Trusting.

And she would not betray that trust.

'You all know there's been trouble lately,' she began, her voice hard, and sure, as her eyes glanced over all the lives she'd sworn to protect. 'Well, there's more coming. I don't know what, and I don't know when, but I'd wager it won't be long.' Some of the younger ones in the group looked to the elders for reassurance. Some held hands. Others nodded, and offered weak smiles. 'Arthur Dudley was taken by the Thames men tonight. Saint Nick, was taken by the Thames men tonight,' she continued flatly, watching the realisation dawn in everyone's eyes. 'Everything that was his, will be dismantled. Which means, someone will come to dismantle us. I won't run. I will fight with all I have to ensure this house's safety. But that will mean, surrender. Tonight, at least. It will mean welcoming whoever comes with open arms. It will mean embracing our enemy. Anyone who isn't up to the task, or who simply wants out, you are free to go. Quickly, quietly.'

She waited, and watched as questions, doubts, fear, swirled in everyone's eyes.

But no one moved. Anyone who hesitated, stood ready a moment later. Her heart swelled, and she prayed again that their trust in her would not be the greatest mistake of their lives. She prayed that she had this right, that this plan, this idea, would work. But it was the only thing that made sense; it was the only way.

I know men, Arthur.

'Very well,' she smiled, nodding. 'Then we wait, together. Bill, your men are to lay down all their weapons on the tables. You stand ready, but do not move unless I give an express order. Service, you ensure there is food and drink ready, set out, and remain here. I want no one anywhere but here. As for everyone else... Be ready to greet our guests as only you know how.'

Taking a deep breath, she nodded, taking a good, hard look at all those who depended on her.

I won't fail to protect you. You, I won't lose.

And Arthur, wherever he was... She would find him. She

would get him back.

Just stay alive my love. I will come for you.

The Devil himself would not stop her.

∞

'Good evening gentlemen,' Lily said calmly, the hint of a smile on her lips, her hands gently folded together before her. Her calm steadiness, her confidence, it was the only thing keeping everyone else sane, she knew. They'd waited, perhaps half an hour, before screams, the sounds of pistols and explosions rocked and echoed through the night.

There had been gasps, and reassuring murmurs, but she hadn't moved from her spot facing the door to the entry hall. The tension had been nigh-on unbearable as they'd waited another minute or two, and then the door had crashed open. And then, everyone had taken a collective breath, which they still held, as they waited to see what their fate would be.

While they wait to see if I can ensure we survive the night.

The band of men that had rushed through the door froze in astonishment at the scene before them, pistols and bludgeons and fists raised, ready to strike, but unmoving. At the forefront of them was Winston, snarling like a rabid dog, blood, lust, and vengeance in his eyes that turned her stomach. She knew she should've seen it coming, seen him coming, and sent Joce away, but it was too late.

Fuck. That worm is not what I need right now.

And he wasn't the leader, so she would just have to find another way to keep the vermin in check.

Forcing her smile to be even brighter, she stepped forward. This was it, the moment that would change everything, and she had to be strong, and unwavering. She could feel her people's fear like a pulsating wave behind her, even as they stood as proudly as she did, and it fed her, gave her courage.

You can do this. This is what you were made for.

'Welcome to my house,' she said, raising a brow.

'Ye're gonna get what's been comin', bitch,' Winston snarled, making a move to come for her.

Unwavering, unflinching, she remained steadfast, and a moment later he was pulled back by his collar as another man stepped through the mob.

Silas.

Head of one of the most fearsome Whitechapel gangs.

Though she had never set eyes on the man before, he was easily recognizable by the scar that ran from his neck to his chin, and the multi-coloured wool suit that had become his calling card. Of about her height, wiry, and handsome in a gaunt, pale, sharp-featured manner, he fancied himself a gentleman, a dandy, a criminal of the more refined sort, as Arthur had been. A wave of relief washed over her.

For a man like that, could be won over.

It was what she'd prayed for, what she'd hoped for. Though she knew he likely took his orders from someone else, something in her mind whispered that this was more than a simple war between rival criminals.

And if there was one sure thing about criminals such as he, it was they always looked out for themselves, above all.

Lily met his deep blue gaze steadily, and smiled even more. His head quirked as he surveyed her, and the scene beyond, all her workers, standing still and welcoming in their most appetising attire, afraid but refusing to cower. All her men, standing unarmed, and quietly. Food and drink, ready to be served.

Time to make a deal.

'Interesting,' he said, his voice low, but unmistakably deadly and cold.

'Perhaps you might indulge me for a moment,' Lily said when his eyes met hers again. 'In my office.'

'Ye're finished,' Winston snarled, lunging forward again.

This time Silas' arm came up to meet his chest.

Winston stopped, clenched his jaw, and looked up at the man pleadingly.

'Ye said this place was mine,' he whined on a whisper, trying, it seemed, for some reason to be discreet as he coaxed the other man to let him loose. 'Ye said I was in charge now.'

Fuck that. Over my dead body.

Which will likely be the case unless you get this done.

Raising an eyebrow again, Lily looked down at the loathsome idiot with all the disgust she could easily muster, then turned again to Silas, letting her annoyance, and impatience with the beast he held back shine through.

We have a mutual loathing I think.

You are an intelligent man, she willed herself to say silently. *Give me a moment.*

'Lead on, Miss Lily,' Silas said, inclining his head, a grin twitching at the corner of his lips. She bowed her own head in return, and turned towards the stairs. 'You lot stay here. No one moves, no one comes in. Parish, with me.'

Damn.

Winston was coming along.

No matter. She would see this done.

She had to.

'May I offer you a drink,' Lily said once they had reached her office. She made her way towards the desk, gesturing at the drinks cart as she passed it to stand behind the demonstration of her place and power.

'No, thank you,' Silas answered for them both.

Smiling that pleasant smile that might as well be etched on her face now, she turned to them, and gestured to the two chairs before her as she settled onto her own.

'Please, do have a seat.'

'This ain't no fuckin' tea party -'

'Manners, Parish,' Silas warned in a voice that might've cut through glass.

Arthur's danger had always been... Leashed. Hidden.

Silas' was on full display, woven into his being as much as Arthur's, but somehow, more volatile. More... Inevitable.

Stop thinking on Arthur, Lily scolded herself, whilst with gritted teeth, Winston dropped in one of the chairs, Silas slowly taking the other.

'Well now,' Silas said, studying her, tapping the arm of the chair distractedly with a long index finger, on which sat a rather impressive silver band. 'You have your moment. What is it you want, Miss Lily?'

'I want things to remain as they are,' she said simply.

'Now why would I allow that to happen,' he asked. 'Why would I keep you here, when I have a man ready to do the job, and your loyalties lie with the old king of Shadwell?'

'Because you and I both know that man is dim-witted worm,' she retorted, gesturing to Winston who yet again made to leap at her before Silas raised a hand. *Good doggy.* 'Because this is the most successful establishment for miles, and that is because of me. I built this place, I made it what it is, in less than a year. He would run it into the ground in days, whereas I would make you just as much money as I made the old king. If not more.'

'You did not address the question of your loyalties,' Silas remarked, looking up at her through surprisingly long dark lashes.

'I didn't think I needed to explain my motives in entertaining Saint Nick to you of all people,' she said lazily. 'I courted his favour to get what I wanted,' she added with a shrug. 'And I did. Now he is gone, and there is a new champion in town, and that is that.'

Silas examined her for a long moment, then finally, seemingly convinced, nodded.

Time to seal the deal.

'I may not know everything, Mr. Silas,' she said. 'But I know enough. I know that whatever the reason for this change in leadership, the aim is not chaos, and destruction. It is power, and control. And I know, as I know you do, that the people of Shadwell, just like the people of Whitechapel, will only stand for blood, and violence, for so long. That was Saint Nick's strength, and the Ghost's. They offered protection, a sense of safety, and normalcy to the people who live here. The people who have families here. They offered prosperity, and power, to the others.

Blood, even, to those who long for that. The people of Shadwell may be used to living with terrible things,' she smiled, willing her voice to charm, and enchant, and convince. 'Only if that is all you offer them, without end, soon they will revolt. You need allies, friends, who can step out and reassure them that all will be well. That life, will resume its natural course.'

'And you wish to be such a friend?'

'I do,' she nodded.

'In return for remaining in your seat,' he grinned.

'Of course. And protection for my workers,' she said. 'In return for which you get the same percentage Saint Nick received. And peace. To do whatever it is you and whoever it is you and the others report to, wishes.' Silas' eyes narrowed at that, and she shrugged. 'I may seem a harmless little woman, Mr. Silas,' she smiled, leaning forward, but putting the deadly strength she had behind every syllable. 'But I have lived in this world long enough to know one should be prepared. You have orders, to subdue me, keep me in your care should your employers need to make use of me. You can still do that, and make a tidy sum. I won't run. If I meant to, I would have already. But know, that otherwise, you may take this place tonight, but you will not take me. And I will make you regret it. I will make it my purpose to take you all down, and discover precisely what it is you and your master are after.'

'I could kill you right now,' he breathed, leaning forth too so they were a mere foot apart.

And yes, there was death and threat in his voice, but also, interest.

'You could try,' she grinned.

They held each other's gaze for a long moment until finally he smiled broadly, and leaned back.

'Very well,' he said.

'No -'

'Enough,' Silas snapped, and Winston froze as if he'd been struck. 'You will be compensated for the part you played,' he assured, and Lily knew. She knew Winston had been the one to set this all in motion. The one who had given up secrets of her house, ways to come in and leave threatening cards. The one who had betrayed Arthur's secret. *I will end you for that.* 'I made a deal, and I am a man of my word,' Silas said, turning back to Lily. 'You will remain at your seat, but you will report to Parish here.' Gritting her teeth, unable to speak for fear of betraying herself and undoing all she had just accomplished, Lily nodded. 'If all works out, we can discuss negotiating the terms of this deal at a later time.'

'Very well,' she managed to get out. 'But I make all the decisions concerning this establishment. And he doesn't come near me, or my workers. He doesn't step foot in this house ever again, unless I expressly allow it. I'll report and meet him elsewhere.'

'Done,' Silas agreed. 'Or be it on his head,' he warned Winston, even as he offered his hand to Lily.

She took it, surprised to find it soft and warm, and they shook on the deal.

I will live another day. My people will live safely another day.

'I look forward to doing business with you, Mr. Silas,' she smiled as they rose.

'And I with you,' he said, inclining his head. 'Now, if you'll excuse us, we must be off. Much to do, and so little time.'

'Of course.'

'I will be leaving some men here this evening,' he said as they made their way to the door. 'For your own protection naturally.'

'How thoughtful,' she smiled. *Entirely expected.* 'We will take good care of them.'

'Winston will meet you in the morning,' he continued, turning to face her again. 'To go over everything. The Queen Anne's?'

'I will be waiting.'

'Good evening to you, Miss Lily,' Silas said, bowing ever so slightly. 'It has been a refreshing pleasure.'

'Good evening, Mr. Silas.'

The two departed down the hall, and Lily waited until she

heard the main door close, voices loud and boisterous fading away before she finally breathed.

In a moment, she would go down, and do as she'd said, make sure her workers took care of Silas' men. But right now, she needed a few seconds, just to breathe, and to find her footing again. The fear which had been gratefully gone from her heart swept back in with a vengeance.

She had won a battle.

Now, she had to find a way to win the war.

This isn't over my love.

I will come for you.

XXII.

A t least there were other mourners, Arthur thought, as the reverend droned on about Heaven and resurrection, and the glorious, beautiful, end of days. At least, Morgana had people who would remember her, fondly, and pray for her, and shed a tear perhaps for her. Here, in this little village he'd found for her, full of green, and peace, and everything they'd never had before in their lives, she had lived a good life. A full life.

He had been able to give her that for a time, at least.

Morgana had thrived here, been a strong, vital part of the tiny community. Helped others. Been happy. Gone to church every Sunday, found her faith again. She'd had friends, and people who had loved her. That was something he supposed.

Something, which would, perhaps, in time, mitigate the utter loss he felt. The gaping hole inside him. Where what was left of a little good had resided. The knowledge that her death had not been his fault, had not even been due to an inability to get her proper care, should've been a comfort too. Only it wasn't. Somehow, knowing he'd had no power to save her, that for all his money and connections and means, he couldn't have done anything more than what he had, made it worse.

What had he thought? That becoming St. Nick granted him power over death?

Perhaps.

Though he knew no mortal had such power.

A sniffle, and the closing of the reverend's bible brought him back to where he was.

At his sister's grave, a black spot in the snow-covered, glittering landscape surrounding it. Surrounding her. He couldn't have asked for a more beautiful day to lay her to rest. The winter sun shone brightly, warm, his mind knew, not that he could feel it. Even the cold numbing his feet, ankle deep in pristine white powder, he didn't feel it. All he felt was numb, and incomplete.

The sadness, the anger, those had faded now. Instead, was emptiness, a hollowness he'd always feared, but that had now finally come to consume him as he'd always known it would. Morgana, she'd been his tether, to the world, to life, to humanity. And now...

Now she too was gone.

He had nothing left. Nothing but money, and power, and lies. When Arthur Dudley died, perhaps there would be mourners. Perhaps, if he died with his name intact, they would mourn the man who had tried to make Shadwell better. But they would mourn that man. And that man, was not him. He was a construction. A lie. No one would mourn the soul he bore inside his flesh. No one knew the soul inside his flesh.

Well, one person did. Somewhat.

One person knew the lie was just that.

One person might in fact mourn him.

Perhaps.

For even she did not know him, all of him.

The thought soured in his belly, leaving a bitter aftertaste in his mouth as the others, wraiths clad in black, moved around him. Leaving final blessings for his sister, saying words he didn't hear but nodded to. Until he was alone, entirely alone, and the gravediggers began reversing the work which must've taken them the night. Pouring the soil back into the hole, burying his sister, finalising the task of taking her from him.

Goodbye, Morgana, he thought, when they too had finished, and gone, and the sun had nearly finished its descent into the horizon, casting the world into fiery tones.

'May you find peace, and joy. I love you,' he whispered, before finally, turning on his heel, and making his way out of the graveyard.

And it was then, as he stepped into the shadows cast by the trees lining the churchyard, as he felt the cold again, biting through, and making him shiver, that he realised, he didn't want to be alone.

He didn't want to die alone.

In that moment, Arthur realised that he still had time, to change his fate.

And he knew right where to start.

∞

Some might argue that despite all he'd done to change his fate, Arthur hadn't in fact succeeded. That he would in fact, die alone. Here, in fact, in the cold, damp, putrid bowels of Newgate prison; or perhaps tomorrow, or the day after, in some other disgusting part of the place. Only Arthur knew they would be wrong. That he had changed his fate; or rather, that a woman had changed it for him.

Given him love, to hold on to, to keep close, to keep him warm and see him through his final days. It didn't matter that she would not be beside him, holding his hand. She would be with him, until the end, and there were no words to express his gratitude for that.

Arthur was pulled from his half-delirious reverie by another crushing blow to his ribs. Grunting, trying to breathe through the pain, he wheezed as his body swung from the ceiling, his bare toes dragging across the floor, wet with a rancid melange he didn't want to identify, blood sliding down his arms from his shackled wrists.

The breath told him his ribs weren't broken - *yet.*

Despite how desperate his situation might look - it wasn't near as bad as it might've seemed to someone looking in. This was the easy part. The beginning. He hadn't even been here a full day, he knew, and the fact that he knew that was good too, because it meant his mind hadn't broken yet.

These blows, this basic form of torture, it was to wear him down. Soften him. Keep him on the brink of rationality, keep his body in fresh pain, until the ones behind all this were done with him.

Until they realised they would need answers from him, and then…

Then it would get much worse.

Right now, they were playing with him. Asserting dominance, reminding him of his place. Demonstrating their power. But when they discovered what they thought was within reach was gone, then, it would become something else entirely. They would attempt to break his mind, and he would likely, eventually, succumb. He hoped he didn't, that he could remain strong, keep his lips in check, but not many men could withstand what awaited him. So he would make peace with that if he succumbed eventually, before his body gave up and released him, but he would buy all the time he could.

For the pieces he'd put into place to be set, and secured.

And above all, for Lily, to be safe, far, far away.

Then, he would let go.

And perhaps, Morgana, you will be waiting for me, if I am so lucky.

Though in truth, he doubted it.

XXIII.

Who in the bloody Hell is Guinevere Nicholas, Lily wondered, staring at the name on at least fifteen property deeds before her. After ensuring everyone's well-being, and even meeting Winston for a despicably long ten minutes during which she'd endured more threats, and revolting promises, she'd returned to the house, then snuck out again. She'd come to St. Nick's lair, to save his papers, to try and make sense of it all. To understand what had happened, why, and how precisely she could save him, and the empire he'd built.

He'd had the answers, she knew that in her heart.

He'd known, what was happening, and why. *That*, she was certain, was what he'd been hiding from her. But when she glimpsed the name on the deeds, she wondered if she'd been rather blind, and foolish, and trusting, and altogether an idiot for believing in a man who apparently was very close to another woman.

Named Guinevere, just to further the insult.

No…

Guinevere is me.

And if she was going to untangle this web, she needed to stop being stupid, letting idiotic emotions like jealousy cloud her mind. Arthur loved her. Was faithful to her. She knew that; trusted him. Just as she knew that passing thought and tinge of jealousy had only surfaced to protect her. How much easier would it be to believe that of him, than to stand here, in his home, at a loss of what to do to get him back?

Tossing the deeds aside she continued her search, emptying the safe, and she stumbled on at least twenty others, along with ownership papers for business holdings, this time in the name of Percival Egerton, Earl of Brookton. More in the name of his wife, Margaret. Frowning, she looked closer at the papers, and noticed the date the transfer of goods had taken place.

April 14th.

She checked the first ones bearing Guinevere's name, and saw the same date.

Three days before he was taken.

She quickly went through the rest of all there was, and found the same.

He had bestowed his empire on others, in its entirety.

He knew something was coming for him.

Yes, but she'd known that already. Sensed it.

This is more than that.

He knew someone was coming for...

For all that was in her hands. And he'd left it all to her; to her and the bloody Ghost of Shadwell. So it would be safe.

Fuck you, Arthur, she cursed, tears spilling from her eyes.

How could he do this to her? And without a word? He had promised to share, to be her partner, and yet he had done this all behind her back. He had known something was coming, and he had prepared for it. Prepared his *empire* for it. Not himself, and not her.

Fuck you.

What the Hell was she supposed to do now?

Think. Think. Think.

Sucking in a deep breath, she closed her eyes, wiped her cheeks, and rose.

Pacing about the study, she forced herself to piece together the shards of information.

Properties and businesses. He wanted them safe.

Out of his hands, and those of his other self. Both names had been on the deeds, his own, and Nicholas Martin, the respectable name behind which hid St. Nick.

But why?

He knew they would come for him.

Not just him - St. Nick. And the other gangs.

There had been trouble at Arthur's properties. Residents being threatened, pressured into leaving. St. Nick's operation had had more trouble than not the past few months. There was always trouble, but never like this. The other ruling gangs nearby would've been likely candidates for the role of *enemy*, had they not fallen the same night he had. Anyone with control over the larger parts of Wapping, and Rotherhithe had also been taken down.

By those from Whitechapel, Limehouse, and Bermondsey.

The war that had raged last night... They'd all heard it. The screams, explosions, pistols, that had rent through the night before Silas and his men had come, had carried on, for hours. And the sounds had come from further away; not that it had made them any easier to block out. Even with the forced revelry they'd staged to keep Silas' men happy... They had heard too much.

And this morning, when she'd gone to the Queen Anne... The streets had been quiet. Oh, people were still there, doing what they had to to survive, but too many were silent. Or speaking to each other only in hushed whispers and in dark corners. There had been too many men in the streets she'd not recognized, but she'd known they were the new order.

But why now?

Why would they wait until now to take him in? To take them all down?

Because they had to have Arthur Dudley arrested for something. And they had to take down St. Nick, who controlled the majority of the area.

Something such as being a criminal leader. Perhaps they had intended to find something else, only to stumble on his identity as St. Nick, and felled two birds with one stone. They had found something that would make the property revert back to the Crown, to then be sold to the highest bidder.

He was betrayed.

Winston.

Not now. Focus. Why the properties?

Not the properties. The land.

What had one of the girls told her?

Think. Think. Think.

Amelia. It had been Amelia. Early February. She'd been entertaining a... An architect? No, an engineer. An Oxford lad who had been sent to Wapping to...

Measure something?

Sighing, she rubbed her face, and forced her mind back to that night when Amelia had come to report in.

What is the bloody use in gathering secrets if you cannot call them to mind?

Not measure. Evaluate.

The tunnel.

The bloody tunnel under the river.

It would be *the* new way to get goods and people across the river. There had been talk about it, but nothing concrete other than a few purchases of land in Rotherhithe. The project had been a dream for years, but now, things were coming to head. Deals had been signed. Moves were being made to get the work in progress. Funds were being collected. She'd read about it and wondered what man would think of next.

This was it; why someone had taken over.

Someone who knew it was finally coming, and knew a while back. The trouble had begun earlier this year, before news of investors and shareholders and meetings. When measurements and evaluations were being taken and land emptied to ready for construction. Someone had known it was more than a dream, and they wanted to control everything around it; probably controlled the majority of investments in it as well.

Someone powerful then.

Someone well off enough to pay leaders of gangs to invade

territories not theirs, and risk everything. Someone close enough to the top to see the bigger picture.

Bloody Hell.

There was no possible way she could discover who had been at work behind the scenes - at least not in time to save them all.

What she could do...

What she could do was make sure their plan didn't succeed.

What I can do is start the war.

Yes. She would harness this rage, this pain, and she would wield it. She would use the power she had, of being invisible, of being underestimated, and she would take back what was hers. And St. Nick's.

Only, I will need a bigger army than that which I have.

Best get started then. You don't have much time.

No, she didn't.

Because whatever they had in store for Arthur, it would get much worse when they discovered their brilliant plan had failed, and that they had lost what they needed so desperately.

Hopefully, by then it will be too late. And I will be ready for you.

∞

Having secured all the papers she'd examined back in the safe, Lily left the study, and was about to make her way quickly, but very, very carefully back to the house when she heard the unmistakable noise of someone else in the cellar. She froze, terror in her heart, but determined to meet whatever came with bullets and knives, and whatever else she had to take them down.

Had she brought them here? She'd thought she'd been careful enough coming here, disguising herself as a beggar, taking more detours than even Arthur had. If she'd brought them here...

Never mind, 'tis done, she scolded herself, slipping behind the cellar door. She waited, taking out and cocking the two pistols she had with her, ensuring the blade in her boot, and that in her bodice, were easily accessible.

Time slowed to a painful crawl as she waited, each sound amplified as if resoundingly loud, when she knew, whoever was down there, was doing all they could to be quiet. Still she heard the shuffling, the slow, steady steps up, up, up, until...

The door opened and she threw herself against it, not quite managing to send whoever was on the other side flying back down into the darkness, but still managing to squeeze them tightly between the door and frame.

A cry sounded in her ears, and then a painful breath before -

'Miss Lily, please!'

That voice...

She knew that voice.

'Harrow?'

'Aye.'

Carefully, slowly, she removed her weight from the door, and peeked her head around it.

And there he was, Mr. Harrow himself.

But how?

'What are you doing here?' she asked dumbly, as Harrow seemed to shake off the pain, checking various places for cuts. Luckily she'd only bruised him it seemed. 'How do you know about this place?

'Saint Nick told me,' he said, straightening. 'I came last night lookin' for you, but you weren't here. When I slipped into *Miss Lily's* a while ago, you were missin', so I figured you'd managed to get here, just as he'd said you would.' Her mouth gaped open, her mind blanked, and her loss of volition must've shown, for Harrow chose that moment to take her pistols, then her arm gently, and lead her back to the study. 'I'm goin' to take you somewhere safe.'

'What are you talking about Harrow?' she asked, frowning.

'I'm takin' you away, somewhere safe,' he repeated reassuringly, offering her a weak smile as he left her by the door, dropping the pistols on the desk as he went for the safe.

She watched as he began to turn the dial, and all at once, her mind and volition returned as she realised.

You bastard, Arthur.

A thousand thoughts and emotions flooded her at once, *anger, annoyance, sadness, despair, love,* and she pushed back the lump in her throat, focusing on the man currently available to be taken to task. She rushed over to Harrow, and managed to slam the safe shut again just as he opened it.

He turned to her, intent, and took her shoulders in his hands.

'It'll be alright, Lily, I promise,' he said soothingly, the tone utterly grating and infuriating. As if she were some child to be *taken care of.* 'The arrangements have all been made, I just need to get you out.'

'Arrangements have been made,' she hissed.

'Yes. Now please,' Harrow urged, letting go of her to turn back to the safe. 'We need to be quick. We should've gone last night -'

'I'm not going anywhere, Harrow,' she said quietly, but with grim resolve. He turned to say something, but she glared at him, and he held his tongue. 'I don't give a rat's arse what he arranged; I'm not leaving.'

'They'll kill you -'

'No,' she said with a bitter laugh. 'They won't. I made a deal with Silas last night. Or did you think I'd just been hiding in the shadows all night whilst my house was taken over?'

Harrow's eyes widened and he backed away a few steps, as if everything in his belief system had shattered before him.

'No...'

'Oh don't be stupid, Harrow,' she sighed. 'I made a deal to save my neck, and my workers'. But that doesn't mean I'm just going to sit here and abide by the terms of it. I'm staying, because I'm going to take them down, all of them. I'm going to take back what was Arthur's, and I'm going to get him back.'

If it was possible, his eyes widened even more.

Shaking his head, he started pacing about.

'You don't understand, I gave him my word, there was a plan, and -'

'What did you say, Harrow?'

The man froze, the realisation of what he'd let slip widening his eyes.

Bastard.

So not only had he made the arrangements she'd known about, the deeds, *her*, he'd gone to Harrow, to the Ghost, and made larger ones. He'd brought in someone else, told someone else, *everything*, and she... Had been left in the dark, to be taken care of.

Bloody trust and partners, indeed.

'Harrow!'

'It ain't up to me to tell you,' Harrow said, regaining some of his composure. 'All you need to know, is that it's taken care of, and that you need to come with me -'

'I ain't comin' with you Lionel Harrow,' she seethed, wanting to scream but knowing she couldn't afford anyone to hear this. 'I'm takin' Shadwell back, and I'm gettin' Arthur back too.'

'You're mad, this is madness, you can't, you don't know what you're up against -'

'Men of the West, trying to take hold of the areas close to the planned tunnel,' she said simply, and he stopped again, too shocked to even express any surprise now. 'Worked it out, yeah,' she added bitterly. 'What was the plan, Harrow?'

He remained silent, and she raised a brow.

An instant later, he was talking.

'Keep the peace, avoid bloodshed,' he began. 'The Ghosts, and any of the bosses in Rotherhithe and Wapping who'd listen were to go to ground. Make sure transition happened easily, and that we'd be ready when the time came to fight. He said, the men in the West might get control of this place, but they'd not get what they were really after.'

The land.

Her land now, and that of the Earl and Countess of Brookton.

'They won't,' she agreed. 'Why didn't he fight, prepare?'

'Were too late,' Harrow shrugged. 'He came to me, about a month ago. Said there was no time for that, no time to find out who was comin' for us, and all he could do, was make his time count.'

Make his time count.

Oh God.

Stifling a sob, Lily clutched her belly and forced herself to breathe, grief and heartbreak tearing through her as she realised she'd been wrong.

Winston didn't give him up.

He gave himself up.

That is why his eyes were so clear last night.

He made his peace.

So that's how it was? He would fight for others, but not himself?

Not for them, for what they had?

'Bastard,' Lily spat. No matter. If he wouldn't do it, she would. He'd made a promise, and she'd hold him to it. 'Well, that plan was shite. And we're makin' a new one.'

'You can't do this, Miss Lily, please, I gave him my word I'd take care of you -'

'I can, and I will, Harrow. Look at me. Look at me,' she repeated forcefully, and he did. 'He didn't know who was comin', but we bloody well do now. At least those around here. So I need your help. We need to gather, quietly. The gangs' hold on Shadwell is still loose. If we act fast, we can take it back. Gather the Ghosts, and the bosses who listened, whoever was highest up in their enterprise if they didn't. Find a safe place, for us all to meet. Tell them I bring tidings of Saint Nick. You want to hold fast to your promise to Arthur? Then you'll have to follow me.'

'Lily -'

'Say one thing,' she dared him, fire flashing in her eyes. 'Say one thing about how I am a woman. Or a whore. Or too young, or too little, or too sweet. Say one thing about why I can't do this.' Clenching his jaw, Harrow shrugged, and looked down at his feet. 'All those reasons, Harrow, are precisely why no one will see me coming.'

'If you lose...'

'I have already lost everything,' she said simply, and he looked up at her. After a moment, he nodded. 'If I lose my life, then at least it will be fighting.'

'I told him you'd not go quietly,' Harrow smiled. 'Suppose even I didn't know how true that would be.'

XXIV.

In a supreme show of confidence, Harrow had left it up to her to devise whatever plans came next. After their little confrontation at St. Nick's, they'd left, separately, carefully, and Lily had returned to the house. Had it only been this morning?

Yes...

Time had stretched again, but it was a good thing. When she'd returned, she'd checked in with all her workers again, and gone about her business, as if nothing had changed. Silas still had men at the house, and everything needed to appear normal. But in the back of her mind, she was planning; trying on plans as other women may try on gowns.

There were certain variables that could not change.

The bosses who took control must be taken care of. Permanently.

And all at once. But coordinating such an attack... It had taken men with greater means and foresight months. She had...

Not long.

She couldn't be sure how long she had before Arthur was taken from her.

That was another unchangeable variable.

I must get Arthur back.

From Newgate.

His whereabouts had reached her ears - not through whispers - but steady voices all around. The word had been put about quite clearly about where St. Nick was, and where he would remain, until his time to meet the hangman came. His capture was a masterstroke for the Thames men - and the other bosses - and even the papers were awash with the news that the *'Terror of Shadwell'* had been taken down.

If only they knew...

There would be a trial, eventually, when all the ends were neatly tied with what the puppet masters needed from him. A sham. Then, an execution.

Soon, but not yet.

Still, she had to act quickly.

I need to get in, and out of Newgate.

Then, out of London.

Another unchangeable variable.

Once she freed him, she needed to get him somewhere safe. Until...

Who knows.

Until things were quiet enough. Until... Their hold was strong enough. They would have to rule from a distance, but then, Arthur had managed to wield power in secret for twenty years.

We'll manage. And if not, we'll build something new.

Sighing, Lily rubbed her eyes, and leaned back in her chair. She'd sat behind her desk, account books open before her, in case anyone came looking. But the work had all been done, not that there was much to do considering the previous night's events.

A hundred different plans had formulated in her mind, then been discarded; a thousand options and possibilities thrown to the wind until all she was left with was the best plan she could think of. She didn't like it, too much could go wrong, she could lose so much, and so many could get hurt, but it was the only way she could see success being even a remote possibility.

And I have to ask so much of others.

Speaking of which...

'Come in,' she said, when Bill's knock sounded.

He strode in, closing the door, then planting himself in his usual spot.

Lily could almost feel the Spring air swirling off him, and she straightened, readying herself.

'He found a place,' Bill said, handing her a slip of paper which bore the address of an abandoned stretch of ropewalk not too far away. 'Says they'll be there, five in the morn, day after tomorrow.'

'Thank you,' Lily nodded, holding the paper to the flame of her lamp, watching it catch before tossing into a silver tray beside it.

'What's the plan, Miss Lily?'

Something foolish and dangerous that could get us all killed.

'We're going to throw a party, Bill,' she said, with false joviality. 'We're going to take care of the big men, and then get others to rid the docks of the rest.' He nodded, waiting, knowing there was more. 'I need to ask you something, Bill. And I don't want you sayin' yes because you think you owe me. You don't,' she promised firmly, eyeing him for a long moment. 'Whatever way I look at it, I'm going to need someone inside the College,' she continued finally, using the unlikely moniker some clever idiot had devised for Newgate. 'Someone I can trust with my life. And Arthur's.'

She shrugged, hoping he could see her desperation, her apology, and her fear for him.

'I'll find a way, Miss Lily,' he said without hesitation. 'I will,' he promised, when she made to speak. 'Bob'll take charge here. I'll be waitin', for whenever you come.'

Lily smiled - it was as if he too could read her mind.

Once he found a way in, he would need to remain there, giving no clue as to where he'd come from and who he reported to. She nodded, a weight lifting from her heart from the knowledge that he would be there.

'Words cannot express my thanks, Bill.'

'No thanks needed, till it's done, Miss Lily,' he smiled wryly.

'Fair enough.' She smiled back, and studied him for a moment. 'You weren't surprised, were you, that Arthur was Saint Nick? Did you always know?'

'No,' he admitted seriously. 'But made sense. And made more

sense as to why he tried to keep away.' Lily nodded. 'Ye got a plan to get in yerself?'

'There's someone I need to see,' she said, the hope that her idea would work, colouring her voice. *Because if she doesn't help, no, I have no clue...* 'Someone I'm hoping has enough sway to get me in without me needing to get arrested.'

'Aye, best not resort to that. Ye be careful, Miss Lily,' he said gently after a moment.

'You too, Bill.'

With a nod, he was gone, leaving Lily to wonder if it was all worth it.

If Arthur's kingdom, if he himself, was worth all the lives she was putting at risk.

To her, *he* was. The love she'd found with him, was. But then he'd done so much to ensure everyone else was safe, and now she was risking it all, and why? Because she was stubborn? Because she was determined not to lose the best thing in her life?

Because I am determined not to let them win.

Not to let them control any of our fates.

Because I cannot lose someone else.

Her parents, Kit, so many friends over the years... She couldn't lose one more person. And if the new bosses remained, if the new order came, well, it wasn't just Arthur she'd lose. Yes, there would be bloodshed if she attempted this, but how much more would there be if she just stood by and let them take control again? Let them change the docks for the worse, when she, and Arthur, and Meg, and the earl, and so many others, had worked for years to change it for the better?

I can't stand by.

And if that was wrong... Well she would live with it.

All she could do, was fight. Make her choice, stand by it, and ensure anyone who followed her unto the breach knew what they faced.

There was no time for doubts.

I can do this.

∞

For never having visited *The Emporium* before, it seemed oddly familiar to Lily. Perhaps it was merely because she had entered through the back, and the back halls of any home, any house, could be quite similar. Simple rugs, wood floors, pewter sconces. Same narrow corridors and stairs. Same burly men guarding the doors and dark alleys.

At any other time, she would've asked to visit the main rooms, of which she'd heard so much; indeed she'd ask for a tour of the house which had inspired her own. But this night was not such a time. Tonight, she was here for one purpose, and one purpose alone.

To beg for help.

It was a gamble, to hope that somehow because of their shared occupation, she might find sisterly understanding here, but right now it was all she had. *The Emporium* was known for entertaining people from the highest rungs of society, and all Lily could hope was that the mysterious Madam E would therefore wield power, and secrets, that could help her.

The fact that the office she was let into, silently, by her burly, but finely dressed guard, resembled her own in its dark, rich furnishings, and walls of books and ledgers, bolstered her courage. Perhaps they were more similar than not. Perhaps her odds were better than she imagined.

But then do not all offices of powerful people resemble each other?

The snick of the door lock prevented any further doubts or musings, and Lily turned, careful to be as composed and assured as she could be, considering the dark beggar's clothes she'd needed to wear again in order to get here without being spotted by the wrong people. The guard at the door had taken some convincing that she was indeed who she said she was, and it was a miracle already she'd made it thus far.

A good portent.

Or at least, so it had seemed until now. For now, before her stood not the fashionable, buxom and sensuous madam she'd heard so much of, and expected, but yet another guardian. Though this one was higher in the ranks at least, or must be judging by the plainer, yet expertly tailored, brown wool suit. Though ensconced in the darkness of the doorway, where the dim fire and lamplight barely reached, Lily made out fine, sharp features, dark, close-cropped hair, and glittering ice-blue eyes. Tall, and lean, something about his presence set her more on edge.

He is dangerous. Like Arthur, in a quiet way.

But no matter. She would convince this gatekeeper too.

'You seem disappointed,' the guard said, in a quiet, almost amused tone.

'I thought...' Lily sighed, deciding to be honest. It was really all she had now. 'I thought I was meeting Madam E.'

The guard's head quirked slightly, and the shine of teeth appeared as he smiled.

Oh.

Lily knew her surprise was apparent, but she couldn't help it. Madam E was notorious, and well-known by, well, everyone. Or so, it had seemed.

The Madam E we know is merely a mask...

For him.

'*You* are the true Madam E,' she breathed.

'Not quite what you expected,' he drawled. 'I'll hand it to you, Miss Lily, caught on quicker than most. Though I'll ask you keep this knowledge to yourself. Very few know of my true role here, and I should like to keep it that way. Name's Mr. Ames,' he said, taking a step into the light.

Lily's eyes studied him a little closer as he extended his hand, and she realised the true head of *The Emporium* was, as some of her own employees were, someone to whom gender was not a binary concept.

She took his hand, and shook it.

'Thank you for seeing me, Mr. Ames.'

A nod, and he strode to stand behind his desk, settling in his seat of power much as she would.

Lily followed, though she hesitated before taking a seat.

Mr. Ames gestured to one of the plush leather armchairs much like her own, and she settled in with a small grateful smile.

'I'd offer you a drink, but honestly, if you're all set on pleasantries, perhaps we could simply proceed to the part where you tell me why it is you're here.'

'I've always been an admirer -'

'Flattery is dull, Miss Lily,' he said, raising a brow, his icy eyes piercing through her, shattering her confidence quite a lot.

'I'm not trying to flatter you. It's a fact. Your house inspired my own.'

'And...?'

'And... I know your power,' she said simply. *Or at least, I hope you have the power I imagine you to...* 'Your connections.'

'Ah,' Mr. Ames breathed, inclining his head slightly, understanding softening the harshness of his gaze.

'I need to get into Newgate. Quietly.'

Mr. Ames whistled, leaning back in his chair, arms folded across his chest.

'This have anything to do with Saint Nick being a recent addition?'

'Yes.'

'And what is it you're hoping to do?'

Lily knew the next words would seal her fate, one way or the other.

Taking a deep breath, she reminded herself why she was doing this.

What she would lose if she failed.

'Get him out,' she admitted.

'Why?' Mr. Ames asked flatly.

Fantastic.

But what had she thought? That she could simply come here and ask what she would, and no one would ask that seemingly simple question, *why?*

Perhaps if she'd been faced with a less piercing gaze than Mr.

Ames', she might've felt less like a stupid ninny telling the truth. Only it was the truth. And perhaps she was a stupid ninny for engaging on this path for something as intangible as *love*, but so be it.

In for a penny...

'I love him.'

Mr. Ames' gaze dropped from her own, lost in his thoughts.

She tried to read them, tried to read him, but her observational powers failed.

His face was a blank mask.

After a long moment, during which Lily's heart pounded, and her breath stilled, moisture slicking her palms, he sprang up, and strode to the drinks cart by the hearth.

He poured a good measure of whiskey, then turned, eyebrow raised, and she shook her head. Still, she waited, afraid to move, to speak, to make any sort of noise which might pull him from what had to be consideration. Shrugging, he downed his drink, poured another, and strode to the hearth, staring at it with such fervour it made her nervous.

Finally, she could keep her words leashed no longer, doubts assailing as to what Mr. Ames was thinking.

'I know that sounds foolish,' she sighed. 'To people like us... But I can't... I can't just let him die.'

There.

She'd said her peace.

Let him think what he must.

Only she wouldn't lie.

'Had you come to me a month ago,' he said finally, still gazing into the flames. 'I'd have laughed in your face.'

It took a moment for Lily's mind to make sense of the words.

'But not now?'

'No,' he sighed, downing his other drink, and turning back to her. 'Not now.' He strode back to the desk, setting his glass on the cart as he did, and resumed his earlier position. 'It also happens that I have an interest in seeing those you go against thwarted myself.' Lily burned to ask more, *who, how, why*, but she refrained. *Questions for another day. Stick to the plan you have. There is no more time.* 'I can get you in. But it will be on the debtor's side, and you will need make your own way to Saint Nick, wherever he may be. And then, it will be on you to get yourselves out. But with someone like Saint Nick… I doubt even a king's ransom would pave your way. You go in, there's no telling if you'll come back out.'

'I understand.'

She did.

It was as Mr. Ames said. In other circumstances, she could've paid every guard from door to cell, and been told to take her prisoner and with many thanks for her generosity. But some very powerful men had put Arthur in there, and they surely had much invested to keep him there.

Lily would have to trust that once inside, Bill would have found a way to Arthur, and back out.

If not, they were all dead.

'Very well then,' Mr. Ames said, tearing her from the depressing thoughts. 'I will send word when your way is cleared. Won't be but a few days,' he added, before Lily could ask. 'Not much time to prepare.'

'Thank you,' she breathed, rising, and offering her hand.

Words were not near enough, but they were all she had for now.

Mr. Ames rose, and they shook on their strange little deal.

'Miss Lily,' he said, when she turned for the door. 'I am an admirer of yours too. If we should all survive the next months, we should speak again, you and I.'

'I will look forward to that, Mr. Ames,' she smiled.

Lily left the way she'd come, unaccompanied now, and strangely…buoyant.

Perhaps this was a fool's errand.

Perhaps she and Arthur would not survive it.

But she had, they both had, a better chance now.

Her plan was coming together, in some small measure.

And now, to convince more follow me.

There was still much more work to do, but her confidence had returned, bolstered by Mr. Ames' aid.

I can do this.

XXV.

Rather than disguise herself in beggar's garb again, for this early morning appointment, she had chosen the severely cut, starched dark wool of widow's weeds. Standing in the shadows, Bob at her side, at the far end of the abandoned ropewalk, she was glad of it. The men she faced now... It wasn't their reputations, as dangerous cut-throats and savvy businessmen, as smugglers and pirates and den keepers and murderers in some cases, which made her wary.

It was her own desperation, clawing at her heart.

Because this was it.

The final piece of her plan.

One wrong word, one whiff of hesitation, and they would tear her apart like wolves.

So yes, she was glad to have chosen the stiff and sombre attire. It kept her shoulders back, her spine straight, and in a strange way, it reminded her of what she was doing all this for.

So that I will not have to wear mourning clothes for Arthur.

For more friends.

For what this place was, once.

Taking a deep breath, she watched them all for a moment, no one speaking, wraiths at the edge of the single lamp set between them. Four men, one being Harrow, while the other three were representatives of the three largest local *businesses*, who had been supplanted with the recent change of power in the docks.

Three men who Arthur had let live all these years, their business practises not as viscous as others'; three men who he'd warned, and three she could live with doing business with.

And if she could convince them, get them on her side, others, still in the shadows, some smaller concerns; others, remnants of those who had not heeded Arthur's warning, would follow.

Three men to convince. 'Tis nothing.

Someone from Hook's enterprise, though he himself was killed.

A representative from Barrowman Bill - still alive thanks to Arthur's warning - but not this trusting it seems.

Waterman Tom came himself.

Once enemies, rivals, now together in one room, they eyed each other cautiously, wondering, she knew, if this was all some trap. Some of their men, what was left of their once grand little armies, stood in the shadows, just in case, and others she knew, along with Ghosts, and her own men, kept watch discreetly outside.

Time to go, Lily thought, as bells rang out the hour of five across the city.

They did not have long, not if they wished to remain unnoticed.

With confidence, and courage, and a reminder to herself that she was every bit as dangerous as the rest of them, and infinitely more charming, she strode to them from the shadows, the heels of her boots clicking ominously against the damp stone floor, and echoing against the vaulting edifice.

The men waiting straightened, tension filling them as she joined their little circle.

'Gentlemen,' she greeted quietly, her eyes noting each representative. 'Good morning to you all.' Quiet murmurs, narrowed eyes, and slight shifts were her response. *Well, you didn't expect to just smile and for them fall at your feet...* 'I won't prevaricate. We don't have much time, and the last thing we need is to be seen together. You're all here because none of you are pleased with the recent turn of events,' Lily said, her gaze travelling over each man again.

They needed to look in her eyes, and see her worth.

Just as she needed to see theirs.

'Don't matter whether we like it or not,' Barrowman Bill's man, one of his lieutenants if she wasn't mistaken, growled. 'All of us here have been decimated. Even those of us who heeded Saint Nick's warning. We couldn't stand against them if we wanted to.'

'That's where you're wrong.'

'You got an army we don't know about girly,' the Hook's man said.

Though whether the new man would take the old boss's moniker was a question for another day.

Focus. Come now, you knew this wouldn't be easy.

'I will,' Lily said evenly.

Waterman Tom, a wizened and weather-beaten slip of a man, narrowed his eyes while the others laughed.

Harrow looked to her, silently asking if she needed help, but she only smiled coyly.

'You don't want to hear my proposition, please, by all means,' she said, gesturing towards the door. 'You don't want to follow me? Please, go. Enjoy living under the thumb of Silas, and Foxy, and Charmin' Charlie. Enjoy serving them like dogs, and seein' none of the profits. Seein' their men havin' your women, and takin' your spoils. Because once I tell you all how this is going to happen, you're in. Anyone even thinks of opening their damned trap, other than to those I say you can, and I'll slit your throat myself.'

Something in her tone told them she was neither incapable, nor would it be her first time taking a life.

They all stood a little straighter, while Bill's man nodded.

'Alright,' he said. 'We're listening. What is it you're offering?'

'I'm offering a chance to take back what's ours,' she told them with a faint shrug of her shoulders, as if she cared not one jot what they decided. 'I'm offering you all your territories back, and those that belonged to the ones now gone.'

'And Saint Nick's?'

'Nick's will be his again,' she decreed, daring them to laugh. But they didn't. Only waited. 'And mine. I'm getting him out.'

'Out of the College,' Waterman Tom scoffed. 'Ye're mad.'

'Entirely,' she shrugged again. 'But I'll get him out. We'll lay low once I have, and when things have calmed, we'll be coming back here. And if anyone thinks of takin' what's ours in the meantime, my offer from earlier stands. Of course, if we don't make it out, well, then, *maybe*, you can carve up what was his.'

'What's the plan?' Hook's man asked.

'Silas, Charlie, and Foxy will be taken out,' she told them, stepping back to cross her arms. 'I'll take care of them. What I need is everyone else to take back what was stolen from us. Make them regret ever steppin' foot in our house.'

'There's still the matter of that army,' Bill's man pointed out.

'We have an army,' she smiled. 'All those that remain of each of yours, and those that remain of the dead men's packs. And Nick's. We have the Ghost's army. And mine. What,' she said, grinning like a cat that got the proverbial cream. 'You didn't think I was just some helpless, unprotected madam?'

She laughed, and they all hung their heads a little.

'The Ghost? But he's -'

'Our ally. In this, at least,' she promised.

Her eyes went to Harrow, as did the other men's.

The ghostly representative nodded in agreement.

There would be peace between prey and predator - for a time, at least.

'Still not enough,' Tom said.

'Aye, so it isn't,' she agreed. 'Which is why we'll get more. We'll enlist every man, and woman who suffered loss the other night. Every man and woman willing to fight for what's theirs. You all know who they are. You've drunk with them, talked with them, worked with them. Men and women who will not stand for Shadwell, or Wapping, or Rotherhithe, to become anyone else's but that of their own. Of those who have lived, and loved, and bled there.'

'Ye're gonna start a riot, girly,' Hook's man said, only this time not mocking, but with awe.

'Thames men ain't gonna like that,' Tom noted. 'And the men in the West.'

'They will when things settle, profits flow again, and the ones who were, are back on our payroll.'

'When?' Bill's man asked.

'Preparations are still in motion,' Lily admitted. 'I have to ensure the fine new gentlemen in our houses will accept my invitation. I will send word when all is set. In the meantime, you gather yourselves, everyone you can find, *quietly*, along with a healthy stash of weapons.'

'Very well,' Tom said, speaking for them all after a glance to the others. 'Ye've got yerself a deal.'

He offered out his hand, and she took it.

The others followed suit, and as she shook their hands, she let the feeling of having succeeded rush over her again, if only for a second. And she also made sure they looked her in the eye again, and saw, *felt*, the danger she would be to them if they failed, or betrayed her in any way.

As they quietly made their way out back into the twilight of dawn, she prayed yet again that all this would work.

'Tis no more the time for prayin'.

Now 'tis the time for doin'.

'You didn't tell them about the gentlemen from the West,' Harrow pointed out, sidling up to her once everyone else had gone.

'They don't need to know,' she said simply, turning to meet his gaze.

'Might've wound them up more.'

'Might've tempted them more to take what isn't theirs,' she pointed out. 'You've got men on them, yes?'

'Of course. As do you, I imagine,' he said, casting a curious glance at Bob.

'Of course.'

'I'll be waiting for word as to a date, Lily.' he nodded. He made to leave, but stopped himself, and leaned in closer, though not threateningly, only to not be heard by Bob. 'I hope you know what you're doing. A great many lives are in the balance. And I think, you would not like the enemies you'll be making if you fail, including his lordship.'

'Harrow, if I fail, I will be dead.'

'Fair point,' he smiled weakly, before stepping back, slipping his hat back on, and departing in silence.

Bob and Lily waited a few minutes, then left the opposite way, carefully making their way back to the house unseen. All the while, the same thought repeated itself.

Oh how I do hope I know what I'm doing.

XXVI.

The grating of metal on metal, the clanging of keys, and the screeching of the opening door on stone, pulled Arthur back to the brink of consciousness. He'd been dreaming, he was sure of it, not that his mind could remember any of it. Only, he felt a strange sort of warmth inside, and considering the ice-cold damp of the forgotten dark cell he'd been lying in for...well, he wasn't quite sure how long, *a few days at least*, that was the most logical explanation.

Not that he had much logic left.

A shred of it, along with a shred of himself.

It hadn't taken them long to understand what he'd done; how he'd taken away that which they so desperately sought. They'd worked him harder, more viciously, and Arthur knew when the door opened, it would only begin again. His little reprieve, his little dream, born simply of his fall into continued unconsciousness, would be over.

Trying to summon what remained of his strength, he drew in as much of a breath through his mouth as his sore, thankfully, *still not broken yet*, bruised ribs would allow. He could taste the putrid air on his tongue, though it felt almost a reprieve from the thick iron of his own blood. The only eye which could still open fluttered to half mast, and he stared at the soiled dirt of his cell; soiled with his own filth, and that of others before him. Lain as he was against it in a corner, he could almost see every speck of dirt, every fleck of ancient rushes, every rat dropping, even in the low glow of the lamp now being carried inside his cell. He pushed himself to feel not only the pain, but also the cold, the slither of wetness against his body; to hear the echoes of cries, and shouts, and doors, and locks, even the distant hum of the city, rumbling towards him. Everything brought him back to, if not the time, the place at least.

It brought him back to his body; and to what was left of his mind.

Now here is something different, he thought weakly, when not his usual assailant's broken and disgusting leather boots, nor his jailor's semi-polished black ones, came into view, but a neat, impossibly clean, and polished pair did. A silver, ornate little buckle twinkled at him, taunting, from the edge of the wool hem of expensive trousers.

Now begins the torture of the mind.

Here was one of the puppet masters' representatives, or perhaps even one of the masters themselves. Though he doubted any would sully themselves thus - not solely coming here, but mainly, doing their own work themselves.

They are not so desperate...

Yet.

'Mr. Dudley,' a clear voice, just as polished as the damned shoes, said brightly. 'Good day to you.'

Arthur didn't move, didn't make a sound; not that he thought for one second the new man thought him still unconscious.

But he had so little strength left; he needed it to keep his mind and lips in check.

'For Chrissake, Jeb,' the man sighed, addressing his usual assailant, who must've been creeping near the door, just out of Arthur's eyeline, for he heard some shifting coming from the vicinity. 'I told you to get him talking, not to make it impossible for him to do so, you idiotic brute.'

'Sorry, Mr -'

The idiotic brute was silenced before he could utter a name, not that a name would be any use to Arthur.

For I shall never live to tell the tale of it.

'Just get out,' the gentleman bit back.

There was more shuffling, and then, silence.

'My sincerest apologies, Mr. Dudley,' the man said after a moment, though there was no regret in his voice, only disappointment for how hard his task had now apparently become. 'Good help is so very difficult to find, as I'm sure you know. Mr. Dudley,' he continued after a long moment of silence. 'I will need you to make some sort of sound so that I know you understand me. I cannot bear to repeat myself, it is most dreadfully dull, and should you wish to remain lying there comfortably for a little longer, I suggest you cooperate.'

Arthur measured his choices, then grunted softly after a time.

'Excellent. Now, to business,' the visitor said brightly, rocking slightly on his heels in excitement. 'I think you know why I'm here, since my...colleague,' he murmured distastefully. 'Asked the same question I am about to. Where are the deeds and titles?'

He didn't have enough in him to tell the man to go back to Hell where he'd been spawned from, so he took a page from Lily's book, and did his best to shrug.

'Quite,' the man responded.

The next moment, he was depositing the lamp he'd carried in to the floor, and crouching into Arthur's eyeline, careful to keep his clothes far away from the floor, but also that his eyes were visible. From what Arthur could tell, he was rather tall, muscular, with jet-black hair greying at the temples, and shimmering grey eyes not unlike his own. On his right hand, a gold signet ring glinted at him, much as the silver buckle had.

A sickening, foreboding whisper of a smile notched the lines surrounding his mouth.

'You know how this ends, Mr. Dudley,' he said softly, almost... *Sweetly?* 'There is no way out of this for you. All there is left to decide, is how you leave this world. How long others are allowed to live. And in what conditions they are allowed to do so.'

Lily.

The man nodded, reading his thoughts.

Arthur bit back the cry of rage, frustration, and fear, that would take all the strength he had with it. He'd known this would come. He'd known his association with Lily would threaten her safety when the truth came out, but selfish bastard that he'd been he'd not only continued to see her, he'd been seen out in public with her.

Harrow.

The memory, of a promise made speared through him, cutting through the panic.

Yes, he'd known all that, and taken precautions. He'd known they would use her against him, and so he'd made sure she was out of danger before they could get to her.

What if -

NO.

He had to trust in Harrow. One of the only people he had ever trusted in his life, difficult though it had been. He had to stand fast. Had to trust that she was safe.

The gentleman's eyes narrowed as they caught what must be some expression of defiance.

'Interesting,' he murmured. 'I wonder, if you would continue to refuse me what I wish if I were to bring a piece of her here,' he mused. 'Perhaps a lock of hair, or a finger...' *Trust in Harrow,* Arthur repeated to himself, visions of those possibilities stirring the bile within him. 'Or perhaps it is simply that you don't care? I had found it rather surprising a man such as you would form an attachment. And her resistance to Mr. Silas was rather... Non-existent.'

Arthur focused hard on not betraying anything else.

On continuing to repeat his prayer, *trust Harrow.* He would not, *could not,* consider the alternative. That Lily was still in London, under the thumb of that vermin.

'I even heard she was throwing a party for him,' the gold and silver gilded gentleman grinned. *Trust Harrow.* 'For all those who served us. But then, she is rather clever. Had you as a protector. I wager she knows well how to survive. Even heard she had something to do with that Gordy fellow kicking the proverbial bucket some years ago. Anyway,' he sighed, pulling himself back to the moment, the glint of *admiration was it?*, gone from his eyes. 'Enough of her then. I mean, I shall still try my luck with bringing a piece of her here for you, just to ensure I've tried all avenues, but in the meantime, I see you are tiring. And I should let you think a while. If not about Miss Lily's fate, then that of others. Your tenants, for instance. Those children and mothers in the foundling home you helped build. Anyone, really. My employer requires those papers, Mr. Dudley. They wish for things to be all in proper order, you understand.'

Arthur grunted, and the gentleman nodded, before rising out of sight.

'I will instruct my colleague to leave you some time,' he said, a brush of flesh on fabric telling him the man was brushing off some imaginary dirt. 'To consider everything. That party I spoke of is tomorrow evening. A perfect occasion for Mr. Silas to acquire what I need.' *Trust Harrow.* 'Rest well, Mr. Dudley. I will see you soon. I hope the time will provide you with some clarity.'

The polished leather and silver buckle faded into the distance.

The scraping of the door, clinking of keys, and grating of metal into the lock, neatly bookended the visit.

Arthur forced another deep breath into his body, and forced the pain in his heart away.

Trust Harrow.

For if he did not...

If he did not and this gentleman returned with a piece of his heart in hand...

Then I will have to give them everything.

XXVII.

Word had come two days after her meeting with Mr. Ames. True to his word, and warning, she had but three days to prepare. Three days to prepare for her entry into Newgate, as the supposed wife of one of the imprisoned debtors. Three days to prepare a plan to get Arthur out from there; trusting that Bill would somehow find her, and lead her to him. Three days to prepare a party for the enemies at her door and in her house.

Three days to prepare their deaths.

Those three days seemed to both a blessedly short time; and yet as if a century.

Blessedly short, for she wasn't sure how long Arthur would last in that place. Surely the men in charge of this whole scheme had learned of his relinquishment of the deeds and titles by now, and were working him for their whereabouts. Soon...

Soon they would come knocking again at her door, she knew that too.

So, really, it was good that it was only three days.

But those days seemed to stretch into infinity. With concern, with fear, with all the preparations to be made in secret. So many were involved with every passing hour, that all it would take, was for someone to be seen by the wrong person. For one word to be whispered a little too loudly. And the jig would be up. Every second she feared Silas would appear again at her door, and bring an end to it all. Still, she did all she had to.

Bob brought word to Harrow, who would bring it to the others.

Sunday morn. When the bells of St. Paul's ring three. A red cloth will hang from the house when it is done.

She visited Sarah, who would provide the means to get out, and away from Newgate thanks to her talents with a needle.

She sent out the invitation to the new bosses, promising a night of celebration, and revelry. A gesture of loyalty, and acceptance of the new order.

She spoke to her workers, one by one, offering them the same choice.

Stay, or go.

If they stayed, she would be asking them to do something beyond what anyone should. Take a life. Or at the very least, aid others in doing so. She would be asking them to put their own lives on the line; their very souls.

If they went, she would see they had enough to get them out of the city, quietly, to begin a new life elsewhere.

Three took her up on the latter offer. Three more of her youngest and newest, she forced to go with them. She had them disappear, two each day.

She tried to get those closest to it all, Joce, Winnie, Jack, and Mary, to leave too.

They wouldn't have it.

They, along with half of those others who remained, volunteered to do the worst of it.

So she chose her people, chose her weapons, and made the final arrangements.

She made arrangements for her own departure and stay outside the city, and put things in place so she and Arthur could rule from afar. She set up an escape plan for everyone in her house, should things not go as planned, at *any* point. So far, the old bosses remained true to their word, making their own preparations, keeping silent, but once her part had been played… There was no telling what would happen.

And she could not, *would* not, just blindly trust them with the lives of so many. If she did this, she had to be confident that no matter what, the people she put in danger, at least had a chance if things went awry. It wasn't much, and it wouldn't save her soul when judgement day came and trumpets sounded, but it would help her sleep at night until then.

Or so she hoped.

Doubts still assailed her, even as she knew she could proceed no other way.

She couldn't just let Arthur die, and she couldn't let men who thought themselves above the rest, decide the fates of everyone around her. Already, within days, things had changed here, and not for the better. There was fear, and grief in the air.

No more.

Not if she had it in herself to do something about it.

Which she did.

And so, just as the last barrels of wine were delivered to the house, Lily closed the door to the secret passage that had served her well these past days, and went to her room, to begin the final preparations for this, if not long, much awaited party.

Time to get dressed and become Miss Lily once more.

∞

'Good evening, gentlemen,' Lily said, brightly, and seductively, as the contingent they'd all been waiting for with bated breath appeared in the foyer, not very much unlike like last time. Only this time, the weapons they wore were stowed, and there was more lust, than bloodlust, in their eyes. *Perfect.* 'Welcome to Miss Lily's.'

Smiling, she let her gaze travel over the large party. They were all here.

Perfect.

Charmin' Charlie, with his handsome looks, crooked smile, and stevedore's build.

Foxy, with his rat-like features and suit that looked to be from his boyhood.

And of course, Silas.

Winston, too, which for once, she was glad of, and a contingent from all their enterprises. A show of force, of power, as was their arrival as a group, altogether. Or perhaps, that was simply a play between the three - each one unbending to a hierarchy among them - neither wanting to arrive first, or last.

Whatever the reason, she was glad of it. They could begin now, and looking at the numbers, she knew this evening might just be a success. Perhaps a couple more than expected, but as long as the principal players were taken out, the rest could be taken care of easily enough.

She smiled, and Charmin' Charlie was the first to approach.

'Miss Lily,' he said, attempting to emulate a formal bow, succeeding only thanks to the impish grin he sported in return. 'Many thanks for your welcome. 'Tis a good thing to see you so… Acceptin' of the new way of things.'

'Aye,' Foxy agreed, stepping forth not to be outdone. His eyes searched hers, and there was a wariness she would need be mindful of. *Will have to warn Winnie to be extra warm.* 'Quite a surprise this party of yours.'

'A good one, I should hope,' she smiled sweetly.

'Let's hope so,' Silas said, quietly, without moving. There was something in his eyes too… *Doubt? Discomfort?* She didn't think it because of the party, but something else, which his next words confirmed. 'Shall we get this entertainment started? Though if you would favour me with a word, Miss Lily.'

'Of course,' she said, before turning her attention back to the others. 'Please, do make yourselves at home. My companions wait in the salon with drinks, and delightful dishes. I'm sure you will all find many things to your taste.'

Though Foxy sent her another wary glance, none hesitated before turning to make for the direction she indicated.

Silas watched them go, waiting until they were alone in the front hall.

'Is there something amiss?' Lily asked when they were, and

still, he didn't move.

He turned to her, his eyes studying her for a long moment.

It didn't make her uncomfortable, but rather it seemed as if he was trying to make sense of a riddle.

'No, Miss Lily,' he assured her, back to his usual self. 'I simply hoped we could speak, later this evening. We have some important matters to discuss.'

'Of course.'

He was lying, but why?

And why not speak now? Not that she cared, because later, in this case, for him, meant never.

'Partake of the merriment awhile,' she said, slipping her arm into his, and guiding him towards the salon. 'I have someone I think you will be most interested to meet.'

Her gaze met Amelia's as they entered the room, where already the rest of the men were indulging their every whim, and the woman approached, as only she knew how, hooking Silas' interest in seconds.

'Silas, meet Amelia,' she crooned, releasing her hold so Amelia could take over.

'A pleasure, sir,' the woman said huskily, sidling into Lily's place. 'Won't you come sit by me and have some wine?'

'Aye.'

With one last look for Lily over his shoulder, Silas followed the woman who would be his doom to a corner of the room laden with a fountain of wine and towers of delicacies.

So it begins.

∞

Five minutes. Lily stared at the clock on the mantel, and took in a deep breath, aligning her heartbeat with the ticking of the ornate mechanism. She said a silent prayer to whatever old god watched over nights such as this, Mars perhaps, or even St. Michael, saint of all warriors, that they win this battle; that as many lives could be spared, would be.

With a nod, she went to her desk, and from beneath it extracted the pistol and knife she'd fastened there. She'd hoped never to have to use them, and even now, in some strange way, she hoped she didn't. Slipping the knife into her garter, and concealing the pistol in the folds of her diaphanous gown, she admitted to herself that the thought was cowardly in a sense. Hoping that the actual blood would be on others' hands; that she would not need to jump into the fray. But at the same time, she knew the blood of anyone who died this night would be on her hands. On her heart, and on her soul.

And that will be quite enough to bear as it is.

Giving herself a tiny moment to accept that, she smoothed her fingertips against the cool wood of the pistol, straightened, and finally set forth.

She descended to the main rooms, checking as she did that all her men were in place; not that she doubted they would be. They stood, seemingly unarmed, and bored; but she could see the tension within them. The coiled readiness.

Not long now.

Passing the smaller entertainment rooms, she glanced in, happy to see the orgiastic tableaux therein. The hours of drinking, and eating, and pleasure, had worn her enemies down into a dissolute stupor, and when the chimes rang two, they would be in no shape to even register what was happening.

Onwards she went, reaching the main hall just as the old grandfather clock posted there rang out, the symphony of smaller timepieces across the house echoing with it. The atmosphere within seemed to change then, as if the house had been struck by lightning. The moans of pleasure, the lilting quiet remnants of music, the laughter, all of it took on a sinister note, before it changed altogether.

Before it became muffled cries, grunts, and ultimately, silence.

Lily went to the salon's doors, where the majority of lesser men had remained, and where now, they met their deaths. Her workers were quick, and had she not known what was happening, she might've mistaken the scene. She might not have noticed the rivers of blood, the eyes full of lifelessness. Those few men who had not been in the company of one of hers, alone with a bottle or food at the edge of the room, were swiftly dealt with by her own men, coming in to clean up. Quietly, all of them, with blades, and ropes, and hands.

A few glanced to her, and she nodded, more appreciative than she could ever say, for the sacrifice they had all just made.

Silence met her ears from the rest of the house as she backed away, heading upstairs again, this time to check on those appointed with the riskiest task: dispatching the leaders. As she ascended, the sounds changed again. Industriousness crept into her house apace, shuffling and shifting; rustling and whispering.

The bodies were taken care of, swiftly, quietly, as with the rest. They would be laid to rest, in secret; dignity in death was not something she would refuse, no matter their crimes. She may be executioner tonight, but she was not judge.

Lily reached Winnie's room first, to find Bob already disposing of Foxy.

'You alright, Win,' she asked, glancing in to find the young woman washing her hands.

'Aye, Miss Lily.'

A nod, and Lily was moving again.

Later, she would speak to them all one last time, check on them, before she left.

For now, she needed to ensure it was done, so the others outside could begin their work.

Mary's room was next.

There, she found her and Jack depositing Charlie outside the door.

Please let it all have been so easy.

So it seemed it had been, as she checked the rest of the rooms where some of the seconds-in-command had taken their ease; and met their deaths.

At Joce's room, she stopped a moment, when she found her sitting on the bed, looking utterly dazed, staring at the wall,

Winston's blood still on her hands.

Kneeling before her, Lily set a hand on one of Joce's.

I should not have asked this of her.

'I'm sorry, Joce,' she whispered, her heart clenching at the sight of the tear running down the other woman's cheek. 'I should not have asked -'

'You did not ask,' Joce said fiercely, finally meeting her gaze, a frown creasing her brow. 'I said I would do this.'

'Joce -'

'I'm crying because it feels good, Miss Lily,' Joce choked out. 'I've been afraid, for weeks. That he would come back. For me. I'd thought it was love, but it wasn't. I see that now. It was twisted, and not right, and now I am free, and he will hurt no one ever again.'

Lily searched her eyes, her heart still full of concern, but she saw the truth in Joce's gaze.

'No,' she said quietly. 'He will not hurt anyone again.'

Joce nodded, and Lily rose.

'You should get cleaned up now,' she said, kissing the woman's forehead. 'I will come see you again before I leave.'

'Thank you, Miss Lily.'

'Thank you, Joce.'

Pushing away the mix of guilt, relief, doubts, and self-recrimination that she could deal with later, *much later*, Lily headed up to check on Amelia.

And Silas.

∞

As soon as Lily reached the door to Amelia's room, she knew something was wrong. Grunts, the sounds of breaking glass, and the woman's moans reached her ears, and her heart pounded within her chest.

Of course Silas wouldn't go fucking quietly.

Glancing down the corridor, she noticed she was alone. The others on this floor had been taken care of, her men were disposing of the bodies, and she wouldn't get her workers involved in this. This was one mess she would clean up herself.

Pulling back the hammer on her pistol, her knife readily accessible, she slammed open the door, and raised the pistol as she strode in without thought nor hesitation.

Her eyes scanned the room quickly, or rather, what was left of it, and found a half-naked Amelia and Silas struggling in the debris of the washstand to her right. He had her pinned, knocking the hand which held her dagger against the floor above her head. Amelia was kicking and kneeing any bit of flesh she could, but it would end badly, quickly. Luckily, both were too involved to notice her arrival.

Taking a deep breath, Lily aimed, praying she hit Silas, and made to pull the trigger.

Only just as she did, a body slammed into her, knocking her to the ground, the pistol thankfully not firing as she fell.

Stunned, and confused, for it was unmistakably a woman that had thrown her down, Lily dropped the pistol and instead grabbed hold of a fistful of golden locks, curling herself around her assailant so she couldn't escape.

They fought for supremacy as they rolled and tugged and clawed, Lily desperately trying to reach her knife. There was a loud thump in the distance, and she prayed Silas hadn't killed Amelia. Finally, she managed to grab her knife, and pin her own assailant down, ready to plunge the blade into whoever the madwoman's side was.

And then, two things happened at once.

'Kit, no!' Silas screamed, just as she caught sight of the girl's face beneath her.

Her sister's face.

∞

Lily was frozen, her knife in mid-air, ready to strike her own flesh and blood. The same flesh and blood she'd been searching for, for years, was here, right here, right now, in the middle of a massacre, beneath her. Both her and her sister's eyes widened, and they lay there for a moment staring at each other in surprise. Questions assailed her mind as all breath left her body, and a myriad of emotions rose within. Relief, fear, joy, despair; all mingled into one as everything else but her sister faded away.

That cost her, as in a moment Silas had grabbed her up and tossed her against the wall.

'Silas, no,' her sister yelled just as the man made for her, murder in his eyes. Lily stared between them, her incomprehension growing. 'She's my sister,' Kit pleaded, grabbing hold of his arm as he yet again made to lunge. 'Please, don't.'

Silas looked about as bewildered as she felt, staring between the two women with a deep frown.

Lily noted he had quite a few scrapes and cuts, his right eye was cut just beneath the brow, and there was a nasty gash in his side. At least Amelia had done some damage.

Amelia...

She glanced over to where the woman lay and saw the rise and fall of her chest.

Thank God.

A slamming door sounded from down the corridor, and Lily came back to the room.

Her sister was still clinging to Silas, who had manoeuvred himself before her, as if to shield her. And in that moment, no matter how incomprehensible, how heart-breaking, how terrifying, she knew what she had to do.

Trust my enemy.

'You have to go, Kit,' she managed to say, though it was the last thing she wished to.

But she had to get her out, and right now...

Right now, despite it being the very, very last thing she would ever have imagined doing, she had to trust Silas to help.

'You keep her safe,' she said to Silas, straightening from the wall, raising her dagger. 'You keep her safe, and you get her out of the city, and your life is yours. There is nothing more you can do here tonight. You lost. Everyone else is dead, and by all accounts, so shall you be. So take this chance. And if you touch one hair on her head, I will flay you and feed you to the fishes.'

Silas regarded her carefully, then nodded grimly.

'Lily -'

'No, Kit,' she said harshly, though all she wanted to do was weep, and pull her sister into her arms, and never let go. 'You have to leave now. We will be together again. I promise. I never stopped looking, and this time, I will know where to find you.'

Her sister nodded, tears falling from her cheeks, and Lily prayed again to whatever powers that this be the right choice.

'Come on.'

After checking it was empty, she led Silas and Kit quietly down the corridor, then up the back stairs to her office.

Once they were safely inside, she pulled on the lever behind the ledgers, and the bookcase swung out, revealing the secret passage.

'It will lead you out into the next house over,' she told Silas. 'There is a bag of clothes, food, and money in a barrel in the cellar. You have just enough time to get out, unseen, before the rest begins.'

'I'll keep her safe,' he promised, pulling Kit into the passage behind him.

Kit dug her heels in and threw herself around Lily.

'I love you,' Lily whispered, tears rolling down her cheeks. 'Do you remember the inn, at the crossing of the roads, ten miles from home?' Her sister nodded. 'Go there. I will send for you when I can.'

Her sister nodded again, then let herself be pulled into the passage.

Closing the bookcase again, closing the door on the sister she had found again just moments ago, sending her off into the night with that man, was the hardest thing she'd ever had to do in her life. She felt the cost of her choices, all of them, good and bad, all the choices she had ever made, in that instant. She felt the cost of the path her life took now, and might've sworn one of

Lucifer's fiends laughed as he came up to collect the due for her soul.

But she couldn't stop now.

And she couldn't risk Kit getting caught in the crossfire.

She would finish what she started, and she would get Arthur back, and then…

Then she would find Kit.

And true to her word, if that bastard laid a finger on her, she'd feed him to the Thames.

XXVIII.

April 25th, 1824

The sun hadn't risen yet, though the first signs of its imminent approach coloured the receding black and purples of the night. Only hours since it had begun, and now, it was over. It was not so quiet out here as it had been from the vantage of her room. Here, the eerie silence still reigned, only it was punctuated by horrific cries.

Cries of loss, and pain, and pursuit.

As she stepped out of the house, Lily could smell it on the air, taste it, the blood and powder, mixing with the smell of the river. She inhaled deeply, taking it all within her; it was, after all, her doing. She would not back away from it. Cower from it, regret it.

Head held high, she stepped down onto the street, and glancing around, she noted the signs of her success. Bodies, smoke, and the visages of the people caught in the middle, peeking from windows and doorways with fear and awe. Some triumphant, others accusatory.

My doing.

Yes.

And she would own it.

Straightening, she set back her shoulders, picked up her skirts, and took off her bonnet and veil. She would let them see who had done this. She would let them see who was to blame, or thank, as they saw fit; who was now the Queen of Shadwell.

With infinite intent and pride, Bob, and Sarah behind her, she marched on through the streets, showing them all. She marched on, as some screamed, and jeered, as others cheered and doffed their hats. She marched through the streets and alleys, up to the High Street, and along it.

Perhaps one day, when she was burning in the fiery depths, she would regret this.

Perhaps one day; but not today.

As she settled in the carriage that awaited her at the borders of her new kingdom, she felt nothing.

No regret, no fear, not even any hope.

It isn't over yet.

Once it was, then she would feel. She would feel whatever she had to feel then.

For now, she would simply do what she had to, and she would get her saint back.

∞

The carriage finally ambled to a stop, and Lily glanced out of the window to find the ever-foreboding, grey, dismal, seemingly impassable walls of Newgate before her. The whole edifice, even in the light of this surprisingly bright Spring day, seemed a thick, dark mass; a hellhole where humanity itself ceased to exist. Even the birds seemed to avoid it.

Somewhere in the back of her mind, she knew that was the architect's intention, to make it terrible and terrifying, but there was also truth in the image of a hellhole.

Not that it will stop me going in there.

Sliding the veil back over her face, she waited for the door to be opened, then stepped down, taking Bob's proffered hand.

'You know what to do,' she said quietly, her eyes taking in all there was to her surroundings.

The prison, naturally, offset from the rest of the surrounding area by its sheer dominating size and appearance. The street itself was busy, even at this early hour, which was good, for it meant that in a short while, it would be even more so as the city properly awakened. Even the front doors themselves were already busy; visitors, prisoners, guards, runners, all manner of officials, mostly entering, but some also hastily departing, looking much the worse for wear for their visit, whatever the purpose. A sense of relief seemed to dance on the faces of all those who left, and Lily shivered, knowing she was woefully unprepared for what she would find inside.

How I will find him. If I even can...

If Bill did not hear of her arrival, if he did not find her, if he had not found Arthur, if news from Shadwell travelled too quickly here, if any of this failed to work -

Stop it. Chin up. 'Tis only a grim place. You've seen worse.

She doubted it.

Still, it helped her screw her courage tight.

'We'll be ready,' Bob said quietly, shutting the door, and making for the back of the carriage again. 'Ye be careful now, Miss Lily,' he added, as he jumped onto the postillion, and the carriage started off down the street again.

A nod, and she turned back to the prison.

They didn't have much time, and she would not waste any dilly-dallying. Chin high, shoulders back, she marched imperiously to the debtors' door, and joined the mercifully short queue to enter. She focused hard on ignoring all those around her; the sounds, the sights, the smells. The cries of desperate prisoners, being led in, never to leave. The angry shouts, or desperate pleas of those come to visit. Some laughter even, from the guards, or even some visitors. People from all walks of life, maids, kiln-workers, gentlemen, and ladies, like herself, or at least as she presented herself today.

A widow, or at least, a woman in mourning for her dissolute husband with too many debts who wishes to be discreet.

Finally, after a short time, slowly advancing ever closer to the imposing white door, she had her turn. Imperiously, but quietly, she murmured the name Mr. Ames had given her. A list was checked, and she was ushered in. Lily breathed a sigh of relief; still aware of the fact that this was only the beginning. And getting in, was easy.

Gettin' out's gonna be the tricky bit.

Forcing herself to ignore the oppressive, reeking atmosphere, she moved on, throwing her name about like some pass from the King himself; along with a few guineas here and there. It did the trick, advancing her further inside.

Carefully, she watched everything around her, noting guards, doors, and twists and turns taken as she was passed along, from this guard to that, given directions here and there; waved through, walked through, and shoved through so many doors, until finally, she stood in a tiny, but well-enough appointed room, for a prison that is, where her *husband*, awaited her.

He was dressed plainly, and his clothes showed a lack of constant care, but he, and indeed the cell were clean. A bed with several blankets and a pillow sat in one corner, a minuscule desk and chair in another, and papers were tacked along the wall above it. The man looked up from his work as she entered, the guard simply depositing her there on his way to some other forsaken place as the door here was not locked nor even closed. A nod, and the man returned to his work, leaving Lily to simply...

Wait.

And pray.

∞

And wait she did, though thankfully, not for long. The scratch of her *husband's* pen, underlining the maddening noises from the rest of the prison; voices, shouts, the clank of keys, and thudding of doors, only had to be endured for perhaps a quarter of an hour, before heavy steps sounded behind her.

Ready to offer up her supposed name and more guineas, Lily turned, only to be faced with the most welcome sight.

Bill.

Had the corridor beyond not been bustling with activity, she might've leapt up and embraced him tightly.

Instead, she simply smiled, and went to him.

'God am I glad to see you,' Lily breathed. Bill nodded, offering up a tight, but welcome smile. 'How did you know?'

This had been the one part of the plan she'd doubted the most.

Because it meant trusting that Bill would find a way in; and find a way to hear of some woman's arrival.

It meant trusting he'd know when to come for her.

'Mr. Ames sends his regards,' Bill said quietly, before turning his attention to the corridor. Lily offered up a silent thanks to *The Emporium's* owner as Bill took a step closer. ''Tis good to see you, Miss Lily. Trust last night went well enough?' She nodded, and he smiled again, admiration that made her heart soar in his eyes. 'And I expect ye got a plan?'

'Aye.'

'Then let's to it, Miss Lily,' he whispered. 'He's in one of the forgotten ones, and last I 'eard shouldn't be but one guard. They's expectin' somethin' from Shadwell, and some toff supposed to be in this mornin'. Worked 'im over pretty good, ye should be prepared for that too.' Unable to speak, the fear of what she'd find rising again, Lily simply nodded. 'Come on then.'

Bill gestured towards the corridor, and before they slipped into it, Lily turned back, and deposited a few guineas on her husband's desk, for which he inclined his head gratefully.

With that, Lily turned to Bill, and then, they were off.

To the forgotten ones.

∞

If anyone wondered what a well-appointed widow and a turnkey were doing together, or indeed, what they were doing further in the deepest bowels of Newgate; they didn't say, Bill's uniform deterring anyone looking to ask questions. Quickly, as discreetly yet confidently as they could, they descended further into the most terrible corners of the prison.

The tales that came from Newgate had always been

horrendous. The stories told of a place beyond even the worst nightmares; and every so often some reformer or radical or that would come in, and dedicate a pamphlet to the despicable happenings and conditions. But because of the unbelievable wretchedness of it all, it made it hard to believe. To comprehend.

Not so now...

Not when the air changed, thickened, with rot, and death, and damp, so much so that she had to lift up her veil to breathe. When the walls seemed to close in on them, even as the ceilings seemed to fall. When light became a rarity, until it was only the lamp Bill grabbed up that penetrated the darkness. When the cries and screams that pierced through the thick walls sounded so unearthly; as if those hellish demons had risen up to visit here themselves.

The room she'd seen upstairs, indeed, the clear, sunlit rooms and corridors of the upstairs altogether, seemed Heaven itself compared to this. There had been rumours, always, of these forgotten rooms, like *oubliettes* of the past, where those in power or indeed anyone with coin enough could make their problems disappear to, but admittedly, Lily had never imagined it would be somewhere she would ever see with her own eyes.

But it's good, she told herself, as they advanced even further. *'Tis good for it is removed, and quiet.*

It would make this easier.

Right.

Ahead, Lily spotted a circle of dim light, and just as she did, Bill stopped.

'Ye stay here,' he whispered.

Lily did as instructed, waiting in the chilly, cloying darkness as Bill and his light advanced further.

His, and another voice echoed on the walls, as did the blow that sent the other man to the ground.

A whistle, and she stepped blindly forth, chasing the light.

'Alright, miss,' Bill said gravely, straightening from where he'd been filching the other man's keys. 'Let's get this done.'

Lily nodded, and Bill went to open the door.

Taking one of the lamps in hand, she stood behind him, and cringed as the door scraped against the stone floor.

Bill stepped aside with a grimace, and Lily rushed through, unable to stop the gasp that escaped her when the light reached the corners of the tiny cell, more disgusting than the worst rookeries, and she saw the figure curled up against the wall.

Her heart nearly broke, and she wanted to be ill, but she pushed back the hot tears, and simply strode forth. She'd known it would be bad, but this...

He'd been beaten to within an inch of his life - what looked like several times. If she hadn't known it was him, she wouldn't have recognized him. His chest rose jerkily, as if he could barely breathe, and the state of him...

If any of these wounds weren't infected, she would be surprised.

'Oh, Arthur,' she cried, rushing to his side, setting down the lamp, and running shaking fingers along his arm. 'Oh, my love...'

What have they done to you?

And will I be able to get you out like this?

XXIX.

So he was to be blessed with another sweet dream before the end. Arthur thanked whatever god had decided to grant him this small mercy after all, and let himself fade into the sweet warmth of his love's gentle touch. The enchanting lull of her voice. He could feel Lily's warmth seeping into him as she touched him, stroked his arm ever so softly. He could smell her, the glorious freshness of her chasing away the horror of this place. It all felt so real...

Because your mind is finally breaking...

Though if that is what this meant, he was glad of it. He could face the gold and silver gilded gentleman again; he could face anything after this. Sighing, his heart and soul at peace, he felt himself smile a little, as he drifted further into the dream.

But then, it was not so sweet.

The touch became harsh. Shaking him. Jostling him so that everything hurt, and his mind screamed at him to wake up.

Not only my mind...

'Arthur,' Lily's voice hissed. 'Arthur I know it hurts, my love. I know, but please, you must wake. We cannot do this with you unconscious. Please, Arthur! Wake up!'

With a jerk, Arthur was pulled back to the reality of his cell, and he knew for certain he had lost his mind.

Because it was impossible. It couldn't be.

She can't be here...

'Lily...'

'Arthur, oh God, thank you,' his love exclaimed, and he saw her now, too clearly despite the haze of pain, and one eye unable to open, for her to be imagined.

'Not...possible,' he gritted out. 'Harrow...'

Trust Harrow.

That is what had gotten him through the hours since that gentleman's visit. Only now it seemed, the gentleman had spoken the truth, and he'd been wrong to trust Harrow, because now she *was* here, and they would all die -

'Harrow tried, Arthur,' she said gently, smoothing some of the locks plastered to his forehead away. 'But I couldn't just go. I will tell you all later. Right now, I need you to help us. Bill is here,' she smiled, and sure enough, her giant appeared, crouching in the light, a grim look on his face. 'We don't have long.'

It took a long moment for Arthur to process all she said; to understand it.

She's come to rescue me. She is not here by the gentleman's hand.

'How...?'

'Later,' she promised. *God she truly is here*, he mused, staring into the depths of her amber eyes; darker today than usual, and filled with a strength that seemed to fill him. 'I need you to sit, if you can, and we must get you changed, and cleaned a bit, and then, Arthur, I will need you to leave here on your feet. We will help, but we cannot carry you.'

Arthur nodded, and focused on her words.

I will find the strength.

Slowly, with hers and Bill's hands helping him, he was raised to sitting, his back against the wall. The pain was, if possible, worse. Everything stung, and throbbed, and ached, and his head felt as if it would explode. He closed his eye for a moment, and heard Lily mumble something about clothes, then Bill shuffle away as Lily rustled about.

Something cool met his lips, and his eye fluttered open again.

'Here,' Lily said soothingly, tipping a flask of what he first thought was water, then realised was coffee, so he could drink.

He did as ordered, and when she was satisfied, she closed the flask, and hid it away in a bag that had seemingly appeared from nowhere. 'Now, we must clean you up a little, and get you dressed again.'

He nodded, shoring up his strength for what lay ahead, and if he was honest, too dazed, and still disbelieving that any of this was truly happening to make any remarks.

Quickly, but tenderly, Lily undressed him, murmuring gentle words whenever he groaned or winced in pain from the movement. Then, from her magical bag, she extracted water, a pair of scissors, and a towel. She cleaned him a little, first his body, then his hair and beard, and he let his eye drift close again as she did, surrendering to her loving nursing. A tear slipped from his eye, which she kissed away.

How to explain the feeling in his breast now?

It was hope, bright and glorious, along with shame, and pain, and fear, and exhaustion. It was relief, and terror, all mingled, and he let himself feel it now, for soon, he knew he would have to get up, and get out, if he wasn't to get them all killed.

Lily, extraordinary, unbelievable creature that she was, had come for *him*. She had risked herself, and God knew who else, to come save him, and he would not fail, if only so that he would not have his worst nightmare become reality. If only so that he would not lose her, in this, the final hour.

I will not fail her.

'I will clean you up better later, and tend to the wounds,' she said, bringing him back to the room. 'But for now, we need them. I only needed you to look as if you'd actually come to work in one piece today.' She offered a tight, but reassuring smile, and he frowned. 'You work here,' she explained, just as Bill reappeared, handing her what he guessed were his jailor's clothes. 'And you were viciously attacked.'

He nodded, as she stowed away her implements, and began the task of dressing him again, whilst Bill took his soiled garments and put them on the jailor he was to become for a short while.

When all was done, Lily crouched before him again, utter resolve and strength radiating from her.

'Are you ready, my love?'

'Yes,' Arthur croaked.

With a smile and a nod, Lily and Bill each grasped one of his arms, and dragged him to his feet.

I'm ready.

XXX.

'Rest a moment, Miss Lily,' Bill said quietly when they reached the top of the stairs. Not quite a blind spot, for eventually, someone would descend, but as good as any other in this place. They leaned Arthur against the wall, and all gathered their breaths. It had been a long, and arduous journey up from the cell, but they had survived it. 'We need to be quick after this, so take a moment.'

Arthur could barely stand, let alone walk, and he seemed to drift in and out of consciousness even as he continued forth. She wasn't sure how much longer he could last, and she cursed herself for thinking he'd be in any shape to walk out of here.

She should've thought of something better, something smarter-

'I'll make it, Lily,' Arthur breathed, pain, and exhaustion in his voice, but also the determined strength that had made him into the man he was.

She looked into those eyes that had taken her from the first, and knew they would make it.

We will. I believe.

'From here, 'tis straight, then left,' Bill told them. He'd decided this was the best chance they had, of the three possible exits. She was glad she'd had eyes posted on all of them; at least there had been some genius in her plan. 'We'll have t'pass through the yard but a little, then through the turnkeys' room. Don't ye stop for no one. Just keep wailin' and howlin', and we'll be out in no time.'

There was a tightness to his voice that belied the show of confidence, but Lily ignored it.

There was tightness, fear, in all of them. Her hands were shaking and sweaty, her blood pumping and her heart racing until it felt it would simply stop. But together, they could do this. All they needed, was to be bold. To march right out there, and show no hesitation, and they would be free.

We can do this.

Taking a deep, steadying breath, Lily nodded.

Together, she and Bill took Arthur between them again. With a glance, they stepped forth, and began the final stretch of the seemingly impossible journey.

As soon as they emerged from the shadows of the stairwell, Lily and Bill both began shouting. Bill - cursing and screaming for *help*, for *vengeance*, for a *'curse to be laid on the varmint who attacked one of them'.* Lily - she cried in despair, in fear, in horror. She let all the emotions already in her breast take hold - drive her to behave as a caricatural hysterical female.

At once, other guards and visitors pooled around them, drawn by the scene. They shouted and screamed and called for help, ebbing and flowing from beside them like a strange tide. Some asked questions, some offered to take Arthur from them. But Lily and Bill pressed forward, muttering words like *infirmary, got 'im,* and mumbling incoherently in answer to *'who did this?'.*

On they pressed, as panic and anger grew around them like flames. Through a door, into a yard, the sun briefly shining hope and light onto them. Through another door, though then the questions grew in earnest.

And the objections.

'Not the way to the infirmary.'

'Where ye goin'?'

Still, they evaded it all, Lily's cries resounding even more shrilly as they shoved through a contingent of turnkeys, the panicked group in their wake a welcome distraction. More came and went. More shouts. Lily focused on the feel of Arthur, on simply putting one step in front of another. She didn't see anything around her, not the people, not the room; nothing.

Not until Arthur tensed against her, and she glanced up, focusing on the point ahead.

The door.

A gentleman in the door.

The look in the gentleman's grey eyes.

He knows.

'Run,' Bill shouted, dropping Arthur, just as the man before them shouted, 'Stop them!'

Lily nearly collapsed under the weight, but she gritted her teeth and tightened her hold around Arthur's waist, then barrelled forth, the momentum from before mercifully keeping her travelling through.

The blur seemed to return then, but not because of a lack of focus. Rather, because of the intensity of hers. There were fiercer shouts, and Bill was clearing the way. There was the crunch of bone on bone, and bodies flying out of the way. There were hands grasping, clawing at her; but all she forced herself to feel was Arthur.

On, each step a mile or so it seemed, until finally the door was there, and they were through it. And there were the smells she had prayed for, *food,* and another door already ajar, and she could see the hive beyond it.

Two more doors.

Pushing her body beyond what she'd ever believed it capable, she thrust them onwards, feeling the resistance from behind them fading.

Two more doors.

The corridor was narrow, but might've been a canyon; until it wasn't. Until they had reached the other side of the chasm, and they were through this door too. Lily turned slightly once they had, her thoughts on Bill, waiting to see him come barrelling through so they could lock it, and push through together to the final doorway.

And he was there, only he wasn't.

He was across that chasm, holding back the stream of pursuers.

'Bill!' she screamed. Their eyes met, and she knew what he would do even before he did it. 'No, Bill!'

But the bastard smiled, and nodded, before shoving the door shut.

Before shutting himself in with the wolves that would tear him apart.

She screamed, her heart breaking, wishing she could stride back in there and save him, but knowing they would all be dead if she did. Bill had sacrificed himself for her, and she would not dishonour him by refusing his love.

With a cry, she shoved the door to the kitchens shut, and thrust a nearby chair under the latch.

It wouldn't hold long, but she didn't need it to.

'Move!' she yelled, extracting a pistol from her pocket, and waving it about as she dragged Arthur onwards. 'Move, now!'

The shocked mass of workers there stared at her warily, but did as they were told, and she rushed through the giant room, through the labyrinth of tables and ranges, and people and food, and detritus, until finally, it was there.

The last door.

Somehow, she would never be able to recall how, Lily managed to wrench it open. The light was blinding for a moment, and the air was intoxicating, though it was not much less foetid than inside the wretched place. For the tiniest moment, they froze, there on the doorstep, before the noise and bustle of the street, now fully awoken, rushed forth to meet them.

It washed over them like a wave, pushing them forth.

And there was a whistle, on the air, and familiar faces were before her.

Their hands grasped her and Arthur, and guided them hurriedly forwards even as the echo of shouts and threats and alarum bells sounded from behind. But she and her love were in a thick crowd now, a crowd of friends and allies, being whisked forth.

Pistols were shot, and screams, and then panic gripped the street.

An explosion rocked them all, nothing to hurt anyone, but enough to distract. Smoke drifted on the wind, and the world around them blurred again, everything moving so fast she could see nothing but a whirl of colours.

And then she and Arthur were shoved into a tiny hack, which began to move before the door had even shut behind them.

Now, to get out of the city.

∞

Even if she knew it wasn't over yet, Lily forced herself to take a moment, to stop, and breathe, and *feel*. To feel the rush of excitement, that they'd gotten this far; that she'd gotten Arthur out. To feel the heartbreak at the loss of Bill that she still couldn't quite comprehend nor accept. To feel the wrenching joy of having Arthur beside her again, even in his current state.

Straightening in the tight, mouldy confines of the hack, she turned to him. He was breathing jerkily again, but he was breathing. His head was swaying and bobbing with the movement of the cab, leaning back against it as he was. But he was here.

He is alive.

Taking his hand in hers, she lifted it to her lips, and kissed it, not bothering to push back the swell of tears that streamed down onto her cheeks.

'I'm sorry,' Arthur groaned, opening the one eye he could, and turning to face her.

'Why?' Lily frowned.

'Bill,' he breathed, that crack in her chest widening a little more. 'Anyone else hurt because of what you did for me.'

'These were my choices,' she told him, tightening her hold on his hand. 'Mine, and mine alone. Anyone who followed me down this path, it was their choice. We did the best we could to avoid people getting hurt. That's all any of us can ever do,' she said, her voice cracking.

It felt true; it was true.

And they had done all they could to avoid others not involved getting hurt. No one was to be killed, and they'd made sure that no prisoners in Newgate would be harmed in riots, or taking the blame for hurting *a turnkey*, even though the options had been considered. The distraction outside Newgate, an exploding cart, had been placed so that it would harm no passers-by, or even guards. Everything that would follow, it would simply be distractions and sleight of hand.

Like this, she thought, as the hack slowed, then stopped, and the door was wrenched open.

Lily released Arthur's hand reluctantly as they were quickly shuffled out of the hack, and into the back of a cart full of market detritus. As they were, she heard the unmistakable sounds of their continued pursuits.

Whistles and shouts; the watch, guards, runners, even a few *good citizens* joined together to find them, and bring them back to where they belonged. Among them were some of her own people, dressed as lawmen, dressed as helpers, to move the rest in the directions they wanted them to. And there were shouts of victory too, not from her own people; and laughter, jeers at the pursuers, and good wishes for St. Nick.

'*Don't ye forget us at Yuletide!,*' someone even jested, which brought a smile to Lily's lips as she lay down close to Arthur and they set off again, this time in another direction.

There was no more speaking as they continued on. Arthur would drift away, her holding his hand, until it was time to switch conveyances. Five more times they switched; during the third Lily changed Arthur's clothes yet again, best she could, and discarded both his borrowed uniform and her widow's weeds. They would be tossed somewhere quiet, where they would be easily enough found, and trigger a nice long search.

It wasn't until they were in the well-fitted, but simple, and indiscernible carriage some six or so hours later, and bumping along a well-travelled, but quiet path in the countryside, Arthur now fast asleep, that Lily finally allowed herself to accept that they'd done it.

We made it out.

We are alive.

For now, at least.

But tomorrow, she would face all that she must. The reality, the consequences of her choices. For now, she would simply sit with her love, and be grateful that they were together again.

To whatever saints or gods watched over us this day, thank you.

Take care of Bill for me.

XXXI.

Bramble Hatch, Kent, Two weeks later

It had been a long time since Arthur had been completely powerless. Life, and he himself, had made sure of that. Even in that wretched cell, he'd still felt he had a sliver of power; if only for a time before he was broken, to remain silent. He'd had the power which came with knowledge; and withholding it.

All his life, or at least all that of it he'd been able to think in such terms, he'd believed, strived, *ensured*, that he would only ever be truly powerless again when he was dead. Because living without power was a death sentence in itself; he knew that well enough.

Yet, here he was, powerless.

And much like the loss of hope, it was unlike anything he'd ever experienced.

For the past fortnight, his life had been in Lily's hands, and in the hands of those she'd decided to put her trust in. Even if he'd wished to object, he couldn't have. In one way, he hadn't been broken in that cell. He'd kept his lips shut, and been saved before the gilded gentleman could finish the work. But in another way, he had been broken. He was not the same man who had entered that wretched place; in fact he wasn't quite sure who this man was that Lily and her people had stitched back together, with grit, and love, and determination.

He didn't remember much of his first week here, flashes of amber eyes and pain, sharp and stinging, pulling him back from nothingness for a few moments. After that, the snippets of memory grew longer.

Lily's soothing voice murmuring things only his heart could hear. Broth and porridge and water and laudanum. More pain, as his wounds were stitched and cleaned and bound over and over.

The sweaty haze of a fever. More darkness. Golden hair in rays of sunlight piercing through. The snip of scissors and coolness of washing.

It had felt like floating between two worlds again; that of the living, and that of the dead.

Consciousness, and something else.

There had been moments of panic, where he'd woken from the endless void of a dream, tangled in memories or simply completely without memory of anything at all.

But then, the most wondrous thing would happen. He'd be told he was safe, and he would believe it. He would feel how safe he was, and he would know he could rest. If only a little longer.

That, is how Arthur discovered the beauty, the awe, of powerlessness.

Even in the past days as his mind had returned from whatever edge it courted, that feeling had remained. As questions began to swirl; objections, curses, gratitude, confusion, all rose at once as memory and coherence returned. Even as he lay, well, half-sat yesterday, while Lily recounted all that had happened since the night he'd said what he had truly believed to be his final farewell. He'd not said anything, not even looked at her, just stared at the worn oak chest of drawers set between two windows before him. Stared as motes of dust swirled from one ray of sun to the other, until the sun disappeared altogether some hours later.

It wasn't that he had nothing to say, or indeed, that he couldn't look at Lily; only it was all so very much to take. To fully comprehend.

To make peace with.

When he'd made his decision, put in place his plan, made

what he believed to be his final preparations before he left this world, his legacy in some way, he'd been certain of so much. Now, it felt as if all of that, everything he'd been, had been picked up, thrown against a brick wall, and shattered into a million tiny shards. He was angry, and restless, and happy, and grateful, and most of all, he was in awe. In awe of Lily, of her love for him. Of what she'd done - *for him.* He was lost at sea, Lily his only point of bearing, and yet, because of that, he was not afraid. He knew that whatever came next, they would face it together.

Arthur heard the door open and close gently behind him, and he turned from the picturesque view of sand and sea beyond a wildflower garden, to find his love beaming at him, surprise in her eyes and a tray of food in her hands.

'You are not in bed,' she grinned.

'Took me at least an hour to get all the way here,' he said, his own smile growing, his voice still shaky from disuse. Indeed, it had taken a great deal of time, effort, and planning, to make it all six feet from his bed to this window. 'But I couldn't lay there any longer.'

'Here,' Lily said, as if shaking herself from a dream - perhaps the same one he would dwell in forever now. 'I brought breakfast; let us enjoy it by the fire.'

She bustled over to the tiny table and chairs set a few feet away, and lay down her tray before glancing at him expectantly.

'I will manage Lily.'

Nodding, but poised to leap at a second's notice in case he changed his mind, she waited, eyes like a hawk's, as he shuffled to her and lowered himself into a chair with a groan.

Lily hesitated, and he could tell she wanted to fuss over him, but instead she contented herself with serving him tea, and a plate of the most delicious fried bread, eggs, and ham. They ate in silence for a while, until Lily's nervousness was so thick he could barely breathe.

Arthur realised then, not only how profoundly the whole experience must've affected her, but also, how his silence and lack of response must've cut deep. He set down his fork, and leaned over to grasp her hand, ignoring the sharp pain in his ribs as he did.

Her eyes fluttered closed, and a weight seemed to lift instantly from her shoulders.

'I did not have the words yesterday, Lily,' he said softly, and her eyes opened again to meet his. 'I don't think I truly do today either, but I doubt I ever will. What you did... For me... You saved me, Lily. Before Newgate, from Newgate... I never believed...'

I never believed I could be loved as you love me.

'I thought you'd be angry with me,' she admitted quietly with that little shrug of hers.

'I am, in a way,' he agreed. Honesty, partnership, they'd promised, and he'd hold to it. 'That you did not go with Harrow. That you put your life on the line for mine. You might've been killed at every turn, and that would never have been worth it.'

'For me it would've.'

'Let's agree to disagree on this point.' He smiled, and she nodded. 'So... What now?'

∞

Laughter filled the air, and belatedly, Lily realised it was her own. It was all just... So much. To be sitting here with Arthur, alive, and safe, and mostly healed, physically at least, simply eating breakfast, and talking, as if all was normal in their world... It was heartbreakingly refreshing.

So many times these past two weeks, despite forbidding herself to, she'd doubted. Doubted that he would survive what he'd endured, then the fever that had taken hold.

Doubted that he'd forgive what she'd done.

That he would still want her after what she'd done.

The weight of all it had taken to accomplish what she had, was nearly suffocating at times. Word had come from London at a regular pace since they'd arrived here, in this little coastal hamlet a few miles from Margate. Their coup, or countercoup she supposed, was holding fast. None but those engaged in the bloody battle had perished, and her people were safe. That, had been a relief.

Understatement of the millennium.

No innocent lives on her soul.

There had been some noise from the authorities about the unrest, but it had calmed when they realised those now in power wouldn't be overthrown; and that St. Nick was not in London. And naturally, that their pockets would remain handsomely lined. So, a tranquil, fragile peace, had returned to the docks.

If the greater power behind the initial plot was unhappy, no one knew nor heard. There hadn't been any further moves to take power again; nor to seek vengeance. But then, news travelled that the owner of *The Emporium* had created quite a stir among the high and mighty; so perhaps whatever Mr. Ames had been up to, whatever persons he wished to see thwarted, had been. Lily hoped that he was safe, wherever he was, and that someday soon they might meet again.

So yes, a tenuous, uneasy peace was holding in Shadwell and beyond, and her daring rescue of St. Nick had aided in ensuring her own position was secure, even from afar. She and Arthur had become something of a popular legend now, which felt rather unreal truth be told. Perhaps, if so much hadn't been sacrificed, she might've been able to enjoy it more.

The confirmation of Bill's death had come shortly after their arrival here. Tending to Arthur had helped distract her from the grief, but in those moments she wasn't actively tending to him, because he slept, or the doctor she'd engaged for a tidy sum took over, she felt his death keenly. His sacrifice, keenly.

From what the reports said, he'd managed to get hold of a pistol during the fight, and ended himself before he could be questioned or hanged. She supposed it should be a comfort that his death had been swift.

It wasn't.

But she would remember him, always. As the good man, the good friend, he'd been, and that was something she supposed. As was the fact that she was now sitting as she was with Arthur, *safe*, thanks to Bill. He would've been happy about that. He would've smiled that crooked half-smile of his if he'd seen her, laughing again.

As for Arthur's question…

'We wait, for a time,' she said. 'We remain very sought-after people, so for now, we remain here. After that… It is up to you, Arthur. Your kingdom is yours if you want it. But if you prefer to leave it all behind, that is possible too.'

'After all you did to take it back,' Arthur said with a slight frown. 'All you lost… You would be ready to leave it all behind?'

'I did what I did for Shadwell. Not just for you. Because living in the thrall of those men…'

'I know. I am sorry for Bill, for your loss. He was a good man.'

'Thank you. He was. And he gave me such a gift… All I ever really wanted, was you, Arthur. I told you that once before,' she shrugged, and his hand tightened around hers. It felt as if the vice-like grip her heart had been caught in these past weeks eased, shards of light breaking the chains that bound it. 'And I stand by that. If you'll have me that is.'

Truth was, Lily needed to hear him say it.

There was so much love in his eyes, and his touch settled her soul, but this once, she needed to hear the words, because yes, she still doubted.

'I'm a man of my word, Lily,' Arthur grinned, picking up her hand, and settling a gentle kiss on her palm. 'I promised you a life. I never thought… I would have as much time as you've now given me. But I do, and I would not have it any other way. I love you; I have said it time and time again, but I will say it a thousand times every day if it takes that for you to believe me. I am in awe of you, of your strength, and your determination, and I cannot imagine what I have done in this life to deserve such a woman as you, standing by my side. I do know, that I will do everything in my power to deserve it from this day forth.'

It wasn't until Arthur's hand came to her cheek and wiped them away that Lily realised tears had fallen.

She nodded, speechless, then, unable to contain herself any

longer, she rose, settled between Arthur's legs, and embraced him tightly. Not too tightly, for fear of aggravating his injuries, though they did not prevent him from wrapping his arms around her waist and holding her with nearly all of the strength he had once possessed.

After a very long moment, so alike, and yet so different to that one in the street, the night he'd been taken, when they simply existed, and breathed together, they loosened their hold on each other.

Lily swept her hands over his features, still bearing the marks of his trial, but nearly all healed. There would be scars, seen, and unseen, and though they would never disappear, they would heal.

Gazing down into the swirling silver that had enchanted her from the first, she felt sure, that whatever did come next, it would be everything she'd never dared to wish for, and more.

'I love you, Arthur,' she breathed. 'And that is not something to be *deserved*. It simply is. And we shall both give thanks for it.'

Arthur nodded, took her hands, and kissed the knuckles.

'You know, the choice is also yours, Lily,' he said after a moment. 'To live a quiet life, away from it all, or to go back. You found your sister, which I admittedly cannot quite believe.'

Neither can I, she thought. With all that had happened, it seemed like a strange dream, yet the reports from the watcher she'd sent to ensure her sister's safety had confirmed it was not a dream, but real. 'And I know you wished for a life with her too. As part of this little family we have become. I also understand the risk of a life such as the one we would lead if we chose to remain at the head of our kingdom. You know I do. I would understand if you wished to keep her far away from it all.'

Lily nodded, and kissed his cheek tenderly.

'I have given it much thought,' she said, and it was true. When she'd not been consumed with thoughts of everything else, she'd spared a moment to hope, to imagine what the future might look like if Arthur made it, and wanted her still. 'I waited so long to find her again, I cannot imagine a life without her in it again, just as I cannot imagine a life without you. You once said you did not think you would be yourself, without living as Saint Nick. I did not think a quiet life would be your choice. And truthfully, how I found her, *who* I found her with... I have resigned that I cannot make the choice for her. Though I would like to have her in my life, and though I would like to keep her safe from the world we dwell in, the truth is, she has become her own woman since we've been apart. And so, the choice must be hers. Her entanglement with Silas does complicate matters, and I admit I have many thoughts on that, but I cannot force her down any path. I wish to get to know her again, and for the time that we are here, I hope we can do that. I was waiting to speak to you, but I think soon I should call for her. We all have much to say to each other, and whatever happens, I believe, I *know*, the future will be bright, so long as we are all together. And, I know that once you are healed, if I ask you to teach Silas a lesson, you will,' she grinned.

'Have no doubt. Kit shall be my sister too,' he added seriously. 'Once you find a minister to pay well and marry us.'

Lily's eyes widened, and she searched his face for any jest.

'You mean it?'

'Of course I mean it,' he said, almost affronted. 'Forged papers are well and good for many things, but I admit to being quite traditional in this respect. I should like to make you my wife, in truth, and put a ring, which I might have to engage some of your friends to find for me, on that finger of yours.'

It was such a small, simple, seemingly insignificant thing in the grand scheme of things.

To be married. To be a wife, to have a husband, when they were already entwined, their souls tied together by the invisible yet unbreakable bonds of love. And yet, Lily was sure her heart exploded then, becoming some manner of bright shining star. A light, of pure happiness, and wonder, and love, which shone through and chased away all the darkness, doubt, and pain. Her wounds were still there, her sins, still there; but they were bearable. They were...

Worth it. For this love.

And perhaps, that was wrong. But Lily's dreams had not only become true, they'd been realised in a way she'd never allowed herself to imagine. So she would live this life with Arthur, and find a way to make wrongs right again, and most importantly, she would love.

With that resolve in her heart, she lowered her head and kissed Arthur with all that love, and passion; gratitude, and relief. It was raw, and painful, and healing, and full of hope.

For an incredible life.

An incredible future.

An incredible love.

EPILOGUE

T he sound of pattering rain had finally ceased, and a faint glow had begun to chase away the clouds, so Arthur padded over to the kitchen window, and opened it fully to let out some of the delectable, yet stuffy air. As he did, he allowed himself a moment to stare out onto the view that felt something like home now, and take a deep inhale of the fresh, salty air.

However long the rest of his life was, he knew he would always look back on the time here as something special. Restful, and beautiful, and exquisitely simple. Normal, almost. He knew it couldn't last forever, but in a sense, that is what made it so wonderfully enchanting.

Since the day he had, somewhat informally, asked Lily to take him as her husband, it felt as if the black clouds of doubt, and the past, had been lifted. Still, Arthur felt as if he was caught, this time not between two worlds, but between two versions of himself; yet every day the broken parts healed a little more, and formed a sharper image of the man he was to be now.

The talking helped; the talking which never ceased now. Both he and Lily spent most hours of the day laying their hearts, their wounds, their fears, before the other. It would take time, a lifetime perhaps, to heal completely from the past, and from their trials; and perhaps they never would, not fully. But together, sharing, as they were, they could live, and thrive, and become...

Better perhaps.

Better versions of themselves.

That is what he had learned the power of love truly was. It inspired one to be better, not for the other, not for the world, but simply because they could be; in whatever way that meant.

Of course, they had discussed much else. The future; the news which came from London. Things were still holding steady in the East, though Arthur and Lily both felt as if it might not hold too much longer with them out of the city. With peace, came prosperity, and soon Lily's once allies would be likely looking for more territory to make their own; accords and treaties be damned. The operation he'd built up over the years was still functioning, but it wasn't as strong as it had once been. And though the deeds he'd fought to keep safe still were, as far as he knew, the Earl of Brookton's continued absence from the city was... Worrying.

Even for Harrow, particularly since the West, Society itself, was still reeling from Mr. Ames' actions, and revelations, of which they'd heard a little more; and indeed, Arthur could understand how it would unsettle the balance so. It was a lot to process, and he knew Lily hoped someday to meet the true Madam E again.

In time.

Yes, in time, there would be so much more for them to do. For now...

Breakfast, he smiled, turning back to the feast he was preparing for Lily. And for their soon to be guests, he hoped, if they made good time.

Once he was closer to fully healed, Lily had indeed sent for Kit, and Silas, the latter not being what he would call an anticipated guest, but a required one nonetheless. Whatever bound the Whitechapel boss to Lily's sister... Well, they would talk of it. But neither he nor Lily would have it in them to judge, either way, considering who their own hearts had chosen. None of it mattered, really, Arthur mused, transferring the food to warming pots. So long as Lily had her sister here for her wedding.

Tomorrow.

Tomorrow, they would become husband and wife. An odd thing to give import to in times such as these, and yet, perhaps it was the most vital thing to revere in times such as these. A marking, of life going on. A marking of...

Life. In all its incredible glory.

A knock sounded at the front door, and Arthur laughed at himself as he made for it, thinking how the feared St. Nick had become so distracted by talk of weddings that he couldn't even hear a cart, or coach, or horse approach.

Dangerous man indeed.

Straightening his waistcoat, wiping his hands on his trousers, he prepared to open the door. He heard Lily's pattering feet at his back, and he turned to find his heart freshly dressed, and still glowing from the hot bath he'd prepared for her.

Ready? he asked her silently.

Her brilliant smile, and kiss on the cheek, were her answer, and she looped her arm into his as they went to open the door together.

Only, the two people on the other side of it, were not Kit and Silas.

Fear sliced through him at the sight of the strangers, both dressed in elegant travelling clothes, both smiling. A man, tall, with dark curls, coal black eyes, and fine features; and a woman, equally as tall, voluptuous, and looking as fiery as her hair in the sunlight.

Arthur cursed himself for not being armed, cursed whoever was on guard and had failed to stop these two, and he pushed Lily behind him as he prepared to fight...

Whoever the Hell these people are.

Though there was something familiar about the man...

'Can I help you,' he said instead, his voice carrying enough menace to terrify -

Anyone but them, he noted, as the woman smiled cheerfully.

'Do not be alarmed,' she said reassuringly, though Arthur did not feel reassured at all. 'We wish you no harm, and we apologise for incapacitating your...friend outside. He will be fine by the way,' she added, looking to Lily, whose hand relaxed ever so slightly on his arm. 'Only, we needed to speak to you, and he wouldn't have let us through I think.'

'Who the Hell are you,' Arthur growled.

'Oh, how terribly rude of me,' the woman gasped, eyes wide, while the man at her side simply scowled a little harder, as if this whole interview was terribly boring. Though his eyes told another story, as they swept across Arthur and Lily, cataloguing everything, and piecing their wholes into something... *Else.* 'I am Effy Fortescue, and this is Harcourt Sinclair,' she said, gesturing to her companion. *What. The. Hell*, Arthur thought, frowning, knowing his surprise showed but caring little of it. At once, he placed Sinclair, not that he'd seen him much though he owned Silver Bell Wharf with Brookton, for he'd barely ever come to the docks, and then disappeared some four years ago, after actions that had thrown Society into a nice little bit of chaos. 'Good, you've heard of him at least, that will make things a bit easier. We are friends of Percy's, you see, Viscount Egerton, Earl of Brookton, whatever you know him by. And Angelique,' she added, pointedly turning to Lily again. 'Who is well, I should tell you. On her way to America.' He heard Lily sigh with relief, and the woman before them smiled. 'And unless we are mistaken, you are the madam and the saint who caused quite some trouble in London recently. Don't try to deny it,' she continued, speaking before Arthur or Lily could do just that. 'As I said, we wish you no harm. We are here as friends, and allies. There are things, *in motion*, which, if you have the stomach for, we could use your help with.'

The woman stopped, and allowed them a moment to ponder her words.

So many questions, and fears, were growing inside him, *how did they find us, why, are we safe, shall I kill them, what things in motion*, but when he turned to Lily, the noise quietened. He gazed into her whiskey-coloured eyes for a long moment, and when they had reached a silent agreement, she smiled, and nodded.

No quiet life for us.

No, indeed. Whatever this was... This too, they would face together.

Taking a deep breath, he turned back to the unexpected guests, and nodded.

'Best come inside, then,' he said. 'There is breakfast, if you wish, and we have other guests expected soon. I have a feeling whatever you have to say, it best be said before they get here.'

'Thank you,' Miss Fortescue said sincerely, dipping her head. 'And yes, breakfast, would be lovely. It has been a long journey.'

Arthur entwined his hand with Lily's, and they both stepped aside so their visitors could enter.

Looks as though I shall have to cook more breakfast for Kit.

Arthur chuckled to himself, and as they made their way to the kitchen, he realised that whatever this was...

Had some excitement growing inside him.

The time for rest, and quiet, had come, and gone. Kit would still come, and tomorrow come what may, he would still make Lily his wife. But as for the future...

It was becoming distinctly more interesting. And glancing at Lily, he knew she felt it too, the thrill of a life less than ordinary.

Of danger, and intrigue, and sometimes, darkness, yes.

But a life shared.

And certainly never a quiet one.

Neither would have had it any other way.

AUTHOR'S NOTE

First of all, a mighty thank you for reading Arthur and Lily's story, I do so hope you enjoyed it. I would normally say, as much as I enjoyed writing it, but that would be somewhat passing over the difficulty I had in finishing this particular story, though yes, I found much joy, as always, in putting the tales in my head to paper.

I began writing *The Saint & The Madam* in early 2020. By the time the pandemic started, I hadn't gotten very far, and I admittedly was not quite in the right headspace to write such a tale as this. So I let it rest, and beg any series readers to forgive me for the time it took to finish this particular story, and thank you for continuing to read these books. I hope anyone just coming to the *Vixens & Villains* series found a satisfying HEA despite the numerous threads I know I've left dangling.

It is always tricky, putting to paper something so clear, and vivid as this was, in my head. To find the words to describe, and properly handle, such matter as is in this book. To bring to life such characters as Arthur and Lily, who teeter on the line between *hero*, and *villain*. But I've always found those characters to be the most interesting, hence the series itself. As always, I have tried to handle difficult subject matter, with care, sensitivity, and respect.

I will, as ever, renew my plea, that if you, or anyone you know, is suffering from any manner of violence, sexual exploitation, or trauma, that you reach out to any of the numerous charities and organisations worldwide that can help.

On a historical note, the Thames Tunnel did in fact exist, connecting Rotherhithe to Wapping, though it was not, in the end, such a financially successful enterprise as the minds behind it hoped it would be. It was a tourist attraction for some time, then eventually, was transformed into a railway tunnel which still exists today.

I also wish to quickly address the matter of pronouns in the case of Mr. Ames, who would today identify as *non-binary*, though this will be further explored and developed when the character comes fully to life in the next book of the series. Employing *they/them*, though historically accurate, would have gone against character in this instance, for both Mr. Ames, and Lily. Mr. Ames appears thus in this book; it therefore felt right for Lily to employ solely masculine pronouns, though if Lily lived today, I know she would ask, and employ whatever pronouns someone preferred, I think you'd agree.

I will also say that I've used some modern vernacular in this book, not out of disregard for historical accuracy, nor for ease, but simply because the vocabulary for certain occupations has connotations which I was either unsure of, or did not wish to imply.

Regarding my liberal use of the word *whore*, I feel that, as she says herself, Lily would have freely used, and owned the word, to take the negative power others would give it, away.

Lastly, I want to wish you well, reader. We have all faced some difficult times, these past couple years especially, and I hope that my books bring you some light, some escapism, and some hope. Perhaps these times are unprecedented; perhaps they are not.

Regardless, I want to thank you.

Because having readers out there in the world reminds me I am not alone.

I hope reading them, reading this, reminds you, that neither are you.

ABOUT THE AUTHOR

Lotte R. James

 Lotte James trained as an actor and theatre director, but spent most of her life working day jobs crunching numbers whilst dreaming up stories of love and adventure. She's thrilled to finally be writing those stories, and when she's not scribbling on tiny pieces of paper, she can usually be found wandering the countryside for inspiration, or nestling with coffee and a book.

Be sure to keep in touch on Twitter @lottejamesbooks!

BOOKS IN THIS SERIES

Vixens & Villains

Set in Britain in the 1820's, the Vixens & Villains series is perfect for fans of historical romance with a dash of darkness, and danger!

Each can be read standalone, though there are stories which continue throughout the series.

The Rake & The Maid

The darkness in their hearts means they can never love – doesn't it?

Euphemia Fortescue fled an arranged marriage, and suffered the whims and trials of false friends and twisted lords. But as Harcourt Sinclair's housemaid, she found peace and purpose.

Harcourt Sinclair has been planning his revenge for twenty years against those peers of society who stole everything from him. But his single-mindedness will cost him, unless he can learn to trust his least expected saviour...

Redemption, adventure, secrets, desire, and love in Regency London.

The Viscount & The Lighterman's Daughter

They've hidden their true selves - but can they find each other?

Viscount Percy Egerton nearly lost everything in the wake of his friend Harcourt Sinclair's scandal. Not even taking over a shipping company and playing nighttime vigilante has helped him find what he wants most; himself. But when the daughter of one of his workers bursts into his life, he'll soon find everything he ever wished for is within his grasp, if only he has the courage to reach out...

When Meg Lowell is dismissed and forced to return home to Sailortown, she is desperate to find the means to survive, and keep her family from destitution. Clever, and hardworking, she has no fear, that is until she meets Percy, and he threatens her with the most dangerous thing of all; love.

Redemption, adventure, secrets, desire, and love in the docklands of Regency London.

The Bodyguard & The Miss

Their pasts are full of secrets – but will the dark truth set them free?

Angelique Fitzsimmons is not the girl all of Society believes her to be. Only a select few friends know of her scandalous and adventurous self, but not even they know of the terror lurking in her heart. Neither can they ever, which is why she runs away without a word. Only, she wasn't counting on the unsettling guard sent after her...

Will Hardy is nothing if not a man of his word. A year he has endured guarding Miss Fitzsimmons from no one but her reckless self; and so he must again when the spoiled chit decides to run away. But soon, he realizes there is more to her than he thought, and if only he can learn to open himself, they will both be able to find what neither was looking for to begin with. Love.

Redemption, adventure, secrets, desire, and love across Regency Britain.

BOOKS BY THIS AUTHOR

Liminal (Traversing Book One)

I'm pretty sure it's bad form to pick up a guy in a hospital.

Pretty sure it's even worse to show up uninvited at his brother's funeral.

Or let him…have you at the wake.

It's definitely not a smart move to let him into your apartment when he shows up uninvited after you made the reasonable choice to ditch him at said wake.

Still, I let him in.

Because… I'm messed up. And so is he.

Besides, he's also yummy, and we're both adults, and we have needs.

Needs that don't include getting attached, or telling each other our secrets.

Which I know he has. Then again, don't we all?

Except the longer we carry on with this arrangement, the harder it gets to remember the deal.

Even if I know that giving into our inexplicable connection will change my life forever.

And that Edward's secrets will either destroy us, or…

Open the door to a world I never could have imagined.

Rosemary & Pansies

When Flynn Carter is offered a job in Coombe's Cross, she can hardly refuse. Not even if that means working on Hamlet with temperamental director Clive Reid or movie-star heartthrob Jake Thornton. Her tough exterior seemed impenetrable armour enough until she met Jake...

No matter that he is here to save his career from scandal and ruin, his ego it seems hasn't suffered one bit...
But, they must learn to work together if they are to save the show, their careers, and whatever this is that is growing between them...

A sweeping and sweet low-heat contemporary love-story set in the magical world of theatre!

Printed in Great Britain
by Amazon

19583999R00171